The Chatterbox Chip

Janine Marie and JHC

Josh
Love talking
to you about
plot + stories +
D+D
XOX Auntie
Danielle
AKA: Janine Marie

This is a work of fiction. All names, characters, places and incidents are the product of author's imagination. Any resemblance to real events or persons, living or dead is entirely coincidental.

Cover Design by Sophia Shafonsky 2017

Published by MTSMarketech LLC

ISBN: **1534636005**
ISBN 13: **9781534636002**
Library of Congress Control Number: **2016909702**

Thank you for purchasing our book.

A portion of this books profits will be donated to the rebuilding of the British Virgin Islands which were devastated by Hurricane Irma and Maria.

Many Thanks

Janine & Jack

Chapter 1

Janeva Jag had always thought of herself as a strong, self-sufficient woman, but now she wasn't so sure. Almost a year had passed. She was safe in her own home and comfortable bed, yet Janeva could not sleep. The memory persisted, and she dreaded sleep. The nightmares had diminished, but now she had been summoned by the police to relate the event once again. *When will it ever end?* she brooded.

Was it the memory of what happened or the realization afterward that she had almost died? Her twelve-year-old daughter, Katie, still needed her. Her husband, Thomas, was a great dad. But a young girl needs her mother. She thought she had safely stored the event in the past—that was, until the phone call yesterday. Now again in her mind, it replayed like a TV show.

***

The feeling of fear again gripped her. Her brain projected the image of being trapped with Trent in a dark, locked room, with Catherine sprawled unconscious on the floor. Imprisoned in the engine room of the one-hundred-foot luxury yacht *Atlantis*, her hands were bleeding from her relentless banging on the door.

The indigo light on the engine-room wall confirmed they'd been imprisoned now for more than an hour, but there was no other light, and no matter how careful they were, every time they moved, they hit their heads or hands or knees on some part of the engine. Surely someone would hear them, she thought. She gingerly reached down to check on Catherine. Catherine was still breathing, and her pulse was regular. It was her moaning that had lured them into the engine room.

Then slowly the engine-room door started to open, and that flash of light illuminated Catherine spread out on the hard, cold steel floor. The air was putrid; they were breathing a cloud of diesel and engine-oil vapor and sweat. But it wasn't a rescue—when the door was flung fully open, it was Wiffy, pointing a gun directly at Trent and Janeva. They stared at her in fear and stunned silence.

Janeva was sweating, but her initial panic had calmed. "Listen, Wiffy—we are your friends; what's gotten into you?" she pleaded quietly. "You need help, and we will help you; let us go, and we'll help. I promise. Wiffy, please don't do anything that you will regret. You don't want to go to jail."

Janeva was shocked at the change in Wiffy. She seemed to have grown taller, and her eyes now glared dark, black, and hard. Janeva then realized she had never seen those eyes before because they were always shyly downcast. Even more surprising was Trent's emotional collapse. He stayed behind Janeva, protecting himself, and he was shaking.

"Wiffy, Trent is your husband; he loves you. You're a couple. You can't do this. Please think. Put down the gun and let us out, and I promise everything will be all right."

"Wiffy, honey, please just put down the gun; it'll be all right," Trent pleaded.

"Honey? Honey? After all these years, I'm now honey? You served your purpose." Suddenly she reached behind her, grabbed her accomplice, and thrust him into the engine room, slamming him into one of the large 1,926-horsepower Cat C-32A diesel engines.

Startled by his change in fate, after a moment the man recovered his balance and lunged at her, grabbing for the gun. Wiffy calmly arched her eyebrows, moved the gun a trace, and fired. The sound echoed like an explosion in the small engine room. A neat hole opened in the center of his forehead, and the bullet exited through his occiput with a burst of brains, bone, and blood that splattered them all. Stunned, her ears ringing, Janeva was almost paralyzed in shock.

"You killed him," Janeva whispered, and as she said it, she realized that it was Wiffy who had murdered Lorenzo.

Trent, astonished, couldn't believe what he had just seen; it didn't register. "Why? Who are you? What's happened to you?"

"Shut up. I prepared for this some time ago. This yacht is going to explode because there is a bomb in the bilge that I'll activate as soon as I'm on the dock. You might as well know that I got what I needed. He"—she waved her gun at the body—"drugged Catherine, and when Lorenzo rushed in to help…" She smirked. "Timing is everything, and just as I planned, he left his computer on. Unfortunately, he came back, and so Lorenzo had to die. Everyone dies, and now it's your turn too." She knew that everyone in the world with knowledge of her business was in that engine room, facing her gun. *Yes*, she thought, *I will soon be a nice, innocent, rich widow*. She smiled to herself as she backed out of the engine room.

Keep her talking. Keep her talking. Distract her. Appeal to her sense of self-importance, Janeva thought, but as she started to move toward Wiffy, a gunshot narrowly missed her head, and she had to put her hands to her ears to suppress the ringing. Trent had curled himself back into a small ball.

"Got the message, I see," Wiffy snarled; then under her breath to herself, she said, "Max will be proud."

"They'll catch you," Janeva shouted, determined to keep her talking.

"Did you forget that I'm an engineer? Sometimes big boats explode when there is a generator fuel leak." As she slammed the door shut, Janeva leaped for it, but was too late. Wiffy had slid the bolts that locked it from the outside.

***

Janeva was still sweating from reliving the memory. She wondered if the police had any new information. Her mind replayed the story as her husband, Thomas, had recited it.

***

They knew that Janeva was on the yacht *Atlantis*, but it was dark. They couldn't see anything. "Janeva, Janeva!" Thomas had been banging on the locked sliding-glass cockpit door.

"Steph," he said, "keep banging on the door. Greg, go up to the bridge, and if it's open, activate all the lights, and I'll try the side doors."

After a quick search, they met again on the aft deck. "All locked," said Greg.

"Maybe Janeva's not on the boat?" Steph suggested.

That was when they heard the shot.

"What was that?" Steph asked. "It sounded like—"

"A gunshot," Thomas and Greg said simultaneously. "Smash the glass!" Greg grabbed a deck chair and threw it without effect at the glass door.

"Shit, it's marine-grade glass." They knew this glass was designed to withstand storms and crashing waves. Thomas looked around him and asked, "Where would Lorenzo have kept a set of spare keys?

"Hanging plant? No. Under the seat? No. Bar fridge? Under the propane heater? No. Tucked in the hand of the Italian sculpture? *Yes*!"

They got the door open and ran into the yacht. "Split up?" Greg suggested.

"Yes, Steph, you and Greg check out the main cabins. Then meet me on the lower level!" yelled Thomas as he ran toward the midship stairs. Minutes later, all three stood in the small lower-level landing without luck after a quick search of all the cabins. "What's left?" Steph asked.

“Engine room and crew quarters,” Greg said, pointing aft.

Thomas ran to the engine-room door and wrenched at it.

“Damn, it’s locked and bolted.”

“If Janeva’s here and that was a shot, then we’re going to have to break it down,” Steph said, and she tugged desperately on the door.

Thomas and Greg both knew it was a reinforced, fireproof steel door with soundproofing insulation on the inside. Thomas moaned in frustration. “There must be a key on the bridge,” he said, and he ran off.

“We will check the crew quarters,” Greg yelled at him as he grabbed Steph’s arm, dragging her after him away from the door.

The crew quarters were unlocked and vacant, as was the small crew galley, so they ran back to the engine room.

Thomas was back and fumbling with a ring of keys. Finally, one worked. When they had unlocked and unbolted the door, Janeva cried and ran into his arms, behind her a horrific, gory scene.

“My God! What happened?” he gasped.

“We need to get off this boat, now! It’s going to explode!” Janeva yelled, turning to go back and grab at Catherine, who was still unconscious. “Help me!” she cried. Instantly the spell was broken, and Thomas and Greg ran into the crowded room, pushed Trent out the door and into Steph’s arms, and then lifted Catherine between them. Janeva helped pull Trent to his feet, and together she and Steph dragged him off the boat to the dock.

"*No!* Don't stop! Keep going! Go! Go! Go!" Janeva yelled to Greg and Thomas, who had been about to put Catherine down to ascertain her injuries.

"She needs medical attention," Greg was saying.

"She will need more than that when this boat blows up!" Janeva yelled back at him from the end of the dock.

Their disbelief was countered by their vision of the exploded head, so against their judgment, Thomas said, "Now! Let's go." Together they grabbed up Catherine's limp body and ran after Janeva, Steph, and Trent.

Boom!

The boat exploded, and the blast force knocked all six onto the wooden dock planking.

***

Janeva's memories had resurfaced with a vengeance. She was trembling. She worked to calm her mind, taking deep yoga breaths. She had to be strong for Katie, whom she was to take to the police station for more questions later that day.

Chapter 2

"Why do we have to go to the police station?" complained Katie. "I will miss band practice, and I have a social-studies test I need to study for. You know it's my worst subject. This is a waste of time."

"We have to go," Janeva said with a sigh, "because the police told us to. We don't have a choice. It's about Lorenzo's murder, and they consider us to be witnesses."

"But we *weren't* witnesses," complained Katie. "We didn't see anything. *We* were just in the area. Anyway, I told everything to the Canadian police—the, um, Royal Canadian Mounted Police—a thousand times!"

"Really? A thousand times?"

"Well, maybe three times. Anyway, it's a stupid name. They're not royal, they're not mounted, and if they were really police, they'd have solved the murder by now, and we wouldn't have to waste the afternoon at the county sheriff's office."

"OK, OK, please stop whining. Anyway, I kind of like Royal and Mounted; it reflects their history. They are a national police force in a huge country, larger than America. In the early days before trains, cars, and planes, they kept law and order by being mounted on horseback, driving dog teams, and paddling canoes. Plus, Lorenzo's murder was in Canada, and they were trying to do their job, considering that the victim was an American and all the witnesses also American."

Rolling her eyes, not listening, Katie said, "I know; maybe we are suspects!"

"Katie," her mom hissed, "of course we aren't suspects, and probably you are right about this being a waste of time, because there was a confession that solved the murder. So if you are very polite, maybe we'll get out faster. And before you ask, the answer is no, we don't need a lawyer. Let's wait and see what we learn, OK?"

***

"Hi, I'm Janeva Jag, and this is my daughter, Katie. We have an appointment," Janeva said to the blank-faced receptionist. Unlike any office she'd ever been to before, this receptionist did not smile or try to be pleasant. She just gave them a look that implied, "You're guilty of something, and we'll find out."

Janeva was subtly reminded of trying to cross back into the United States from Canada in their boat and seeing the same bland face on the customs agent asking, "How long were you in Canada? Do you have any lemons or limes? How much alcohol and tobacco are you bringing back? Oh, well then, just step off your boat, and we'll check." All the time she was wondering, *Why should America care? Who would buy alcohol in Canada? It's so much more expensive in Canada than in the United States anyway. And by the way, Mr. Customs Man, the lemons and limes are all from California in the first place; it's too cold for them to grow in Canada.*

Jolting Janeva out of her musings, the tired clerk pointed and in a formal tone said, "Right. Just sit over there. I will call you."

Katie and Janeva took the only two vacant chairs—wood, stained, straight backed, and uncomfortable. Janeva saw Katie grimacing, holding her nose, and rolling her eyes. Janeva knew why. It was the smell leaking out from the men on both sides—some powerful combination of stale tobacco, alcohol, dirty clothes, and probably a week without bathing, like a cloud settling around them. *I'm glad I am not a police person*, she thought. She pondered how much of the job was interacting with people who suffered from some form of mental illness.

With nothing to read, all they could do was watch the parade of police officers coming and going, so they did the only reasonable thing, and both pulled out their smartphones, Janeva checking e-mail and Katie on Instagram.

But Katie wasn't concentrating on her Instagram. She was musing about her difficulty at school. Everything she did went wrong. Math and science were easy, and she always had the answer, put up her hand, and asked smart questions. However, instead of being popular, she had been discounted by her classmates, out of the corner of their eyes, as a nerd or geek.

Janeva couldn't concentrate on the podcast she had opened because she was starting to relive the event. Now she wondered how much of the story had happened and how much was her imagination and her memory. The more she told the story, the stronger she rewired her brain to believe and relive the event. *Neuroplasticity, where are you when we need you?* she thought. *Maybe it wasn't Wiffy who was mentally disturbed; maybe none of it happened. It's just a dream, a nightmare.* Then she reviewed what she had learned about the case from the police investigation.

"Janeva and Katie, room number three down the hall," the blank-faced receptionist barked out.

"Why do they call us by our first names?" asked Katie.

"Good question," her mother said.

"I know," Katie replied, inspired. "I think it's because there are always reporters from the media hanging around, and if they can get a last name, then they're able to google the name for a story. So the desk clerks try to manage without revealing the names of people, especially witnesses like us who are really here to help the police."

Janeva answered by raising her eyebrows and nodding agreement as they entered a small, windowless room that had one long desk with a phone and recording device. The only person in the room was a young, tall, dark-haired policeman in standard blue uniform who explained that he was Deputy Sheriff Something-or-Other that they didn't quite get.

Katie gave her mom a puzzled look and whispered, "Did he say his name was Do Good?"

"No, not Do Good, young lady; it's Dugud," the deputy sheriff said. He explained that he was required to review and categorize a collection of past case files whose outcomes either were unsolved or if solved, contained some element of uncertainty. In order to finally close the Lorenzo file, he needed to connect one last time with witnesses. Dugud thanked them for coming, apologized for keeping them waiting, and reminded them that the case involved the murder of an American citizen in a remote area of Canada.

"You previously reported that you'd accused the Wiffy woman of Lorenzo's murder, but there was no confession," he explained. "Subsequently, Wiffy was found drowned. Failure to deny an event is not the same as admitting it, so your implication that she killed Lorenzo is conjecture based on your memory, Mrs. Jag. We have no other credible leads; we have no motive, so your impression is all we have to go on to learn the identity of Lorenzo's murderer. His murder and all the events that you witnessed leave us with many questions."

Dugud went on to explain that this case was just one of an unmanageable stack of old and unsolved crimes he had inherited. The new chief of police was trying to look effective and was probably under pressure from the media or another unknown source, so he was hoping that a new, unbiased view—"That's me," said Dugud—might come up with some new evidence or at least satisfy any controversy and finally close the file.

"I have reviewed your previous testimony and didn't think it necessary to question you and your daughter separately. In fact, sometimes a collective interview activates memories. And just to speed up the process," he said, gesturing to the several stacks of files he had to get through, "let's get on with it, shall we?"

Unlike the reception clerk, however, Dugud was friendly and smooth, sort of like an actor, and Katie liked him immediately. Janeva noted that he was being charming and trying to act like their friend, when of course he was trying to solve a crime. And despite her earlier message to her daughter, she knew they were all still considered to be associated with two murders, and that *did* make them possible suspects.

Deputy Sheriff Dugud addressed most of the questions to Katie. "Why did you choose to go to that particular ocean inlet?"

Katie turned and looked at her mom, mystified.

"Honey, there is no right or wrong answer here. The deputy sheriff just wants to know what you think," Janeva said, prompting her.

"Um, I don't know for sure," Katie answered.

"Like your mom said, I just want to hear what you think."

Katie shrugged. "Well, OK, it isn't a secret. When I grow up, I'm going to be a marine biologist, and my dad loves to sail and is always looking for a sailing adventure with good marine life for me, and so this was perfect. I don't know how he found out about it, but like he said, it was beautiful, with a big waterfall so I could observe freshwater, brackish-water, and saltwater creatures from remote ocean inlets. It's way up north in Canada."

"Hmm," the deputy sheriff mumbled as he absently tapped his pen on the open file in front of him. Then he took a breath and quietly, in an uninterested manner, asked Katie, "And was it a great adventure?"

"Oh yes, it was fun, but then there was that murder, and that for sure was a bummer."

"Yes, I know all that. It's in my file, and I'm sure that's not the adventure your father was planning." He paused and smiled. "Was it?"

Giving him a puzzled look, Katie shook her head vehemently.

"So sailing and anchoring was the real adventure then. Is that all there was?"

"Well, he didn't plan it, but we did get to see a real Indian village and powwow!"

"And was that special?"

"Yes!" Katie reached down and opened her school backpack, rummaged around, and pulled out a crumpled sheet of paper. "I just finished writing a report for school based on our trip, and it's all about the Canadian Indians. Do you want me to read it to you?"

Janeva interrupted. "I don't think this is related to anything, so—"

Deputy Sheriff Dugud looked up and said, "So you don't want me to question your daughter about the powwow?"

"Oh no," Janeva replied. "It's just that Katie is very detail oriented, and, well, you might just get more than you bargained for."

Katie broke in, looking her mother in the eye. "This is a murder investigation, and just maybe my information could be critical." Then she began to read from her school report after noting that her parents had forbidden her from including anything about the murder. "'My Summer Holiday. We hiked to a native Indian village that we thought would be close to where our boat was anchored at Chatterbox Falls. But it was really far, and we hiked for a long time until we finally came to the native Indian village. Canadian Indians don't like to be called Indians or natives and prefer to call themselves "First Nations" instead. Our timing was super lucky because they were having what we would call a party of sorts. They call it a potlatch. First Nations people from all over that part of the Canadian mainland, or what we call the Pacific Northwest, were involved in a sort of singing and dancing that took place in their traditional longhouse.

"'We had a very long hike up a mountain trail through a thick forest; then we had to walk over white chalk beds that were the remains of centuries of clam harvests; then…'"

As Katie read her report, Janeva's mind drifted, remembering the forest. It was thick and heavy with moss and the most beautiful arbutus trees with their crooked trunks and red, flaking bark folding off in layers. She remembered that an ominous and threatening pair of large bald eagles had circled overhead silently, watching their every move.

"'The potlatch was good,'" Katie continued reading. "'The Haida people call it a Nuu-Chah-Nulth, and during the ceremony, they wear masks and chant a prayer to protect them from the diseases that the white man inflicted upon them a long, long time ago and that almost wiped out their nation. So now, they hold a Nuu-Chah-Nulth any time they think their way of life is being threatened. What we saw was everyone dancing to the traditional drumbeat. Not like a school dance, they all joined hands, even the little kids and old people, in big circles and moved counterclockwise and bent their bodies up and down, often chanting a strange song. Finally, when everyone got quiet and still, an elder told the story of their origins at the inlet.'"

Looking up, Katie said, "This part is in quotations because I copied it from the brochure." Then, looking back at her paper, she continued. "'"Many times ago when the earth was in beautiful harmony, a fight broke out between the giant ocean whale and the giant land bear. The bear threw huge chunks of land at the whale, and the whale fired massive high waves of water at the bear, and then, high in the sky, the real lord, the eagle, determined to show them both who was the master of all things, caused a sudden great ball of fire to rocket down from the heavens and smashed into the land. It exploded and caused all the land to burst into a massive fireball, and when the land finally cooled, it left behind a mountain and a great hollow that was filled by the sea." And that, they say, is how the inlet and mountain came to be.'

"The end." Katie smiled, clearly pleased with her report.

"Thanks. I'm sure you do very well in school," the deputy sheriff said, and Katie admitted that she had an A in almost every class. Dugud turned to Janeva. "This potlatch and the Indian village aren't mentioned in the files. Do you have anything to add?"

"Not really. As far as I could tell, the real reason for the potlatch event was a political rally of sorts to raise awareness of a planned pipeline extension from Alberta to ocean tankers. Those tankers would fill up with raw petroleum or bitumen right in that gorgeous inlet as the embarkation point in shipping the petroleum to Asia. Some of the organizers, like the elder who recited the poetic story of their origins, were dressed like native Indians with feathered headdress and moccasin slippers, but when I googled them, I found out that some were well-known environmental activists from British Columbia. One woman, I found out, was a physician who had graduated in medicine from Stanford University in California. So I guess she is now back in BC helping her people."

"That might be important," noted Dugud. "Do you remember her name?"

"Sorry, no; that was a long time ago, but I think that Google keeps a record of everyone's every search forever, so you can probably get it somehow."

"Were Lorenzo or any of you involved in this pipeline venture?"

"Not as far as I know. The pipeline dilemma was interesting, but since we are not personally in any way involved in the oil industry and live in a different country, we didn't think much of this issue. In fact, as your file should show, we didn't even know Lorenzo, so I can't answer any questions about his business interests. He was obviously very rich, and I suppose he might have had investments in the petroleum export business. I get the impression from the news that Asia is in need of imported petroleum, so I can see why this issue is topical now."

"You saw these First Nations people up close. Do you think that any of them were fired up enough to want to hurt or kill any of the people in the yachts?"

"What? Oh no. It wasn't like that at all!" Janeva exclaimed and added, "It was more like an education event."

"Education event?" the deputy sheriff repeated, confused. "Education about what?"

"Bitumen extraction," Katie said, jumping in.

"What?"

"You know, oil from the tar sands," Katie said in a know-it-all way.

"Oh, so they were protesting?" Deputy Sheriff Dugud asked.

"No, not really. Not in that sense," said Janeva, "and they all seemed to be reasonable and to know what they were talking about. I was impressed that they made a kind of balanced case and even had handouts that stated that bitumen extraction, transport, and shipment would certainly influence their coastal marine ecosystems. Some speakers identified possible risks and even what they felt were certain environmental impacts that would happen right there on their coast. But we had to leave long before the potlatch was over."

Janeva felt it important to relate what she'd read—"I gathered that recently there was a minor fuel spill right off the heart of that region they call the Great Bear Rainforest. The Heiltsuk First Nations watched in horror as their seafood-harvesting area was contaminated probably for decades, so we have a better appreciation of their concern."

Katie jumped in. "I looked it up online for my school report. Did you know that in just the port of Vancouver, Canada, more than seven hundred seventy thousand liters of fuel have spilled in the past ten years, so this is *really* important." Then she added that the Heiltsuk spill was just part of a small tugboat's fuel, but the planned pipeline would support 348 Aframax-sized tankers, and each tanker was the size of two football fields. Then she caught her mother's eye and got back on topic, noting that sometimes the potlatch might go on for as long as three days.

"Yes," her mom went on, "so we missed the rest of the event. But thinking back, it was a memorable and interesting once-in-a-lifetime event for us."

"Hmm. That is interesting. Did you keep any of those handouts?"

"Yes, I think so; why?"

"Just in case this is a new direction that might be worth following up. What happened next?"

"Well, that's when I found the chip," Katie said.

"Yes, we are back to the chip." Rubbing his chin, the deputy sheriff flipped through the pages of his file until he found the page he was looking for. He took a moment to review the page and then looked up at Janeva and Katie. "You said in your statement that Wiffy said she had killed Lorenzo because she wanted computer information and that maybe it was related to the chip."

"I've gone over and over the event endlessly, and it's the only explanation that makes sense."

Janeva then recounted the whole event from her memory. Katie didn't have anything more to add.

"You are aware," said Dugud, "that we are always restricted in the information we can divulge while an investigation is ongoing, but in cold cases like this, sometimes we stimulate the memory of a witness by reviewing and sharing some information. Hopefully, something in the investigation might trigger a memory or a forgotten clue. I need your collaboration and assistance if I'm going to make progress on this Lorenzo case, so if you agree to help, then I'll share some confidential information with you."

Dugud glanced at each of them and continued. "Confidential means you must not discuss or disclose it until the case is resolved and we grant you permission. This is both to assist our investigation and to protect you. In any case that involves murder, we must assume the possibility that witnesses could be at some degree of unappreciated risk. Certainly, we do not want to expose any of the people whose evidence we are compiling to any amount of risk. Do you both agree?"

Katie and Janeva nodded.

"There are some intriguing and confusing aspects of this case."

Now this is actually becoming interesting, thought Janeva. She leaned forward and said, "Like?"

"Well, for example," said Dugud, "Lorenzo's office had already been ransacked and searched before we did our forensic search of his office and possessions. But regarding your chip, we found no evidence that he or anyone in his company used or was involved in making microchips. We explicitly inquired, and the employees denied any knowledge of microchips, so it's not clear whether that chip is another bit of the puzzle or, as we'll discuss later, just a coincident discovery."

"Can I ask questions?" Janeva interrupted. "Of course we want to help, so what else did you find in the office?"

Dugud scanned the inventory and replied, "We did find a large, high-powered microscope and some robotic tools that can be associated with microchip manufacturing, but the company had other uses for that technology. Whoever ransacked the office was careful not to leave any clues and, we suppose, might have taken any evidence that could lead us to solve the crime. Our investigation did not find any useful information. The office was a dead end, just like the chip. In review, as you know, Lorenzo's murderer is assumed to have been the Wiffy whose body was found later, and unless we get new and compelling information, we have to further assume that this murder will remain unsolved. Like you, we tried to connect the microchip to the murder, but it appeared to us that they are not related."

Katie looked crestfallen. "But someone went to lots of trouble to make the chip, and it must have been for something, because it flashed."

"What do you mean flashed?"

"Like a spark. It shot out a flash of light."

"Hold on," said Janeva to her daughter. "That was a reflection of the sunset. You know we listened to you about the flash; we all studied the chip for a long time, and not once did any of us see it flash or spark."

"Good point," said Dugud. "We scanned the chip as well, and certainly it doesn't have a battery, so maybe it was a reflection. We did discover a few interesting things about the chip, but again, they had nothing to do with this case."

"Deputy Sheriff Dugud," a deep, resonating voice bellowed as the door opened, "you know that call you've been waiting for…"

The deputy sheriff was already on his feet and folding up the file as he said, “Ask them to hold for a minute. What line?”

“Four, sir.”

“I have to get this call, but I can tell you that the microscopic dot on the chip surface that looked like dirt was, in fact, a microscopic lens, and the flash that Katie saw was almost certainly a reflection. If the chip had a power source, our examination suggested that with photoelectric cell technology, it might have been capable of taking a photo outline or maybe even a picture, but nothing about the chip was special or superior technology. Our experts noted that current chips are already advanced from the one you found. So it’s unlikely it was hidden to protect its technology—in our view, certainly not worth hiding or transporting to a different country. Anyway, whatever the reason for making the chip, it is old technology now and certainly unrelated to our murder investigation. So despite the fact that Katie found the microchip close to the crime scene, even if it was able to take a photo outline of her, it has nothing to do with this case, so here it is.”

“Really? Do you think it took a picture of me?” Katie asked, intrigued.

“Well, no, but as I said, it had a lens, and our technicians reported that if powered, this technology can be used to produce an image outline of your face rather than a real photo. The only other information on the chip was a microscopic bar code that didn’t refer to anything that our investigators could determine. So please keep the chip safe just in case we ever need to see it again, but it isn’t evidence.

We simply can't store everything that well-meaning people bring to us as possible evidence, so it's yours again." With that, he gave Katie the chip, and with a quick nod, he left the room.

"I'll show you out," the other police officer said.

"Cool," Katie said as she studied the half-inch-by-half-inch chip. "Do you think this tiny little chip could really have taken a photo outline of me?"

Ushering them out, the other police officer, looking rather overworked, practically propelled them out the door. "I'm sure Deputy Sheriff Dugud will be in touch with you if he has any further questions. Right this way."

"Mom, he said to keep it secret, and then he didn't tell us a secret. I wish he didn't have to leave for that phone call; then he would have told us the secret," Katie said. She stomped her feet in annoyance like she'd seen on TV, and they were led out of the police station.

Chapter 3

Like most self-employed people, the Jags didn't get much time off, and when they occasionally both got a weekend, they were out on their sailboat. When they couldn't get away on the boat, they did the next best thing and met their friends at the yacht club. It was Friday night. Janeva left work early and picked up Katie from school, and they drove to the yacht club, where Katie could hang out with her group of longtime yacht-club friends. The Jags looked forward to an evening of dinner and socializing with their best sailing friends, Greg and Steph.

Janeva treasured this special block of time before the others arrived. Just as she had done as a child, she sat at the lounge window and absorbed the view over the bay. Daydream time. They were members of the yacht club because her grandfather had been one of the founding members when this part of the bay was a collection of factories, sawmills, log booms, and warehouses. Now the yacht club was almost certainly one of the most valuable pieces of waterfront property in the area. She had inherited her share from her grandfather and was one of two hundred shareholders who owned the clubhouse and its property. The other more than three hundred members were not owners, but they all paid the same yearly fee. *What a beautiful place*, she thought, *and it is partly mine.* Of course, she admitted to herself, the Jags could never afford the initiation fee required to join now. The yearly dues and boat moorage were already a financial challenge.

She watched the beautiful sun setting on the flotilla of Friday racers, all displaying the yacht-club burgee on their starboard shroud just below the spreader. As she watched, she saw them all furling their sails, and she recalled a fond memory of herself when she was learning. She could see the crew of one of the sloops balanced in the bow pulpit, carefully down hauling the jib and unclipping the jib luff from the forestay. All the sailboats were attaching fenders and motoring back to their slot in the yacht-club moorage. Sailing was an art that required practice and stamina, but maneuvering the boat back into tight quarters, especially in any wind or current, was the challenge that some thought was the real measure of a skipper. Helmsmen always knew that they were on display as they entered the marina.

***

"There you are, right where I expected," said her husband, Thomas Jag. "I'll find Katie. I just saw Greg and Steph parking, so why don't you find us a spot in the lounge or dining room?"

Thomas also felt at home here at the club. This was the place where he truly relaxed and forgot about work. In the boat, on the water, he was emotionally free from the challenges of earning a living day to day. It did not hurt that the social connections at the club could be subtly related to business prosperity. Katie had grown up at the club, and the kids of other club members were her good friends. In the clubhouse, she chummed around with them in the game room, and she met them at the outstations when they were sailing. Here on the docks, the staff, some who treated her like their own daughter, recognized her. What a difference from school, where she felt excluded from close friendships; here she had real friends.

"It feels like déjà vu," said Thomas, who after finding Katie, sat down, laughing. The group was sitting at the same cluster of comfortable leather chairs and couch they had occupied the Friday before. The group consisted of Trent Braise-Bottom III and Greg and Steph Writeman. Greg and Steph were not only sitting on the same couch they had sat on the week before but also in the same places. They were the Jags' best and closest friends, even though they were powerboaters and the Jags were dedicated sailboaters.

The sailing-powerboating rivalry had been a source of friendly banter between sailors and steamers for more than a hundred years. After a few drinks at the club, it could become a loud, even rollicking source of great amusement. Real sailors bragged endlessly about how little money they spent on fuel, and the powerboaters countered with time and convenience—turn a switch, and they could get to where they were going quickly and go straight where they wanted to go, avoiding the crap of tacking and gybing. Sailboaters smugly noted that, as in life, it is the journey and not the destination that counts. And so the debate went on.

In his day, Greg was an excellent sailboat skipper and racer, and in their younger years, Thomas and Greg had had quite the amiable rivalry as they sparred for first place in the yacht-club racing fleet. They hadn't changed. Thomas, at five foot ten, had thick, wavy, dark-brown hair and a strong, muscular body. And Greg, his opposite, stood half a foot taller at six foot three. He was lean and athletic, with a mop of straight blond hair falling over his right eye that he was always sweeping back. Competitive racing days were now a thing of the past because the Jags had a forty-foot cruising sailboat, and Greg and Steph a fifty-four-foot luxury, diesel-powered cabin cruiser named *Write-Now*.

"Where did Trent wander off to?" Janeva inquired.

"Look to your left," Steph said.

Janeva was dyslexic, so of course, she looked to her right.

"Your other left; he is right over there." Steph laughed and pointed across the room toward a short, rounded man with thinning brown hair and glasses standing at the bar. The rest of them were respectable but casually dressed in nice jeans (ripped jeans were not allowed) or khakis and nice blouses or shirts, but not Trent. As usual, he was in a dark-gray suit and tie.

"Do you think he always wears suits because he is British?" Janeva asked Steph.

Giggling, Steph said, "I do think he does all his shopping at Harrods in London. Could it be his overbearing mother who makes him wears suits?"

"By the sound of things, she is rather domineering, and she did make him move back into that old Victorian house with her after his wife died."

"I wonder if she lays out his suits for him to wear each day." They laughed together.

Trent was an anachronism to the little group of friends. Since the death of his wife, he had hung around, and now they just accepted him as part of their group. Even more surprising was that Trent was not a sailor. He did not sail and even boasted about it. The others rather suspected that he wasn't comfortable on the water, but here he was, always at the yacht club. Through his behavior, Trent hinted that he was financially pretty well-off. Some suspected that his love of the yacht club was more the love of chumming up to many of the wealthy and influential members.

"Well," Janeva said, "you'll never guess where Katie and I were this afternoon."

"Ha," said Steph. "I'll guess that you did exactly what we did the other day and went down to the grubby, stained, intimidating, smelly police station."

"Humph, you're right. Does that mean that you were already interviewed and didn't tell me?"

"It just happened, and the policeman asked us to not tell, but now that we've all been interrogated and cross-examined, let's compare notes. What did he tell you?"

"Actually, the policeman was very nice and not threatening. He asked us the usual questions, but we didn't have any helpful answers."

Realizing that Steph was looking at her quizzically, Janeva quickly summarized. "Katie told him about the potlatch and was a bit disappointed when he informed us that the chip she found and was so protective of, as far as they could determine, was a false alarm and apparently had nothing to do with any of the events. I surmise that they have eliminated all of us as having any relationship to the crime, and, disappointing to Katie, they have discounted that the chip was in any way related to or was even a clue regarding the Lorenzo murder.

"Since Katie found it and the police don't want it, it looks like it will be her souvenir. Judging from the size of the file and the information that I saw him glancing over, it's clear that the RCMP had had us all investigated and that there was a file on each of us even before we even got home from that inlet in British Columbia. We were all subject to investigation as a consequence of that murder, and it's possible that we've even been studied since our return."

"Well," said Steph, "as far as I'm concerned, the murder is solved, the murderer is deceased, the chip is absolved, and I thank God that the Lorenzo thing is finally behind us. It's almost frightening to think that this tragedy in some subconscious way connects us all for life now"—she glanced pointedly at Trent, who was at the bar apparently taste testing different wines—"just because we were all at the same place at the same time as a disaster. Instead of remembering an adventure, a great time boating, and a vacation, all we remember is a ghastly murder."

After an uncomfortable pause, Thomas redirected the conversation. "What is it about you guys with powerboats who keep talking about how good any voyage was?" he said with a grin. "It's the journey, not the destination. I think you are really just a bit envious. No halyard or jib sheets—just diesel, exhaust, get there fast, and contribute to climate change."

"Give us a break. Enough anti-stinkpots rhetoric. Are you coming sailing in the Caribbean with us or not?" Greg demanded.

"What are you talking about, Greg?" Janeva asked.

"Where have you been, Janeva? Catherine, Lorenzo's widow, offered us the use of her catamaran in the Caribbean this February. It's docked now in the British Virgin Islands. Are you guys in with us or not?"

"What? I don't get it," Janeva stammered, confused. "They had a catamaran?"

"You know she never liked boating and would only go out on *Atlantis*, their hundred-foot yacht, but her husband, Lorenzo, loved sailing, and he kept a forty-foot catamaran in the Caribbean. I understand that he and his buddies would fly down in the private jet and explore the tropical islands."

"And she has offered it to us?"

"Loaned, not offered. Catherine has no use for the boat and wants to sell it, but she has never even seen it and doesn't know what condition it's in or anything. So, quid pro quo, we get a free vacation in exchange for testing the boat out, taking some photos, doing an inventory, and reporting back to her on its condition and the possible need for servicing or repair, so the broker can estimate its sale value."

The timing was good, because Thomas had been working so hard that he was close to exhaustion. It was a good exhaustion brought about by the unexpected growth and success of his company. His company built and designed 3-D printers, and his brand seemed suddenly to have become very popular—though actually, it had been a consequence of months of hard day-and-night work. Thomas had been flying around the globe and working long hours in response to customer demand.

Thinking about Thomas's company, Janeva reflected on Katie's sudden enthusiasm for 3-D printing. Maybe it was a ploy to win her father's affection; 3-D printing was her father's passion and his business, and now his research into the technology was certainly paying off. Why had Katie undertaken night after night to get her father to instruct her in the magic of 3-D printing in order to make a cross to hang on a necklace? It had made her realize that her daughter was growing up. Katie came home excited about all the different kinds of 3-D printing in her father's little factory and had designed and constructed her own cross using selective laser sintering and fused deposition modeling. It seemed simple, but it took Katie more than twenty false attempts before she built the cross just right.

"Thomas, you have been working so hard…maybe we should consider it," Janeva started to say, but she was interrupted by Katie, who had lagged behind because she was walking and texting at the same time. It was a skill her mother had yet to master, and Janeva was always amazed at how she managed it. Another of her many skills was selective hearing; she was not one to miss an opportunity.

"Yes, let's go, please, please, please!"

"Now you've gone and done it," replied Thomas, putting his arm around Janeva and grinning.

Katie thumped down into the large leather armchair and warmed to her subject.

"Please! If Greg and Steph are going…"

"And how do you know that Greg and Steph are going?" Janeva asked her, as she had been several minutes behind them and couldn't have heard Greg's initial comment about the Caribbean.

"Steph told me. They are going on their way to Haiti," came the smug know-it-all reply.

***

Greg was a highly qualified and sought-after physician, and his wife, Steph, had been an environmental blog writer until she inherited a considerable amount of money. They later both quit their regular jobs and devoted their skills to volunteering for health organizations, such as Médecins Sans Frontières and the World Health Organization. This coming week at the yacht club women's committee luncheon, she was giving a speech about understanding earthquake preparedness. Steph hoped it would drive her fund-raising efforts and that the yacht club members' donations would help fill the container of medical supplies for Haiti. Greg and Steph needed to supervise the filling of the container in Florida, then meet the container in Haiti a week later to escort it through customs and supervise its unloading, and then get it to a primitive health-care facility that certainly did not resemble any American hospital. It didn't make sense to fly back and forth from Florida, so when they got the offer of a boat and a chance to explore the British Virgin Islands, that seemed a perfect fit.

***

Katie did a quick Google search of the style of boat, reported that it could hold both families, and announced again, "We should go with them." She gave her mother a pouty look that implied she should not have doubted her daughter.

"Um, hmm. Yes, that could make sense. I'm sorry I doubted you, honey," Janeva said, still processing the new information and considering the cost. Thinking of the budget, she knew they'd already had a costly summer sailing vacation. Thomas's company might be doing well, but they'd invested all their savings and borrowed a lot of money to get to this point. Spending more was financially risky.

"When are you going?" she asked, turning from Katie to Greg and Steph. But before they could answer, she turned back to Katie. "We really can't take you out of school."

Again Katie was way ahead and replied, "As it happens, it's the same week my school's off for Ski Week." Katie had obviously prepared for her mother's expected negative reasons to stay home. Thomas smiled at his daughter.

"Well, that's convenient, isn't it? What does your father say? Thomas, can you get off work?" Janeva smiled at her daughter

"Hmm." Thomas pulled out his smartphone. "What were the dates again?" *A relaxing trip to the Caribbean might be the thing to help Janeva get over the nightmares that started up again when the police called wanting to review the Lorenzo file*, he thought.

"February fourteenth to twenty-third," Greg replied. "Come on, guys; opportunities like this don't come up every day. The only cost would be meals and travel to the Caribbean, and you must have tons of air miles that you can use to cover the flight."

"So far no trips or major meetings planned that week, so…why not?" Thomas said as he scrolled through screens on his phone. Then he fist pumped Katie in a manner that made Janeva suspect the two of them had planned this all along.

"What is the fist pump for?" Trent asked as he seated himself in the corresponding leather chair to the one Katie was sitting in. Janeva told Trent about the possible sailing trip to the Caribbean, and then the conversation lagged as everyone looked over his or her menu.

Trent took the opportunity to ask, "Why would anyone in their right mind actually consider getting aboard a little floating pod in the middle of a sea that was known to be full of pirates, strong winds, and high waves, and spend a fortune to just get there? Take time off and stay home, or if you must, stay in a luxury hotel, go to Hawaii, and sit on the beach, but…to bounce around in the sea—you've got to be crazy." He looked around for a reaction.

Thomas could not resist and took the bait. "This is a yacht club, believe it or not," he said. "Boats are unique among the works of man. It is believed that no other creation has existed so long with so little change. The boat antedates the wheel, pottery, and even the domestication of animals. Boats are a way of life. They are an escape; they are our magic carpet that puts the sailor completely on his own the moment he leaves shore. Life becomes a matter of weather, gusts, squalls, currents, waves, the set of sails, the distance to a port, expanding horizons, and—"

"Again, enough already," said Greg. "We've all heard the lecture before." Thomas was often trapped into defending boats and sailing, provoked by Trent, and everyone enjoyed a good laugh.

"OK," Trent said. "I guess we're at loggerheads."

"I'm vindicated finally," said Thomas. "Trent can't help but use nautical terms. I do sort of wonder if you know that a loggerhead was a tool for sealing pitch into the seams of wooden sailing ships to plug leaks. Sometimes, red-hot, they were fired into the rigging of an enemy ship. Now to use yet another nautical term, it's your turn to start bowing and scraping."

"OK, OK, I do know that the Royal Navy cocked hat was called a scraper, so here's my servile salute." And he pulled off his pretend hat and bowed to Thomas.

"I don't know why you all spend so much time studying the menu every Friday. It doesn't change!" Katie complained.

"Not true. Sometimes there are specials, and I like to try different things. Not like you, who picks a cheeseburger with trans-fat-covered fries every week," Janeva retorted.

"We're going to check out the buffet," Steph said as she and Greg stood to walk over to the far corner of the lounge, where the large Friday buffet was set up.

Trent finished filling out his chit. The yacht club worked on a chit system, and members would either fill out their own chits or have the staff do it for them and then bill the members at the end of the month.

"Wiffy didn't kill herself, you know," Trent said with a shake of his head.

"Where did that come from?" Janeva asked, confused. *How*, she wondered, *did we go from the Caribbean to menus and buffets to that?*

"Trent," Thomas said gently, "that memory will be with you the rest of your life, but somehow you have to put it behind you. It was a horror that could not have been prevented. It's no one's fault. No one is to blame. You must let it go. Every time this thought arises, you must focus on a different thought."

They all knew that Trent's wife had murdered men, imprisoned Janeva, and exploded the yacht before she jumped off a bridge to her death.

"She was depressed, and we now know that after what happened, she had reasons to be depressed," Thomas noted further. "Depression is an illness, not a choice, and she'd hid it from everyone."

"I know that, but…I know her—I mean, knew her—and she was a fighter. She would never give up," Trent replied as he reached for his dark and stormy, his favorite cocktail—dark rum and ginger beer with a twist of lime—and then turned away to hide the tears.

They all knew Trent's wife as Wiffy, which was such an embarrassing title that they all avoided ever calling her by that name. Wiffy was his term of affection and a short form of her real name, Wisteria, which she'd refused to respond to even as a child. In any case, Wiffy had impressed them all. She had an innate understanding of mathematics and a PhD in physics. She had taught engineering at the university and seemed to be an attentive listener even to those who were not in her academic league.

Despite those credentials, she also came across as quiet and modest. After she had died, though, there were rumors that she was even more than she seemed and that she had a secret life in the information game. This was especially hard for Janeva to believe, and certainly, she could not think of Wiffy as a female James Bond, but events and her recurring terrible dreams exposed Wiffy as some kind of psychotic murderer. There was nevertheless a rumor that Wiffy had somehow acquired secret information about certain research, businesses, and maybe even the military, and that she had passed the information along to some mysterious other party. Corporate secrets, new science, nanotechnology, drones, and nuclear subs were all just speculation, but of course, the more they or anyone pondered, the more intriguing it all became—and probably equally unrealistic.

The accepted explanation of her death was that she committed suicide. But the most terrifying moment in Janeva's life was when Wiffy had held her at gunpoint, and then to Janeva's horror, she had witnessed Wiffy shoot and kill a man, for no apparent reason. Everything, the whole event, was now a confused blur. Who said what, who did what, and where? Now the memory was just part of a completely bad dream.

After the murder and the explosion of Catherine's yacht, Wiffy had disappeared. She was the subject of an unsuccessful nationwide police search. Rumors and false sightings were common for a short time, but they did not find any substantive clues to her whereabouts until her body was dragged out of a river months later. The coroner concluded suicide. The forensic evidence included some footage from a highway bridge entrance that had closed-circuit TV. It showed, in retrospect, a nighttime figure of a person who certainly resembled Wiffy and was interpreted as probably being Wiffy walking purposefully onto the bridge. The police believed this was the place where she committed suicide.

This bridge crossed a deep river canyon and was some miles above the place where her body was subsequently found.

"Thomas, you know there was someone else involved. Who was paying her; who was forcing her?" Trent continued. "And Janeva, you also heard her say the name Max. Who is Max? There is more to this. Wiffy was smarter and more accomplished than me—maybe more than any of us. Max might be a clue. Wiffy couldn't kill and certainly wouldn't kill unless she was under enormous pressure. Somehow the police and even we are missing the full picture."

"I agree with Trent. I don't think that Wiffy was a criminal mastermind," Janeva agreed.

"Janeva, it's over!" Thomas said. "The case is closed. Don't go looking for trouble. Forget it. Now is the time to put this behind us. Don't encourage this line of thought; it will only bring back old and terrible memories. I'm tired of talking about this," Thomas growled and shook his head of dark, wavy hair in frustration as he glared at his wife. No one ever said anything, but from experience, they all understood that Janeva had to be redirected quickly, because they all knew she harbored a secret obsession for crime detection. This wasn't the first time that Thomas had to remind his loving wife that not everything they didn't understand was a clue to a conspiracy. Janeva, her friends believed, could turn the simplest life event into a theoretical police investigation.

Frustrated, Janeva couldn't resist replying, "Listen, Thomas, I heard you, and I know you think I'm paranoid. But we were, in some unexplained, totally random way, associated with a series of horrible crimes, and no one yet has come forward with any answer about why. What was it all about?"

Trent said, "There's another clue, and it's the bar code on the chip."

Janeva looked over and shrugged. "So what?"

Katie, who had designed a cross holder for the chip using one of her dad's 3-D printers and was wearing it on a necklace, pulled the chip out. "I don't see any bar-code numbers," she said as she looked intensely at the chip. "Just the circles and some tiny lines."

"Katie, can I take a look at that chip?" her father asked.

Studying the chip carefully, Thomas asked Trent, "What exactly did the detective say about the numbers?"

Trent replied that the detective had said that someone had put an identification or bar code into that chip, but despite all the study, the forensic team had not been able to make anything out of the code. It certainly didn't help in any way to identify the source or role of the chip. It did not resemble any retail-store code. Their forensic analysis concluded that it was without meaning.

"Hmm…it must mean something," Thomas said, musing. He quickly pulled out his cell phone and held the chip under the table. Although the use of cell phones in the club was considered impolite, teens and twentysomethings generally ignored the request but did grudgingly turn off their volume on their phones. He took a discreet photo of the chip.

Their food arrived, effectively stopping the depressing and morbid discussion about Wiffy, Lorenzo, chips, and bar codes. Katie took her chip back and reinserted it into its center space on her necklace, and they went through the usual ritual of passing the plates around. The yacht-club food was good, but the service could be random. Some of the staff had been around for years and were more like old friends, and they knew what the group liked and how they liked it. However, that evening they were being served by new part-time staff. Two twentysomething servers plunked the dishes down randomly on the table. Katie handed her mother her salad, and Thomas handed her the burger and fries that had ended up in front of him.

"Who ordered the pasta?" Steph asked, and so it went until everyone had what he or she had ordered. Quiet ensued as the group tucked into their dinners.

After the first pangs of hunger had been satisfied, the conversation turned to the general, teasing and laughing about past boating trips and cruises.

Then Katie and Thomas started their regular postdinner debate over what she should order for dessert, Thomas wanting the mocha cheesecake, and Katie, who did not like cheesecake, countering with a flourless chocolate tart.

Janeva laughed and pointed out to Thomas that this was Katie's dessert, not his. If he wanted one, he should order one.

"But I don't want to order a dessert. I just want a bit of the chocolate cheesecake."

"Thomas, I'll order the cheesecake, and you can have a bit of mine if you like," Steph said in her lyrical voice.

"Steph, please tell me your secret," Janeva demanded. "How do you stay so slim?"

"I don't know. It must be good genes." She shrugged and gave her endearing, sweet smile.

Shaking her head, Janeva ordered her big treat: a low-fat decaf latte. *These days*, she thought, *I actually feel pretty good about my weight.* Out loud she said to Steph, "I suppose I could get to my ideal weight if I gave up alcohol and chocolate and bread and everything good, but I want to enjoy life too."

Laughing, Steph replied, "At least you keep in good shape by exercising, doing boot camp three times a week, and then weight training twice a week with your personal trainer."

"You are not helping. I have no idea how you maintain that perfect petite figure without exercising. And speaking of exercising: don't forget my morning yoga stretches and weekend long walks or hikes. Plus, as 'crew' on our sailboat, I hoisted the halyard and sheeted in the jib as we tacked and gybed around, racing all other boats on the water, and that actually is hard work," Janeva teased as she looked at her slim, composed, and elegant best friend. *It's a good thing she is so nice*, Janeva thought.

Laughing, Steph said, "I'm sure it is. Your Thomas loves to race. I'm sure you do a lot of sheeting and trimming the sails to get maximum speed regardless of where you are sailing."

"You know him too well." Janeva laughed.

***

Later that evening, when the Jag family arrived home from the club, Katie pressed her dad about the computer chip. "But, Dad," Katie whined, "your computer company is leading edge; our local police can't be that advanced."

"Katie," a tired Thomas said, "stop it. Deputy Sheriff Dugud told you that experts in computer technology examined the chip. My business relies on software and technology, but we design and make 3-D printers, remember? That is different from chip technology. Whether it's an accident or the plot of a brilliant mastermind crook, I think we can assume that the chip is a false trail; it just misleads everyone, including you. It is a decoy. It is not related in any way to the murder that occurred, and it almost certainly is jetsam from some capsized boat, or it was just dropped by a child. It is not associated in any way with the murder. It's time now to forget it."

Half listening to the ongoing banter, Janeva reflected that on the dinnertime conversation. She thought it was the first time that Trent had spoken about any aspect of the murders or about Wiffy in any detail. It was as if he was finally trying to remove the memory of those terrible thoughts. *What is the connection?* she wondered. Was Wiffy saying "Max" just a figment of her imagination? A casual acquaintance murdered in a remote Canadian inlet had brought her to within a hair's breadth of death.

She wanted it over, but after dinner, almost reflexively, she had said to Trent, "You must have thought about this endlessly."

He had sighed. "Yes, of course. I can't get it out of my mind. We were married. She was many things. We had a good, comfortable lifestyle. Why would she turn to crime? It is just too hard to believe. Why would she want to steal information from a computer? She used computers, but she wasn't skilled. She couldn't search someone else's computer without training and direction. How would she even know what to look for? That wasn't the Wiffy I knew and married and shared my life with; that was the action of a deranged person. Someone was behind it; she was being pushed, threatened. Don't tell me that this case is closed. I don't think we are even close to understanding what really happened."

"Thomas," Janeva said, breaking out of her reverie, "I was just thinking about Wiffy and Lorenzo, and I was wondering if—"

"Janeva," her husband said, interrupting her midsentence. "The police have virtually closed this case. It is over, and we should just put it behind us now. It is no longer any of our business, and past events have proven that it might even be dangerous to get involved. Please stop trying to be an Agatha Christie or Miss Marple. Think of Katie and me, your long-suffering husband. So how about it? Let's just stay out of it. Thank you. The end."

A few moments later, as Janeva was still struggling with an appropriate response to a sentence that ended with "the end," he continued. "In fact, let's just throw the bloody chip away. It has brought us nothing but sorrow and bad memories. Throw it into the composting bin, and it will be buried as fertilizer and gone forever, and we will get on with our lives. We can take a sail in the Caribbean as a eulogy for the damn chip." He nodded, happy with his proclamation.

"You are not going to destroy my chip," Katie said softly but with determination. "I promised Deputy Sheriff Dugud that I'd look after it in case they ever needed to see it again."

That ended the conversation. It was getting late, and Katie took off upstairs to her room. She pressed the chip against her chest protectively. She had hoped to see the flash of light again, but no luck. No one believed her, but still, she secretly believed—knew, in fact—that the chip was important.

Chapter 4

Running a yacht club was a bigger challenge than Betty Rothman had anticipated. Moving down to this lovely city should have been a dream, but Betty was single and alone. Life had been good to her. She had assumed a senior role in a big company, chosen to move here to integrate new technology into the company, made some unexpectedly good investments, and taken early retirement. But her life had been focused on work; she had no family and found retirement boring. Sailing was her hobby, and when she was approached by a recruitment firm to apply for the job of general manager of the local and prestigious yacht club, she couldn't resist. And that was how a few years earlier, she had found herself as manager of the club. She had never explained why she'd given up her previous job, but certainly, her academic and management credentials were impressive and her references outstanding.

A further bit of luck was that she got along well with Terri Turnell, the membership director. Terri had been with the club for years and knew all the members. The membership ranged from real sailors who had a passion for sailing to nonsailors who pretended to be yachties but were really there at a company's expense to win friends—investment-potential friends. Other members were there strictly for social contact.

Successful management of a private club was in part related to intimate knowledge of all the members. Terri could welcome and call them by name, ask about their family or job, or hope that they were over that nasty cold. Betty was impressed that Terri knew them all.

Now, the club was undergoing its scheduled change in volunteer leadership, including the executive committee. Betty was especially eager to get Janeva Jag involved and had selected her as marketing chair. Terri seemed a bit uncertain and remarked that the Jag woman in her opinion was an obsessive-compulsive, detail-focused individual who would probably pry into everyone's business, and she was dyslexic. Nevertheless, despite her misgivings, Terri did not have another person in mind and agreed to at least approach Mrs. Jag to see if she might be interested.

Betty had her own reasons for wanting Mrs. Janeva Jag on the executive committee. Mrs. Jag, she determined, had the skills she needed and was someone she could trust. She wanted a new leadership; plus, she had questions about some of the club's financial details. Both Terri and Betty knew that Mrs. Jag would be attending the lecture luncheon today, so this was their opportunity to initiate the recruitment.

***

Tuesday midday found Janeva back at the yacht club for the club's regular ladies' tea luncheon, an event she usually avoided because it was hard for her to get away from the office. In truth, she didn't enjoy these events. When asked why she did not attend more often, she usually made her pun: "They just aren't my cup of tea." The luncheons, she thought, were great for the yacht-club women who enjoyed a reason to get dressed up and socialize, but she did not have much in common with this crowd. She did not play bridge and was not part of this foundation or that committee, and she had a family and a business to manage.

Today she had made an exception because her best friend, Steph, was the guest speaker. Steph's talk was titled "You, Me, and the Earthquake," and anyone living close to San Francisco or within a hundred miles of the San Andreas Fault was sensitive to potential tectonic-plate movement. So it was going to be a full house. Steph's real reason was to raise money to purchase medical supplies to send to Haiti.

Janeva arrived early, hoping to see Steph and offer her some words of encouragement because she knew that Steph hated public speaking. However, as she approached the registration desk to find her name tag, Betty and Terri greeted her.

"Janeva, how wonderful to see you at one of our events," said Terri in her cultured drawl. Terri, who was in her midforties, looked fabulous as usual in a designer knee-length dress with heels that were so high, Janeva was worried she might break her ankle. Her thick, jet-black hair was perfectly styled in a bob that was longer in the front than the back.

Betty looked Janeva up and down through her stylish glasses. "Janeva would be perfect to chair the marketing committee."

"Oh, Betty, you are so clever," Terri said enthusiastically. "Yes, Janeva would be brilliant."

Betty smiled at Terri and then turned to Janeva. "It's time you got involved with the club, Janeva."

"I'd love to, but I have a company to run," Janeva stammered. She had started her company, Jag Tags, which made custom bag tags, after many years of failing to build a marketing career in the corporate world. Despite her best efforts and (she thought) splendid creativity, she just couldn't spell or really write well. It was not from lack of trying or an unwillingness to look words up, but if you have no idea how to spell a word in the first place, then even the dictionary is a challenge. The one word she had learned to spell was dyslexia, and she knew better than anyone that she was dyslexic. Even with spell check, her inability to recognize words caused her to stumble as she tried to climb the corporate ladder. Less innovative fellow employees who did not seem to contribute much in hard work had climbed past her.

Also, she had to really concentrate in order to read, and she wondered if this disability somehow amplified her passion for seeing mystery around every corner. Fortunately, Thomas recognized Janeva's real gifts and how clever she was, and after their daughter was born, Thomas had helped her achieve her goal of starting Jag Tags. It was the third-best decision of her life, marrying Thomas and having Katie being the first two. Once she was her own boss, suddenly dyslexia did not hold her back, and of course, the first thing she did was hire the strongest speller and proofreader she could find. Then began the manufacturing, marketing, and selling of her product, Jag Tags.

Now she was the proud owner of a small but successful company with a range of clients from posh hotels to weddings and corporate functions. *Posh*, she thought to herself, remembering the conversation from the night before, was another sailing expression for "port out starboard home," which of course was the only way the wealthy would consider sailing to East India in the time of the British Empire and the Raj. Moreover, in her flight of ideas, she started to consider how Katie's new understanding of 3-D printing might be an asset to the company: the modern world through the eyes of a thirteen-year-old. But then Terri interrupted her musing.

"But I heard that you are very proud of your employees and how good they are," Terri said.

"Of course I am, but as you both know, the success of any venture relies on everyone doing their own special thing, and it takes us all to make the system work."

"You enjoy this club, don't you?"

"Um, yes, of course."

"Well, we are in the same situation as your company. The executive committee plays a key role in our club, and it needs a marketing chair to make it work," said Betty. Betty was in her late sixties, but you wouldn't know it. She was an imposing figure with steel-gray hair cut short in tight curls, wearing a classic-cut, rose-colored Chanel suit circa 1960 and multiple strings of pearls. As her hard, gray eyes fixed on

Janeva, the younger woman felt like she was back in grade school.

She was on the verge of acquiescing and agreeing to help a bit when Sara Fontaine walked by and was kind enough to say, "Janeva, what's this I hear about you going to the BVIs for Ski Week? Where are you sitting? I was going to call you. Alexa wants to have Katie over for a sleepover and—"

Janeva interrupted her. "Sara, I know Katie would love that." She took Sara's arm with one hand and accepted the name tag that Mitchell, the yacht-club concierge, was handing her with the other hand. She quickly steered Sara away as she nodded with an apologetic look and mumbled, "I'm sorry, but I have to go now; it's important that I talk to Steph before she speaks."

"Thanks for rescuing me," she whispered as she made her escape with Sara. This sly tactic probably would not have worked except that a large group of women arrived, and courtesy demanded that Betty and Terri greet them.

Janeva and Sara moved into the elaborately decorated main dining room of the club. This striking room always took Janeva's breath away, with its windows looking over the ocean. She paused for a moment to enjoy the view and then took in the room's paneled walls, once again noting the trophies, photos of yacht races throughout the years, and models of various famous racing yachts that adorned the dark wood walls and framed the wall of floor-to-ceiling windows. Padded leather chairs surrounded circular tables, each with ten elegant settings of blue-and-red yacht-club china and designer flower centerpieces.

As a rule, Janeva never drank alcohol during the day, but on this occasion, she accepted the glass of chilled chardonnay and maneuvered Sara to a table in the far corner. Sara gave Janeva a puzzled look, but she was one of those easygoing, relaxed people who are a real pleasure to be with, and she said nothing—just went where she was directed.

"Thank you for saving me from Betty and Terri."

Laughing, Sara said, "Those two are hard to resist! They already got me! I'm now the treasurer in charge of finances. It would be great to have you on board."

"But I don't have time to be the marketing chair," Janeva said in despair. "Sorry, but I can't get involved."

"Good luck with that, unless you can find someone to take your place. Betty doesn't know the word no, and if she has decided you are doing it, then it's my guess you will not escape. In a way, you should be flattered that of all the members, she really wants to work with you." Janeva groaned. Sara continued, "It's not so bad, and Betty runs things very efficiently; meetings are exactly one hour long, and it's really not too much time as long as you do things exactly the way Betty wants them done. And she makes sure you get lots of support."

"But she has me pegged for the marketing chair; that's a huge job. Marketing is involved with every event, and it's a yearlong position."

"If you want to escape after just a year, you'd better start planning an excuse, like the extended trip that Sally, your predecessor, took, or move to Palm Desert for six months of the year."

"Groan—do you have to say it like that?"

"What?"

"My predecessor?"

She giggled softly. "Janeva, you're beat, and anyway, I want you on the committee. It will be fun—you'll see."

"Fine, but shouldn't I start off with being on the Christmas committee or auction committee?"

"Those positions fill up fast because, as you said, they aren't year-round." Sara smiled. "But it will be nice for me to have you at the meetings, and we can have dinner or a drink at the club afterward."

"Oh look, there's Trent," exclaimed Janeva. "How come he's always around and now at a women's luncheon meeting?"

"Good question," said Sara, "I just assumed that he was bored and had nothing else to do and hung around the club looking for companionship." She lowered her voice to a whisper. "I think that the one thing he has in common with a lot of the wives, you know, is that they are indifferent to or even dislike boating."

"I really wonder why he joined the club."

Then, before Sara could speculate and answer, Janeva changed the topic. "OK, if I can't get out of marketing, at least I'll make the best of it. We will plan on dinner and drinks together after the meetings. That will be our reward. Now when does Alexa want to have Katie over for that sleepover?"

By the time Janeva and Sara had finished comparing calendars on their iPhones and had found a date that worked, the room and their table had filled up. *Darn*, Janeva thought, *I missed my chance to wish Steph good luck.* However, she caught Steph's eye as she was being introduced and gave her a thumbs-up.

Steph must have been practicing because she gave a wonderful presentation. She eloquently thanked the women's club and then reminded the audience that they all lived in an earthquake zone.

"It's an illusion that the earth is still and unmoving. All the earth's tectonic plates are moving two to four centimeters a year, and they eventually collide. Just reflect, for a moment, that on March 11, 2011, there was an earthquake that drove a twenty-three-meter—more than a sixty-foot-high—wall of ocean as a tsunami into the Japanese town of Ofunato. More than fifteen thousand people drowned, and this in a town of only forty-one thousand people. The debris from the wave of water that swept the coast of Japan is still, years later, washing up on the coast of British Columbia, Canada. And just to really get your attention, in December 2004, a powerful submarine earthquake struck northern Sumatra, and the tsunami killed more than two hundred thirty thousand people. A few years ago, a devastating earthquake in Nepal actually moved the physical location and height of Mount Everest. Thousands of people were displaced from their homes and many killed.

"Americans gave generously and still are giving to assist the many suffering Nepalese women and children. I'll get back to that," she said, "but I want to talk a bit about what happened after the earthquake in Haiti."

Steph noted that the numbers of injured and killed in Nepal were only a fraction of the number of lives destroyed in Haiti and that years after the event, Haiti hadn't recovered. Years after the earthquake, the Haitians were still suffering from disease and poverty. There are not any words to describe what happens when a disaster strikes a situation that is already in crisis, she said.

"Haiti is right here in our own backyard," said Steph. "The scope of the crisis is simply unimaginable. They are in desperate need of help, and we know that it's possible to restore the country. This presentation is not about climate change, but about what happened first was the earthquake, then the hottest summer in sixty years, and then above-average rainfall that fell on people huddled in refugee camps, who then caught the next affliction: cholera. Cholera already infects five million people a year worldwide, and the number dying in Haiti is already, believe it or not, now in the tens of thousands. Imagine for a moment dying from unabated diarrhea and vomiting. Even surviving it is an ordeal unbelievable to us, but it could happen here if we are not prepared."

Then, using a PowerPoint presentation, she went on to detail how she and her husband, Greg, whom she explained was a physician, were going to use the money raised to provide a full container of medical equipment, everything from medication to hospital beds.

"On the surface, it may look to all of you like the main role of this relief is to provide direct and needed medical aid, but there is an even more pressing and important role that this fund-raising will achieve." She hesitated, making sure she had everyone's attention. "What we have learned is that we really have no idea how to cope with the devastating effects of earthquakes. Even in Japan, one of the world's most sophisticated societies, the consequences persist for years and years after the media has lost interest. We in America are not prepared for the event. Maybe worse, we're not even close to understanding or preparing for the aftermath, for the long-term outcomes of these naturally occurring events.

"Any financial support you give will directly assist the people of Haiti, but please know that my husband and I are committed to studying every aspect of the relief program so that we will better understand and be able to initiate and direct an appropriate and effective relief plan for us. For Americans. And be assured that the risk of cholera is with us. So please open up your hearts and wallets to the suffering people of Haiti—with the knowledge that not only are you saving and bettering their lives. Your dollars will also provide valuable knowledge and expertise for the inevitable San Andreas earthquake, which, I hesitate to remind you, is a part of the future of this region."

After her presentation, the room started to clear, except for the cluster of women around Steph asking questions. A thoughtful waiter refilled Janeva's coffee, and she settled down to wait for Steph. But this turned out to be a mistake, because Betty swooped down and plopped herself into the vacant chair beside Janeva. Inwardly groaning, Janeva steeled herself for what was coming: the big "join the executive committee" sales pitch.

"Where is Terri?" Janeva asked, hoping to divert her.

"She is at the front desk writing a check out for your friend Steph. Why?"

"No reason. It's just so unusual to see you two apart," Janeva said.

Betty smiled and with a soft sigh said, "Janeva, you know I deplore gossip, but I have to ask…" She hesitated, and Janeva waited, wondering where this could possibly be going. "They tell me that you helped the police solve Lorenzo's murder."

"Oh." Janeva looked at her in surprise. "Um, that mystery seems to never stop—"

Betty interrupted her. "Please, if you don't mind talking about it, tell me what really happened. I have a personal reason that I prefer to keep that way, and as I hope you know, I do not gossip. Please assure me that this conversation is between the two of us. It is true that I want you on the club board because I do absolutely trust you and respect your ability. For reasons that I would like to remain totally confidential, anything you can tell me about the murder might help me in other ways. Please," she said again, "I would like to hear the real story."

Janeva thought, *I took time off work to encourage a friend and missed that chance because I was interrupted by being recruited into a job I did not want, and now I'm being asked to recount the story of an event that I am trying to forget. What a bizarre day this has turned out to be.*

Feeling trapped, she launched into the story that she had told the police in Canada. "It was the end of summer," Janeva said, "and we were at the end of our sailing holiday up in Princess Louisa Inlet, a beautiful but remote inlet in Canada, when rain and a windstorm forced us to weigh anchor and moor onto the dock. My daughter, Katie, and I climbed up the forest trail to experience a First Nations potlatch that turned out to be a really memorable event. As chance would have it, because of the storm, there was a group of us who otherwise would never have met, but we were all boaters who had taken temporary refuge and tied up at the same dock. Lorenzo and Catherine were there on their hundred-foot Hatteras yacht, and they invited us all to share dinner with them and their friends, including the Braise-Bottoms, Trent and Wiffy, that evening. This was a holiday, so our next-day plan was to sleep in, read our books, and wait out the storm. That plan was destroyed when Lorenzo's cook/housekeeper awakened us, screaming for help. That is when we found out that Lorenzo had been murdered."

Janeva stopped there, hoping that would be enough for Betty, but the older woman just sat nodding for her to continue.

Fortunately, Steph arrived at that moment, and her presence conveniently blocked any further questions from Betty. Steph was beaming. Her presentation had resonated and caught the attention of a number of the audience members, and she already had some promises of donations. Now, she explained, she was faced with the paperwork, including charity tax receipts and media information. Janeva said her good-bye to Betty and walked with Steph to the parking lot.

Chapter 5

Janeva took a deep breath of the warm, tropical Caribbean night air of the British Virgin Islands. It had been a long, long day. Thomas had spent the week in Florida promoting his business at a trade show and conference and had made the short flight earlier in the day to the BVIs. Katie and Janeva had arranged their own flight from the West Coast. Greg and Steph had also been in Florida supervising the loading of the container for Haiti, so they were all going to connect in the BVIs. And if all the flights had been on schedule, everyone would have met up in Tortola in time to go shopping and have a nice dinner together on the boat, but the airlines had other plans that didn't involve them getting to their destination in a timely manner.

"Thank God you are safe," Thomas said as he hugged his wife and daughter hard. "I've been so worried about you."

"Actually, it was fun, but an unexpected adventure," Janeva said, taking the gin martini that Thomas handed her.

"It's been a very long day, and right now I just want to sip my drink and relax."

"It was kind of scary, and we got rained on," Katie said, chirping in, "and I'm hungry."

"I have just the thing, honey." Thomas disappeared into the boat and reappeared with a bag of popcorn and a soda for Katie.

Finally, feeling settled enough to look around, Janeva asked, "Where are Greg and Steph? Did they go out for dinner?"

Laughing, Thomas said, "No, I've been on my own all day. They are stuck in San Juan for the night. Their flight was delayed like yours, and they missed the last flight out."

"Ha. We were clever and found a ride," Katie said, gloating.

"I'm impressed, but what ferry company did you use? I thought the last one left at four o'clock, and it's ten now."

"Um…it wasn't a company; it was just two guys with fast powerboats who taxied us for cash late at night and in the dark."

"What? Now I'm really glad I didn't know that before. I would have been really worried." Thomas glared at his wife. "You shouldn't take chances like that, Janeva. Especially with Katie."

"But, Dad…it wasn't just us. We were in a group; we were all on the plane together."

"Oh, uh, well, I guess that's a bit better. How many of you were there?"

"Um, twenty, right, Mom?" She looked to Janeva, who nodded in agreement. "But eight went on the smaller boat and twelve on our boat. I made Mom take the bigger boat, and it was the right choice. We would have gotten way wetter in the small boat."

"Good for you, Katie; you have a good head on your shoulders. But how did you end up missing the regular ferry?" Thomas asked.

"Well," Katie said, getting into telling the story, "it all started two days ago when we left our house—"

"Twenty-four hours ago," Janeva said, interrupted her and preempting Thomas, who was looking confused.

"Our first flight was delayed by one hour, but that was OK because I knew we would still make our connection because we were on the red-eye. Mom said the airport would be quiet at nine o'clock on a Friday night, but she was wrong—it was really busy. Snowstorms in the eastern United States had forced the delay of over six thousand flights! Everyone was grumpy and frustrated. It didn't help that it was Ski Week, and everyone was flying somewhere to go skiing."

"How big were the boats?" Thomas asked, hoping to stop the play by play for every event in Katie's last twenty-four hours.

Katie shook her head.

"Um, thirty-foot high-speed powerboats," Janeva replied for her.

"Dad, it was crazy. The boat screamed off full throttle through the dark. We were jumping over big waves; it was like being on a ride. I had to hang on tight or get bounced out. We couldn't even talk."

Katie finished chewing a large handful of popcorn and then continued, dramatically pointing up at the moon. "Look at the moon—it's so cool."

It was a full moon, with gray, thin clouds making wavy lines in front of it. At Thomas's puzzled look, she said, "That's what the moon looks like in, you know, like, *Twilight* or *Buffy the Vampire Slayer*. And when we started our boat ride, just then the moon disappeared, and it started to rain. It was a warm rain, but we got soaked. But we were drier than the group in the smaller boat."

"How did you know that?" Thomas asked.

"Oh, we saw them again when we arrived at Nanny Cay to clear customs. They got the rain and the spray. And they were soaked." She laughed. "Anyway, by the time we finished with customs, it had stopped raining, so we hopped back in the boat. Mom found a towel to wipe down the bench seat cushion again, and we were off full throttle to Road Town. Mom found a taxi, and here we are."

Katie smiled up at him and then yawned.

Thomas put his arm around her and said, "Let's get you to bed. Give your mom a kiss good night, and I'll show you your cabin."

After they left, Janeva sat on the back deck of the catamaran sipping her martini and enjoying the warm, tropical night air gently blowing on her face, bringing with it smells of seawater and the humid, moist smell of soil and night flowers. The colonial-style building lights reflected on the calm water, and the sound of the occasional car or motorbike going by on the road was the only sound other than crickets and water lapping against the hull.

Janeva's head dipped, and she realized she had better get to bed as well; she was exhausted.

As she walked through the galley to the inside sitting-and-eating area, she was relieved to see how clean everything was. Lorenzo's three-cabin catamaran called *Joie de Vivre* was practically brand-new and spotlessly clean. With a contented sigh, she relaxed. The boat was clean. It was another obsession, but she loved clean. She even found the smell of bleach and cleaning products relaxing and thus a good, happy smell. Smiling to herself, she recalled Steph saying, "Most people like smells like lavender or cinnamon, but for you it's bleach."

As there were three in the Jag family—Janeva, Thomas, and Katie—they had taken the pontoon with two cabins and one head and left the other pontoon, the master suite, that had a large cabin, desk, and head, for Greg and Steph. Janeva looked around and was pleased with their cabin: it was surprisingly roomy, with a good-sized hanging locker and shelves. Though once she saw the bed, she uncharacteristically admitted to herself that she was too tired to unpack, so she just changed into PJs and crawled into bed.

***

The next morning Thomas woke her up with a steaming cup of coffee, and after eating a piece of toast alfresco, reclining in the cockpit dining area, and inhaling the salty, warm air, everyone was reenergized and ready to go. Greg and Steph called to say they would be arriving soon. Not wanting to spend any more time at the dock than was absolutely necessary, they all set to work preparing to sail. Janeva stowed away all the beverages and water she had preordered and had delivered to the boat. Thomas and Katie did the boat checkout, filled up the water tanks, and loaded up snorkels, paddleboard, and kayak. They had just finished when Greg and Steph arrived. After hugs all around, Katie showed them to their cabin to unpack.

Twenty minutes later Steph and Janeva jumped in a taxi and headed off to the big Riteway Market, where they spent almost two hours shopping. It took a bit longer than expected, which was related not to the amount of food they had to purchase for five people on a ten-day trip but rather to the fruitless search for their usual favorite foods and staples that just were not available, even in this well-stocked market.

"I know you love to cook because you think it's healthier, and so you make almost everything from scratch, Janeva. But I think you are going to have to let that go for this trip if we plan to eat," Steph said in some frustration as Janeva carefully studied the ingredients labeled on yet another jar of peanut butter.

"But they put sugar in the peanut butter. Can you believe it?" Janeva protested, holding out the jar for Steph to see this latest nutritional atrocity.

"Janeva, you will have to, just for this trip, break your make-everything-from-scratch rule. Because we are going to buy frozen pizzas, loaves of premade bread, and, yes, even mac and cheese from a box," Steph said with an evil laugh as she loaded up the shopping cart. "Why don't you go and pick out some meat?" she suggested and accompanied it with a gentle shove in the direction of the butcher and deli section. After some deliberation, Janeva decided that beef—ground or otherwise, like steak—was very small and crazy expensive, but fortunately, the chicken and fish looked great and were frozen—even better.

Janeva, laughing, told Steph about the price of chicken.

"It's not surprising that chicken is inexpensive. They stroll freely everywhere. Haven't you noticed the constant call of one rooster to another across town?" Steph said.

Eventually, they caught a taxi for another wild ride. Janeva turned to Steph and whispered, "I'm sure that he is driving perfectly normally, but the combination of driving on the left, the jet lag, the frequent honking, and the lack of seat belts is a bit disconcerting. I'm totally disoriented and can't wait to get back aboard *Joie de Vivre*." Joy of living, she remembered, was the expression for a rare quality that simply shone forth in some people, especially in their ability to love life.

Steph laughed and nodded her agreement as she hung on to the handhold on the ceiling in an effort not to slide across the seat and into Janeva's lap.

Back at the boat, Steph put the food away, and Janeva bleached and washed all the dishes.

Thomas walked by rolling his eyes, and Janeva replied, "Lorenzo used this boat for boys' trips. I have no faith that they knew how to wash dishes."

Finally, it was time to leave Tortola and start the British Virgin Islands adventure properly.

Thomas went through his standard predeparture lecture that initiated every boat trip, long or short. They knew it by heart, but that didn't deter him; they had to suffer through the lecture and pretend to learn it again. It was the same old stuff.

"First," he said, "you familiarize yourselves with the location and use of every fire extinguisher and make sure they're current. Do not forget to shake them before you turn them on. And remember, always hold them vertical, right side up, because they won't work upside down. And let's remember the rules, especially you, Katie. We never dive or snorkel alone. Anytime we are in the water, we always wear a floatation vest or inflatable PFD. Close to coral, we wear gloves because the coral is razor-sharp. Because boats come and go and diving can have unexpected challenges, we always carry a line-cutter knife with a release-mechanism sheath when we are snorkeling or diving. Protect yourself from the sun, wear your rash guard, and always twice a day cover your exposed skin with sunscreen."

The lecture went on and on. Katie wondered to herself how many people knew that there were no ropes on a boat, only lines, and that a big risk of sailing was being caught in the bight of a line that suddenly snapped tight because it was sheeted to the clew of a sail, or worse, caught on the prop. Katie nodded enthusiastically that she agreed and understood. She knew if she didn't, she would hear *again* the story about the time her dad saved the boat by diving down with his line cutter when the dinghy line got caught on the prop during a maneuver, and they were being blown into some rocks on a lee shore.

The group chose Peter Island for the first night because it was central and not too far a sail. They secured a mooring buoy, and everyone was keen to jump in the turquoise-blue water for a swim before time for a snack and a cold, refreshing beverage.

After everyone was full and happily enjoying the sun, the usual questions and discussion that marked the group of friends emerged. What should they do now? Have a nap or lower the dinghy down from the davits and go to shore to the beach bar for happy hour? Janeva was not surprised that happy hour won, nor that they were the first to arrive, as promptness was a Jag family trait. But other anchored boats saw them, and soon other dinghies arrived. Much to Katie and Janeva's amazement and pleasure, one of the families that had been on the plane and subsequent speedboat trip the night before also arrived. It was Jeff, who had helped organize the group and, it turned out, was from Newport Beach, California. His blond-haired, blue-eyed wife, whom Janeva and Katie hadn't met the night before, was originally from England and had moved over to be with her matching blond-haired, blue-eyed husband. Their daughter, whom Katie had palled around with at the airport, was only a year older than Katie. The two of them were soon exploring the beach and showing each other moves on the dance floor.

"Do you have a sail plan?" Jeff asked the group after everyone had been introduced.

"We are going to Nor—" Thomas began to answer, but Janeva interrupted him.

"Not really. We are just going to go where the wind blows us. What about you guys?" she asked.

Thomas slid his empty plastic cup over to Janeva with a puppy-dog look that clearly said, "Please would you go and get me another?" Rolling her eyes, Janeva turned and headed to the bar.

"What's up?" Steph asked. She had followed Janeva to the bar. "Why didn't you want them to know where we were going next? Wouldn't it be good for Katie to have a friend to hang out with?"

"I know, but something is weird about them," Janeva replied.

As they waited for the next round of drinks to be made, Steph turned and looked back at the couple talking to Greg and Thomas. "What?" she asked with a shrug.

"I don't know, really, but it's just kind of spooky. At the airport, he asked me where we were going, and when I referenced the places I'd searched on the tourist brochures, he wanted to know why we wanted to go there, and now here he is again and still asking where we're going. And look at their daughter: she doesn't resemble either parent," Janeva replied. Appearances are deceiving, as the saying goes, but their daughter had dark skin and really dark brunette hair, while the parents were both fair skinned and blond.

"She could be from a previous marriage, or maybe she was adopted," Steph replied logically. "Maybe they were just pleased to have another family with a daughter the same age so they could play together."

"Well, OK, you're right; I'm reading too much into nothing. But he seemed unusually interested in our plans and destination; it just feels weird somehow," Janeva replied and paid for the round of drinks.

"Janeva, relax. You don't need to be cautious here. This is a holiday, remember? I think they're just trying to be friends," Steph said seriously and then teased, "So no need for you to get even a bit paranoid."

Chapter 6

"You know you are in paradise when you wake up to the gentle rocking of the boat, the sun streaming in your porthole window, the wonderful scent of percolating coffee. And the first article of clothing you put on is your bathing suit," Steph announced, standing in her bikini as she poured herself a cup of coffee. "What's on the agenda for today?"

"You mean other than sailing, swimming, eating, and drinking?" Janeva joked.

"Good point."

"Thomas is deep into his e-mail because something happened at his office that he is dealing with, Katie and Greg are already swimming, and I'm about to cut up some pineapple and mango to have with my yogurt. Want some?"

"I can't believe it!" Thomas stomped into the galley holding his laptop.

"What's wrong?" Janeva asked.

He ignored her and instead turned on the generator and plugged in his laptop, and then he plopped down on the seat and started typing again.

Steph and Janeva made eye contact, unsure of what to do or say next. Finally, Janeva ventured a question: "Would you like some more coffee or some fruit and yogurt?"

"Huh?" He looked up at her, distracted, and then as the question registered, he forced a smile and agreed to both and thanked Janeva.

Steph and Janeva decided to leave him alone with his laptop, taking their breakfasts outside to enjoy the beautiful morning.

"Where are Greg and Katie?" Steph asked, looking around the water at the back of the boat.

"Let's check the bow."

From the deck, they searched the surrounding water but found no sign of the two missing swimmers.

"We are too far from shore to swim in," Steph said with some worry in her voice.

"Not to worry—look, the kayak is missing," Janeva said after taking a quick survey of the water toys that came with the boat. "It's a two-person kayak; they must have gone exploring."

Janeva went inside to the nav station to grab the binoculars. "I found them; they're over there," she said, pointing and then handing the binoculars to Steph.

Thomas was now in the cockpit sitting at the outside table, his computer abandoned inside. He was glaring at the chart. "So what happened at your office?" Janeva asked him. "If you're going to be grumpy, at least let us know why."

"I'm not grumpy; I'm angry…and I have a good reason." They waited. "My office was broken into last night and trashed."

"What?" Steph and Janeva both exclaimed.

"Why? What did they take?" Janeva asked in alarm.

"It doesn't appear that they took anything, and that's the really strange part. All the desks were rifled, the drawers emptied, and the files scattered, opened, and dumped on the floor. A huge mess. The staff will be cleaning up for days."

"That sounds crazy! What about the other offices in the building?"

"Perhaps it was some kids, vandals, just trying to make trouble?" Steph suggested.

"Do you think it could it be Bruce, whom you let go last month?" Janeva asked. "He was very angry; maybe—"

"I don't know, and speculating doesn't help my mood. But to answer your questions: no one else's office was broken into, there is a twenty-four-hour security guard working at the entrance, and they didn't break either the door or the window, so they must have gotten hold of someone's security card."

"That means—" Janeva started to say.

"Janeva, before you go off on one of your theories: yes, we have looked, and there is no record of anyone using a card to enter the office last night, and no, I don't think it was Bruce, but the police are following up. Stop playing your role of detective; this is real life."

"Maybe I should call Deputy Sheriff Dugud and let him know," Janeva said.

"Why?" Thomas demanded, astounded.

"Well," she said, "we actually know a police investigator. We aren't just the anonymous public, and his role is to link up any clues that might help him resolve the other event. Moreover, obviously you have some valuable bit of IT that someone wants enough to raid your office. Think. What could you have that is so important, someone would risk trying to steal it? Unless you have something really valuable, maybe it's somehow connected to the Lorenzo murder or Wiffy's death. We have to examine the big picture."

"Not again! Janeva, I told you. All those events are behind us now. That is why we are on vacation. Don't pretend to be a detective; please just stop," Thomas said.

Undeterred, Janeva continued, "Do you have secrets that someone wants to steal? It seems to me that your office is friendly and open. Have you turned anyone away who was prying and asking questions? I mean, who would break into an IT office? Why would anyone break into an IT office? If it was your IT they were after, wouldn't they use hackers to break into your systems?"

Thomas threw his hands up in the air and exclaimed, "We're not an IT office. We do not do Internet technology. We do 3-D printing, and we do not have secrets. Our office is just like every other office: bills, receipts, records of instructions, personnel files—and no one steals documents anymore. They just take a photo of them with their iPhone or download them, so who knows what they were looking for or even if they found what they were looking for." Then he stomped off in a snit.

"So much for my attempt to help," Janeva grumbled to herself. She thought again that there must be some obvious reason for the break-in, and the sensible approach was to consider what motive anyone might have. Why would anyone want to see a personnel file, a bill, a receipt? Was there a technological design, some secret process that made the risk of criminal break-in worthwhile? At the back of her mind, she wondered again if the chip business might be related, but she also knew that topic was forever off-limits with Thomas. She decided to wait until Thomas calmed down and approach the issue with him again.

***

When Katie and Greg returned to the boat, Thomas was still irritable and said he felt it important that he return to oversee the cleanup and assist any investigation. Begrudgingly, he admitted that his company did have some important projects under development, as did every successful entrepreneurial company in the world, but that those files and all related information were secure in the cloud and not easily accessed. A phone call to his security advisor assured him that their cloud-computing detecting and deterrent controls had not been breached, and they went further and suggested that he should let them clean up and restore the office and enjoy his well-earned vacation.

So he determined to concentrate on being happy and enjoying his vacation. He mumbled as much to no one, and he shut down his laptop after changing his login password. His laptop could access his secure cloud network, but he could not risk having it fall into the wrong hands. His own employees had now put him in a dilemma so that if he did return, it would insult them and irritate his family and friends. But then, it was his job to make the responsible decisions, be the leader, and take charge. This was his company and the most important project he had ever taken on; how was he to relax in the Caribbean if it was at risk?

He compensated by whipping everyone into action aboard the *Joie de Vivre*. They hoisted the main, and when it caught the wind on the head, they slipped moorage and sailed close-hauled with main and jib foresail to Treasure Point, hoping to find a moorage close to the snorkeling caves. It was a quiet sail, considering the moderately strong wind, and they made their destination and clipped onto a nicely sheltered mooring buoy without incident. They sorted through the mess of gear until they each found a snorkel, flippers, and a mask that fit. Janeva brought out the dish soap to wipe a drop inside the masks. As though not everyone already knew, she explained, “It helps defog them.”

“But I’ll get soap in my eyes,” Katie complained.

“Rinse the soap out in the water before you put on the mask,” Janeva said with a laugh and then demonstrated.

The group slid off the back of the boat and into the warm turquoise water and swam to the caves. Thomas’s impatience had its reward, because they were ahead of the crowd and had managed to snag a premier mooring buoy. It was only a short swim to the snorkeling caves.

Everywhere she looked, Janeva saw spectacularly colored tropical fish. It was fantastic. Instead of rocketing away as if she were a predator, every color and variety seemed to swim up to examine her, maybe anticipating food, she thought.

"Look, Mom," Katie said, swimming up beside Janeva. She pointed to the back of one of the caves and gave the hand sign that said, "Follow me." Together they swam back as far as they could go until they came to the end of a shallow, rounded, high cave with some sort of vine hanging down the back wall.

Janeva and Katie treaded water, letting their snorkels hang from their masks as they admired the vine wall.

"I bet real pirates hid treasure here in the old days," Katie said and pointed to a dark back corner. Together they explored around the edges of the cave, looking for hidden pirate treasure until it was time to head back to the boat for lunch.

After a lunch of hot dogs on the grill, it was time to set sail again. With Thomas at the helm, the group hauled up the main and made way to Manchineel Bay. The bay was packed with boats.

"It reminds me of a busy mall parking lot at Christmas," Greg said. They'd dropped the main and jib and were under power, searching for an empty mooring buoy. They were about to give up and drop anchor when they spied a powerboat preparing to cast off, and they beat several other boats that were also searching for a moorage buoy. They hitched to the last vacant buoy.

"Should we go exploring?" Steph pointed to the shore; the blue water lapped the strip of golden yellow beach, and a cluster of buildings peeked out from behind palm trees and the lush, green, tropical hillside behind them.

"Why not? Maybe there is a good restaurant," Greg said in agreement and started to get the dinghy ready to launch from its davits.

"This is heaven," Steph said to no one in particular as they walked up and down the beach exploring.

"The only thing that would make it better would be a rum punch," Thomas said, giving Janeva a meaningful look as he commandeered a high, round bar-style table set out in the shallow water.

Janeva sighed. "OK, I'll go get this round, but someone else has to get the next," Janeva said begrudgingly. Actually, she was happy to go and get the drinks. The beach-club restaurant and bar was so cute, with its open concept of no walls; instead, it had a high, bleached wood ceiling with exposed beams and struts highlighting the many angles, each with its own slow-moving, dark ceiling fan. Janeva found a place at the bar and was patiently waiting for her drinks to arrive as she took in the architecture and many different vacationers.

Handling Katie her virgin strawberry daiquiri, Janeva carried the drinks to the sandy, palm tree–lined beach. She left her flip-flops on the beach with the rest and waded out to the table, reveling in the feel of sand between her toes.

***

Later, back on the boat, Steph and Janeva made an early dinner of barbecued chicken in a spicy sauce with sautéed mushrooms, onions, rosemary, tomatoes, goat cheese, and a generous splash of hot sauce, and sides of white rice and crispy steamed snow peas with lemon squished on top. It was a perfect Caribbean evening, so the meal was eaten alfresco on the back deck.

The evening's entertainment consisted of watching a large blue superyacht in the distance named *Lady Cécilee*.

Not only was the yacht beautiful, but it also had a helicopter-landing pad. The arrival of a copter caught their attention. Katie, the group photographer, took many photos as the binoculars were passed around. The helicopter made another trip, and the group speculated about why it was making so many trips and where it was going. Maybe they were practicing taking off and landing. On the other hand, maybe this was an exchange of guests, or the owner's group arriving in shifts. Or were they perhaps just sight-seeing, going out to see the sunset?

It was then that the day's salubrious weather started changing from hot, clear-blue, sunny haze to gray. Then the wind started to build, and their calm anchorage quickly changed to high waves. The boat started to pitch, bow to stern, tugging on the mooring float. Then when the wind spun, they rolled side to side in a sickening motion that crashed some loose kitchen utensils onto the galley floor. Visibility dropped to zero, and the pelting rain drenched them as if they had just moved under a fire hose. This was a major squall. Sailors understood this was a part of their reality, and they were thankful to be neatly secured to a mooring buoy instead of sailing between the islands.

"It's so fortunate for us that we managed to secure a mooring buoy, because this cove is relatively unprotected," Steph said from the inside seating area.

"If the storm gains enough intensity," Thomas remarked, "there could be a risk of even the mooring buoy losing its anchorage hold." Thomas never sailed without carefully noting the marine weather forecast. Sailors always kept a close eye on the weather when sailing, but now they were securely moored and had turned off the marine radio.

They had been more interested in dinner than the weather and had not anticipated the squall bearing down.

“Thomas, are you serious about the anchor?” Steph asked, concerned.

“Our anemometer already recorded gusts up to thirty-five knots, and the mooring buoy is only rated for forty knots, so we’d better get prepared,” Thomas replied grimly.

They looked around at one another, all pondering what it might be like to be rolled beam over beam onto the rocky shore or even to crash into another boat.

Chapter 7

As day faded into evening, it become apparent that this was not a gust or squall but a full storm that wasn't going to blow out. Katie was zoomed into a movie on her iPad with earbuds in and seemed oblivious to the storm.

"Help me with the dinghy," Thomas suddenly requested. He had been working on his laptop, replying to e-mails about some business proposal, but every few minutes or so, he would look up and scan the sky and boats around them. Alarmed, Janeva put her Kindle down and looked around to see what was wrong. Even in the fading light, it did not take her long to see what had happened: the mainsail on the boat to windward had unfurled.

"Thomas, what are you going to do?" Janeva, standing in the cockpit, yelled at him over the roar of the storm, which was even louder now with the flapping of the other boat's mainsail.

"We have to help him," replied Thomas as he handed Janeva a line to lower the dinghy down from its davits. "If he doesn't get that mainsail in, his boat will drag its mooring buoy and in all likelihood take us with him."

Janeva looked around. It would be like boat dominoes: there had to be twenty boats anchored or secured to mooring buoys in the bay, and she could only imagine what it might be like if one got loose and shot in some direction with the wind. The wind was swirling, rebounding off the coast, and she had no way of knowing where the storm might take them: thrown up on shore in one direction or swept out through the inlet into the violence of the sea in the other direction—or the worst possible, onto the rocks. Janeva could see the white foam of waves crashing into rocks. *We need to start the engine and make sure everyone is wearing a floatation vest. Where are the flares?* She said to herself.

"Now, Janeva, the storm is building! We don't have much time to help him," Thomas yelled at her.

Instantly she saw he was right. Huge, gray storm clouds were headed toward them. Janeva could feel that the wind was stronger than it had been just moments before and could see that the next wall of gray rain was approaching fast. They were bow on to the waves and pitching, but she was able to uncleat the pulley line and wind it around a winch so she could control lowering the dinghy. They were pitching and rolling wildly, and it was almost impossible to stand. Greg came up from his cabin in response to Thomas's call for help, and together they were able to control the dinghy, freeing Janeva to retrieve the PFD life jackets. She insisted that they all wear one, even Katie. Greg and Thomas managed to get into the dinghy, even though it was slamming against the pontoon hull. They started the small outboard engine and headed into the peaked waves toward the neighboring struggling sailboat.

Janeva and Steph were holding on. The scene that unfolded was riveting. They watched Thomas and Greg make slow, wet progress in their small dinghy, waves crashing over them and bouncing them in various directions. They almost broached a number of times, but they stayed afloat. The mainsail on the boat in front of them farther unfurled, and the violent wind slammed the sail, firing the boat around and rolling it until it was almost swamped. Janeva could see Thomas trying to grab on to the pontoon to hitch their dinghy, but there was no place to grab a pontoon, and the boat was swinging. He missed, and Janeva's heart missed a beat. This was turning into a life-threatening rescue. Why wasn't the woman on board helping? She was just standing there, holding on; her husband was frantically grabbing at the sail that snapped like a whip and banged like a shotgun every time the wind caught it. He was doing his best to keep the rest of the sail from unfurling. Even from where Janeva and Steph stood, they could see he was yelling at her, but they couldn't hear anything over the crashing of waves and whistling of the wind.

"I can't hear what he's saying, but I can guess," Steph said sagely.

"He desperately needs someone to grab the wheel, start the engine, and turn the boat into the wind, giving them a chance to furl in the sail," Janeva replied in exasperation. "What is wrong with that woman?"

Finally, there was a momentary lull in the wind, and Thomas was able to grab the port pontoon and hitch the dinghy onto a deck cleat. Then he and Greg scrambled aboard with surprising dexterity. Thomas grabbed the wheel and started the engine. The woman still stood, paralyzed, in exactly the same spot. Then to Janeva's astonishment, she turned and walked into the cabin and closed the sliding-glass door behind her.

Janeva mused, *I have been married to and boated with Thomas for fifteen years; I'm 100 percent sure he was yelling at her to come and take the wheel so he could get to the mast and help lash down the mainsail.* Greg and the man, who looked vaguely familiar, were already struggling with the wildly snapping clew that cracked like a whip with a force that would cause serious injury if it slammed into them. *He must be livid.* Janeva could imagine the anger and tension in the set of Thomas's shoulders as he worked to lock the wheel so he could go and help with the sail. Why had she gone inside?

Thomas must have succeeded in locking the wheel in place, because as Janeva watched, he went to the mast with some line, grabbed the head of the sail, and was able to tie it to the boom. Greg found the mainsail cover and was able to secure the jib and mooring lines. Job done, they shook hands with the relieved boater and departed.

Boat saved, storm howling, and waves churning, Thomas and Greg embarked once again in the dinghy and made the perilous journey back, this time with the wind, to *Joie de Vivre*. Janeva grabbed the line that Thomas threw and secured it to a stern cleat. Even with both the dinghy bow and stern painters attached, the inflatable dinghy was smashing against the stern, but finally, both Greg and Thomas were able to get onto the stern swim platform and safely into the cockpit. Janeva got towels.

"Who are they? They sort of looked familiar. And why didn't his wife help you?" Janeva screamed at them over the roar of the storm.

"Not now," was Thomas's terse reply. "We need to get the paddleboard, the kayak, and the dinghy safely stowed."

But as he yelled, they saw the paddleboard break free. Janeva grabbed for it, missed, and reflexively jumped in after it.

"Janeva, *stop*!" Thomas yelled to her. "Let it go!" But it was futile. Janeva was already in the water, and the storm ripped his words away. Janeva grabbed the board and swam with it to the lee side, which was calmer, but she was astonished at the ferocity of the wind, current, and waves. Just a fathom from the boat, she suddenly thought, *I am not going to make it.* She was a strong swimmer, but as she swam as hard as she could, towing the paddleboard, the terrifying realization dawned that she was at real risk of being swept away from the boat and out into open water. *Joie de Vivre* had lifelines and life rings ready just for this purpose, and even though they had never before been used, this was their moment. Thomas threw her a line. Janeva had to let go of the paddleboard and lunged for the yellow poly floating line.

"Damn it—it's the reason I'm out here swimming in a storm, after all," Janeva grumbled. The next wave slammed the paddleboard, propelling it like a weapon back at her, and she grabbed it. With the line in one hand and the paddleboard in the other, she let Thomas and Greg drag her aboard.

She was wet and had a bruised shoulder where the paddleboard had hit her, but she had rescued the paddleboard. It was still a challenge to get the paddleboard on board because the wind kept trying to rip it out of their hands. Eventually, the paddleboard was finally safely stowed on the floor behind the outside cockpit table and out of the wind.

Janeva anticipated a lecture from Thomas on her recklessness, so she quickly descended the companionway's three stairs into the starboard pontoon. She hung on with one hand, reached down, grabbed, and started to haul in the kayak tie line. The paddleboard rescued now, they had to secure the kayak, so hand over hand she pulled the kayak line in until it was close enough for her to grab the small, black, plastic handle on its bow. It was one of those things that come naturally to people who sail together. They didn't need practice because everyone knew what he or she had to do. Janeva pulled the bowline, Thomas was ready to grab the bow handle, and Greg was waiting to pull in the stern handle, intending to walk the kayak to the lee side and tie it down until the storm blew out. It would be their escape lifeboat if that became necessary.

They were pummeled by the wind and waves, and their boat and the kayak were rolling and pitching at different frequencies; Janeva couldn't grab the handle. Even with their backs to the wind, they were being soaked and bounced, but finally, she got the handle. Holding on to the deck lifeline with one hand, she pulled as hard as she could but wasn't strong enough to pull the kayak in. Finally, she gauged the next roll and let go of the lifeline, and with both hands on the handle, she took a deep breath and yanked the kayak up to the side where Thomas could help.

"Oh my God!" she said, gasping. There was a face in the water between the kayak and the boat. There was a body swooping up in the white foam of the three-foot waves that were pounding the boat. It seemed to be looking up at her. She was screaming. She didn't even know she was screaming. She stood rigid, paralyzed, lashed by the rain and spray, and leaning back into the force of the howling wind. The earlier struggles of fighting to hold the moorage, assist the loose-sailed floundering boat, rescue the paddleboard, and save the kayak were all forgotten.

Like a horror-movie nightmare, she looked down into the face of a dead person being thrust up toward her and then swept down away from her by the next wave. It seemed to be looking straight at Janeva. A zombie look. She finally recovered enough to take a deep breath. Maybe, she hoped, the person was still alive, but as she looked, it was clear that the skin was pale and the eyes were staring wide open and blank. It was only a moment or maybe a lifetime that she stood motionless, gazing into the eyes of death; then Thomas was at her side. Together, and with great difficulty, they heaved the body onto their deck. Janeva saw that the person had a huge open wound on his or her head and face. Then she realized that it was a woman. The woman was wearing a self-inflating Mustang floatation vest, and she was obviously dead. Janeva stared at the corpse, unable to move or respond.

"OK, everyone, calm down," Thomas said unnecessarily. "Greg, what should we do? OK, it's OK, Janeva," he said, worried about Janeva. This trip was to help her relax and forget about nightmares and death. He decided the best thing to do was to keep his wife busy and away from the body. “Janeva, we need some help here. Get the kayak secured.”

Thomas and Greg carried the body onto the cockpit and headed back down the pontoon stairs. Greg had checked for a pulse and vital signs and confirmed aloud that she was dead and cold and had probably been dead for some time. Even though he was a physician, he said it would not be correct or proper for him to further examine her for other signs of injury. Obviously, she had drowned. The head wound was disconcerting, though. What did it mean? Was it caused by her fall into the water? Maybe she fell and slammed into something so hard and sharp that it broke her skin. When he palpated the wound, she appeared to have a fractured cranium. He was not a forensic pathologist, and he was not licensed to practice here in any case. *What is the right and ethical thing to do?* he wondered.

“We can’t just leave her here like that,” Janeva yelled to Thomas over the roar of the wind.

“Yes, I think that’s probably what we should do. There is nothing we can do for her now,” Thomas replied calmly.

“Umm, well…I guess you are right,” she had to admit after his words had sunk in. “Can we at least cover her? I don’t want Katie to see her.”

“Yes, of course,” he said and then called to Greg. “If you agree, then I think we should lash her to the deck and cover her with the dinghy tarp until the police can assume responsibility. I’m trying on the marine radio band to get the police now.”

With one last look at the vacant eyes and gashed head, Janeva felt a bit unsteady, and her stomach lurched, but she dutifully turned and followed Thomas to finish securing the kayak, lashing down the mainsail, and rechecking the knots. They all knew that any superstructure and especially a loose sail could be grabbed by a gale-force wind and drag a boat to its destruction, so they prepared just in case the wind picked up even more.

Thomas satisfied himself that they would ride out the storm and got onto the marine radio, and Greg wrapped the body in the plastic cover that protected the dinghy when it was towed. They were all suffering now from the cold and wet. Thomas announced that he was getting into a hot shower and recommended that therapy for the others.

The local police were not able to attend until the morning. They were trying to cope with other crises also brought on by the storm. They instructed Thomas to ensure that "the deceased" was secure. This death was certainly not a secret now, because everyone in the marina with the radio monitoring channel one six now knew that a female body had washed up and was being secured by *Joie de Vivre*.

Thomas announced to the others, "I guess we get to spend the night with a corpse." It was supposed to be a bit of lighthearted humor, but it had just the opposite effect. They all suddenly looked like they were weighted down under a blanket of gloom.

Chapter 8

After an almost sleepless night, they awakened to a beautiful Caribbean morning—a clear, blue sky. The sea was like glass—not a ripple or sign of the previous night's storm. Janeva made a fresh pot of coffee and tried to ignore the body under the tarp that was just outside the galley. She took her first sip of coffee, closed her eyes, and pretended that when she opened them, she would awaken from the nightmare of last night's events, and they would just slip off the mooring ball and sail into the blue to their next sunny destination.

As was their habit when anchored, she checked the moorage for anchor drag, but that was unnecessary when they were attached to a mooring buoy. Then she noticed that the sailboat Thomas and Greg had saved last evening was gone. The mooring float was empty, just bobbing serenely in the sun. Had it been carried away by the storm, she worried, or had it slipped moorage and sailed off at dawn? Then it suddenly occurred to her who the couple was and why they looked familiar. They had been on the same snow-delayed plane, and she recalled that they were also in the small group that had gathered to charter the speedboats to get to the islands after the last ferry had sailed.

She was just about to tell Thomas when the police dinghy pulled up beside her boat, and after introductions, two constables came aboard to record the story and to view the body. Fortunately, Katie had transitioned from an early riser to a typical teenage late riser, so she had not yet appeared and was not aware of any of these activities.

After studying the body, the police directed their questions mostly at Greg and Thomas but also carefully recorded both Janeva's and Steph's accounts of what had happened. It took both police officers and Thomas and Greg to transfer the body into the police dinghy. They were all officially required to go to the police station for photo ID and written statements.

"Sorry," the lead police officer said, "but this is a case of sudden, unexpected death of an unknown person, in all probability a nonresident, and there is a lot of official paperwork required. You are all required to attend with us at the station now. We do not want to seem overbearing, but unfortunately, this is not a request. You must follow us." So it was back into the dinghy and, Janeva thought, their second visit to a police station.

"Look," Janeva said as Thomas and Greg started to drop the dinghy that had been securely lashed up on the davits to ride out the previous night's storm, "Katie is only twelve and was in her cabin the whole time. Really, I don't want Katie to be involved or associated in any way with this ordeal." She said this in a pleading tone to the kinder-looking of the two police officers. "Katie doesn't even know about any of this; we purposely kept it from her."

The commotion of loading the dinghy and launching the other dinghy had finally aroused Katie, who appeared, looking sleepy and disheveled, asking what all the fuss was about. "Why is everyone up so early? After all, this is a holiday, and…" But her comments stopped when she saw the police boat and what looked like a dead person in their boat. Her parents appeared worried and fatigued, so she suddenly became very quiet. Looking at his notepad, the officer asked Katie about her recollections of last night, and except for the storm, it was clear she had no information to share. So he agreed that she could stay behind on the boat, but the rest had to come along.

"Thanks," Katie said happily and too quickly.

"Oh no, you're not going to stay on the boat alone! Get a book; you can read when they are questioning us," Janeva said, quickly alarmed.

"Read a print book?" Katie exclaimed. "And I'm thirteen now! Can I at least take my iPad?"

"Right, of course, you are," her mother answered, feeling guilty for forgetting her daughter's true age, but then, Katie had only just turned thirteen. "I know you are a full-fledged teenager now, but bring a book too, just in case."

"OK, people, let's get moving. It is a busy day for us. That was a major storm, and there was lots of damage and activity requiring official police attention," the large, black, Caribbean police officer said, though still respectful and polite.

***

The police station was a two-story, plain cube of concrete painted sky blue with white trim—an attractive, clean, and colonial-looking building somewhat reminiscent of the days when the area had been a British colony. Inside the station's whitewashed walls, the two officers who had escorted them to the station arranged for the body; then they separated the group into small interview rooms and proceeded to question each person individually.

"Please, how do you explain how a body materialized beside your kayak in the middle of a storm?" they asked repeatedly in many different ways. A body appearing in their bay at any time was in itself incredible. But both Janeva and Steph knew the dead woman. It was Betty. Betty, the manager of their yacht club. Not surprisingly, the police were not buying into the coincidence of the event. Thousands of miles from home, two women find the body of someone they know? Janeva began to wonder if they would ever leave the police station and continue their vacation. The questions and cross-examination continued. Another corpse. And she'd not slept. Just lay in bed unable to sleep.

"What boat was she on?"

"I don't know."

"When did she arrive?"

"Again, I don't know."

"Did you know that she was planning to be here at the same time as you were?"

"No!"

"How did you not notice her earlier?"

"Our attention was focused on the boat whose sail had unfurled."

"What boat was that?"

"I don't remember the name, but it was a Moorings Charter boat."

The questions went on and on until Janeva's head ached. She was tired and thirsty. *I cannot take any more questions.* This was not the vacation she had envisioned. Katie was glaring at her from the chair she was sitting on, rubbing her tummy to indicate that she was hungry and waving her iPad around so Janeva could see that it was out of batteries or that she had finished the book. Then suddenly, after what seemed like an eternity, they were told they could go.

"Why did they suddenly let us go?" Janeva inquired as Thomas tried to drag her out of the station.

"Honestly, I don't care! I just want to get on with my holiday," he responded tersely.

Janeva cared, though. She had known the woman, after all—OK, not all that well, but she still wanted to know what had happened to her, so she held her ground and asked again, "What happened to her? I can't just leave not knowing."

The police had not revealed anything to her, but somehow Greg had found out.

"She has been reported missing from the yacht *Lady Cécilee*. Apparently, she had been seasick from the storm and had gone up on deck to get some air and never returned. She wasn't missed at first, as they thought she was in her cabin. It was only this morning when she didn't show up for breakfast that they searched everywhere and finally concluded that she must have fallen overboard in the storm."

"You mean she fell off that big, blue yacht we saw last night with the helicopter? How did you find out?" Janeva demanded.

"The officer who was questioning me volunteered the information," Greg replied with a shrug.

"I still think it's unbelievable that she ended up wedged between our boat and kayak," Janeva exclaimed as they walked down the beach toward the dinghy.

"Coincidences do happen," Thomas replied.

"You know, Thomas, I'm with Janeva on this one," Steph piped in. "It's pretty incredible that of all the boats moored in that bay last night, someone drowned and floated up to our boat, and it was someone we knew."

"And the laceration on her head is also a bit suspicious," added Greg. "I'd like to get a look at that yacht, *Lady Cécilee*, and see where she fell from."

"No, no, no—not again! This is a holiday. We are going to sail, suntan, and drink rum punches, *not* play detective!" Thomas growled.

"But—" Janeva started.

"And we should start right now," Thomas said as he marched up to a beach bar and ordered each of them a rum punch.

"I think we had better order some food too; Katie is starving." Janeva reminded them all that the police had not given them time for breakfast.

"You shouldn't have slept in," Thomas teased his daughter.

"I'm with Katie. We're on holiday, and sleeping in is what you're supposed to do on holidays," Janeva exclaimed and, still with an empty stomach, finished her rum punch.

She felt almost too intoxicated to carry on. *Yes, I do need to eat*, she thought.

"And drinking libations even before the sun is over the yardarm—now that's a record, even for a Jag," Greg added, laughing and shaking his head. "Playing Agatha Christie…sounds like Janeva's perfect vacation. Too bad it's not plausible."

Forcing a laugh to cover up her discomfort and fight off the sadness of death, Janeva asked, "What part isn't plausible? The part where she accidentally fell off a yacht, then swam to our boat to die? Or the part where she was pinned by the kayak I was pulling in during a storm? I don't want to make a bad pun, but it all sounds fishy to me." Janeva rolled her eyes and lifted her hands up in a "can you believe it?" gesture. "If I were still home and someone told me this story, I wouldn't believe it."

"Agreed. A woman from our own yacht club, outside on the deck at night with a PFD in a huge storm, and a passenger on a superyacht, and with a significant scalp wound, death presumably by drowning—it's almost too incredible," Greg said, summing up the situation.

"OK, let's talk it out," Thomas interrupted him. "How well did you know her?"

"You probably never met her because she worked quietly and was purposely unobtrusive, but she was the general manager of our yacht club," Steph said softly. "I'm not surprised that the police are suspicious of the coincidence."

"OK," Thomas said and then interrupted Janeva the moment she started to speak. "Let's review what we know."

Janeva summarized. "The woman who ended up in the sea beside our kayak was Betty Rothman, our yacht-club GM."

"Did you—" Thomas started.

"No, I hardly knew her. Actually I had been avoiding her because she wanted me to join some committee," Janeva interrupted.

"We had no idea that she was coming to the Caribbean, and we do know that she was an experienced boater," Steph continued.

"And that was not a small, unstable boat; it was a superyacht, very stable and like a cruise ship. Most passengers do not get motion sickness on a boat that size. She had a head wound. How did it happen?" Greg added.

"And incredibly, with the whole ocean available, her body floats to our boat," Thomas finished off.

"She was a bit bossy, but she was a good leader," Steph said. "She might have annoyed some people, but it's easy to remove the manager of a club like ours—you certainly don't hit them over the head and toss them into the ocean."

"Demanding is more like her than bossy," Janeva said. "She didn't ask me to be marketing chair—she informed me that I was doing it."

"She isn't all bad. Let's remember that we have a container full of medical supplies for Haiti, and through the women's committee, she helped raise the money," Steph added.

Why, Janeva wondered, *is Steph always so nice?* She groaned inwardly.

"Just for the record, it was the collective women's committee, not Betty Rothman, that raised the money," Thomas added.

"Well, actually, the luncheon was Betty Rothman's idea, and she gave a substantial personal donation to get the fund-raising rolling," Steph clarified. "And no one could deny her ability to run the yacht club and raise money for the causes she believed in."

Sighing, Janeva shook her head sadly and added, "You're right, Steph. I think many of the members will realize our loss and be sad that she is gone."

"Enough about Betty Rothman. It's a police matter now. Let's do our best to forget about it and enjoy the rest of our holiday. Are we going to spend another night here? Or head up to Marina Cay as planned?" Thomas looked around at them all.

"Hey, oh," they heard, and they all turned to look.

It was the blond, blue-eyed Newport family that they had run into earlier.

"How are you?" Jeff asked. "Good? You rode the storm out OK? What a night; I didn't sleep a wink. The wind and waves kept us up all night, didn't they, dear?" He turned and gave his wife an affectionate look and then continued, "Hey, you all know anything about the police boat? Saw it this morning. Man, I wonder if some poor sap fell in or something. Naw, probably just checking to make sure everyone was OK. Where are you going next? No way we are going to spend another night here; the wife here needs to dry out from the storm."

Before anyone could answer any of the string of questions, his wife continued in her British accent. "I know we can't control the weather. You know, I had expected it to be sunny every day; it just never occurred to me that it would rain. I did not bring a single thing to wear in the rain, and these small tourist shops have nothing suitable, just T-shirts and ball caps. It rained so much last night, and it was so windy."

"I hear that there is a hotel at Scrub Island. Do you know anything about it? It's supposed to be very nice, and I bet they have a gift shop," her husband said, interrupting.

"Yes, I'm sure; it's a luxury resort, dear," his wife said.

"Only the best for you, sweetums. I'll book us a villa for the night. Do you want to race up to Marina Cay?"

This was not a conversation but more of a monolog, since he was one of those people who asked and answered his own questions. The group, all stunned into uncharacteristic silence, just looked at him quizzically, waiting for him to continue. How did he know that they had planned to sail up to Marina Cay today? Janeva strained her memory, trying to remember the conversation with the family the other night. Had they ever mentioned or discussed their tentative itinerary?

Thomas, who loved to race sailboats and never resisted a race challenge, said, "Race? To Marina Cay?"

"Loser buys the rum punches?" Greg threw in.

"You're on, boys," Jeff yelled and flicked his blond hair back as he started running down the beach toward the dock where the dinghies were beached. He grabbed his wife by the arm on his way past. "Come on, let's go; we're in a race," he said, and looking over his shoulder, he yelled at his daughter, "Do you plan on swimming?"

"Did you hear that?" Thomas yelled. As he started running down the beach after them, he yelled, "I just opened up a can of whip ass."

"Let's make like a bird and fly," Katie said; then she burst into giggles at the pun.

"What is whip ass?" their daughter yelled back to Katie.

"It's a trophy," Katie called to her as the two groups ran down the beach, sand flying. When they reached the dock, the men started to shove one another to get to their respective dinghies first. Janeva and Steph calmly walked up the dock behind them, helped each other into the dinghy, and then untied the lines. To Thomas's frustration, their overcrowded dinghy lagged behind the other dinghy. Blond Guy had a head start with only two adults and one child. The Jag dinghy, with four adults and Katie, could not get up on a plane and had to push itself ahead through the water. Races were often lost at the start line, and they were already behind.

"Janeva, Katie, move to the bow," Thomas instructed.

"But, Dad, I'll get wet," Katie protested.

"It's ninety degrees out, and you're complaining about getting wet?"

Having no response for this logical retort, Katie joined her mother, sitting precariously on the inflated bow tube as Thomas unsuccessfully attempted to get the small dinghy to a plane.

Chapter 9

Fortunately, because the morning had been spent at the police station, the kayak and paddleboard were already secured to the lifelines, so all that had to be done was to start the engine and untie the two lines that secured the boat to its mooring buoy. Despite their apparent ability to make a good departure, Thomas did not give them time to relax, and he barked orders out like Captain Bligh.

"Greg, Janeva, get us off the mooring buoy. Katie, unfurl the lines so we can hoist the sails. Steph, turn on the electronics."

Then they were under sail and traversing the Sir Francis Drake Channel toward Marina Cay. Thomas sent Janeva to check the chart plotter that was inconveniently located inside the boat at the chart table and not at the helm where he could see it.

"Thomas, I think the boat was searched!" Janeva yelled at him.

So what, he thought. *Who cares? We are in a race.* Ignoring Janeva's message, he called out, "What's our course?"

"Twenty-five degrees north, northeast," she answered, realizing that Thomas had racing fever. Years of marriage had taught her that he was too competitive to let a small matter like the boat being searched impede his chances of winning. Janeva helped Katie and Greg trim the sails to Thomas's satisfaction, and then she quietly slid inside to see if anything had been taken when the boat had been searched.

"Why is the boat so messy?" Katie asked, joining her mother inside. "Dad wants a bottle of water and Greg a soda." Janeva handed her the beverages.

"Katie, Janeva, where are you? We are tacking," called Thomas, aka Captain Bligh.

On autopilot, Janeva ran outside, grabbed the main sheet, and started to wind it around the winch.

"Why are we tacking so soon?" Katie asked. She had wandered out slowly and then with teenage intuition realized she could avoid jobs if she started asking questions.

"Come up here and look around; then you tell me," was Thomas's reply.

Katie did as she was beckoned and then said, "It looks like we might be tied with their boat."

"Actually, they are a tiny bit ahead of us; that's why we tacked to the other side of the channel."

"I still don't get it: wouldn't it be easier to race them if we were on the same side?"

"Visually, yes, but as I said, we are a tiny bit behind them, and we need to get out of their bad air."

"Bad air?"

"Think about it: put your hand up like a sail. You feel the wind on it, right?" Katie nodded. "Your hand is changing the natural course of the wind, so when the air leaves your hand, it swirls around, and if we are in that swirling wind, our boat won't go as fast."

"So does this mean we are going to beat them now?" Katie asked.

"You got it." Looking around, he asked, "Janeva? Where did she go now? The main needs to come in a bit."

"Oh, she's probably down below. The boat's a real mess."

Groaning, he said, "Of course she is. Can you go and grind in the main sheet for me then?"

"But Greg is closer."

"Come on, you're a sailor. I didn't ask Greg; I asked you." Katie went to adjust the sail. She knew better than to argue with that tone, and deep down she was pleased to get the sails just right and to win the race.

In the catamaran, they zigzagged, beating and tacking all the way up the channel, and managed to squeak out just ahead of the other boat as Thomas had predicted. The happiness was short-lived, as the other boat managed to get the last mooring buoy.

"How did they manage that?" Greg asked, amazed.

"What are we going to do now?" Katie asked in alarm. "There are no buoys left."

"We will just have to anchor," Thomas replied calmly. "Janeva, can you go on the bow and get the anchor chain ready?"

Janeva, having finished her cleanup of the boat, had been happily dozing during the sailing race. She yawned and made her way to the bow.

"How much scope should I let out?" she called back to Thomas as she let out the anchor line.

"The depth meter says we are in fifteen feet of water," he replied.

OK, so be it, she thought. Looking around the busy anchorage, Janeva quickly realized that the recommended eight-to-one scope that ensured that any pull would act to force the anchor in deeper wouldn't work, because they could swing too far and collide with another anchored boat. The water was so clear, she could see the bottom. *I'll go with the minimum five-to-one scope*, she thought.

Aloud, she said, "We are in fifteen feet of water plus five feet to account for the distance from the water to the bow, so we'll go with a hundred feet. Let me know when you're ready to tip the anchor."

The chain rode and line were conveniently marked with different-colored ties every twenty-five feet, so Janeva gave Thomas a thumbs-up and, using the windlass remote, dropped the anchor straight down into the water, with Katie looking over the side following its progress.

"Twenty-five feet," Janeva called back to Steph, who was acting as a relay, so they didn't entertain the whole anchorage by yelling at one another.

"Are we on the bottom?" Steph relayed from Thomas.

"Yes, I think so; try some stern way."

Thomas started reversing way slowly as Janeva let out the rest of the anchor rode until she had reached the one-hundred-foot mark. She gestured to Thomas to let him know that all the line was out and hooked to the bow chock so he could gently pull on it and set it.

Janeva moved to the bow of the boat and put her hand on the anchor line to feel for any shake, knowing that an anchor that was dragging or bumping along the bottom would telegraph the shake up the line. Not feeling anything, she did her visual check to see if the water was skipping in the triangle where the line entered the water.

Satisfied that the anchor held, Janeva gave Thomas a thumbs-up and leaned over with Greg's help to secure the bridle to the anchor chain. As she did this, she asked Katie to look around carefully to identify any landmarks on shore so they could see if there was any position change. Dropping the anchor was always easy; the tricky part was knowing that you were securely anchored. Many sailors had found themselves battered up on shore because their anchor had failed to grab the seafloor. A visual location was great unless you were swinging, and the GPS monitor was great, except that it ran down the battery and constantly rang the false alarm, usually in the middle of the night.

The chart said they were lucky enough to be on a sand or mud seafloor rather than rock, and their CQR anchor was perfect. Katie located them by a red flower bush at eight o'clock and a dead tree at four o'clock.

"OK, we'll use that as our visual check to make sure our anchor isn't dragging. By the way, that was a very clever way of marking the landmarks. Go and tell your father. I'll bet he has done the same with the compass."

The anchor set, Greg and Thomas busied themselves lowering the dinghy and putting the kayak and paddleboard in the water for Katie, who was keen to show off her newest move: a headstand on the paddleboard.

Inside the boat, Steph asked Janeva, “Is anything missing?” as she put together some snacks for the group.

“Not that I can see. Fortunately, we had the presence of mind to lock up all our electronics, cameras, and wallets in my travel safe before we left, so there really wasn’t anything of value for them to take.” A travel safe and a medicine kit were two of Janeva’s travel-kit staples. The travel safe was a wire-mesh sack that, once filled, locked shut, and then the wire was pulled around a stable object like, in this case, the mast.

“But they didn’t even take any alcohol,” Steph said as she held up a bottle of rum and moved beer into the cooler for later.

“You’re right. I guess that validates Thomas’s assumption that it was the local police when we were being questioned.”

“I don’t know about that,” Steph replied. “It’s a small island; I suspect that all the police they had were questioning us. I just can’t imagine they had extra to search our boat.”

“I’m sure you’re right, but someone searched the boat, and they were definitely looking for something,” Janeva said, shaking her head.

“Oh well, no harm done, and the boat is all put back to normal now. So let’s put it behind us and enjoy the day.”

Janeva nodded. She knew that Steph, Greg, and Thomas were working hard, for her, to be cheerful and forget about finding Betty’s body.

Chapter 10

After diving off the stern swim platform, they dried off and decided to explore the island and check out the other boats moored around them. Janeva excused herself. She wanted some quiet time alone. She happily sent the rest off in the dinghy and settled down to catch up on her e-mail. After deleting the enormous number of spam e-mails, she was left with a manageable amount of work and "friend" e-mails. From the work category, Janeva quickly answered some pressing questions from Tiffany and Cody, who were in charge of running her small company until she returned.

Jag Tags was not booming, but it was doing OK, designing and selling custom tags for luggage, corporate events, and weddings. Tiffany, Jag Tags' salesperson extraordinaire, was engaged to Cody, the company graphic designer; as requested, Tiffany was sending a daily business update. It sounded like they were managing quite well. Janeva was pleased, and she started to dream of ways she might grow the business now as she typed her response to some questions Tiffany had about a difficult client. Then she forwarded and replied to a few more work e-mails, mostly letting clients know that she was away and connecting them with Tiffany if they needed something before she returned.

Janeva was surprised to find an almost daily e-mail from Trent. Trent always seemed to find and often join them at the club, but he certainly was not a close friend. In fact, he had never been invited to their home. Yet here he was e-mailing her every day, curious about where they were and what they were doing. After her meeting with Deputy Sheriff Dugud, Janeva had asked Trent about Lorenzo and whether he knew anything about Lorenzo's background. She remembered that it had been Trent who had introduced them to Lorenzo in the first place. At the time, Trent said he and Lorenzo had not been close friends but rather yacht-club friends. Janeva couldn't think of anyone else as well connected to the members of the yacht club as Trent, since he seemed to spend all his time there and seemed to be a friend of almost everyone. She guessed that if anyone could dig up information on Lorenzo's activities around the club, it was Trent.

Trent e-mailed that he had found out about Lorenzo's education and was waiting to hear back on some patents that Lorenzo had filed. Janeva replied and encouraged him to continue, but she also wondered to herself why she had this passion for playing detective when this was none of her business, and none of this really had anything to do with her. *Should I tell him about Betty's drowning?* She didn't want to think about Betty's death much less type the words. Somehow that would make it real. She was working hard to pretend that nothing had happened and enjoy the holiday. But her mind raced on with more questions. Why was Betty here? What was Betty doing? Who was Betty? The almost unbelievable coincidence of them being here and finding Betty's corpse seemed too much. She now realized that she did not know very much about Betty. It was almost like some kind of omen out of an ancient Grecian ode. A warning? People end up dead.

She realized that it would certainly seem strange when the club found out about Betty's death and then learned that the Jags and the Writemans had been present and hadn't even informed the club members that their manager had drowned in a boating accident in the BVIs. So she decided to just be up-front and e-mailed Trent, asking him to inform the yacht club. She felt better just to have unburdened herself and disclosed the information. She closed her computer and snuggled into a shady spot in the corner of the dinette as she sleepily looked out at the tropical view of waves breaking over the sandbar. *Take a deep breath*, she told herself, *and appreciate the fragrant flowering shrubs on the island; listen to the gentle rustle of palm fronds waving smoothly on the shore.* The soft clang of halyards slapping and brushing the masts of boats anchored all around sent a message, subconsciously received, that it was time to doze off.

In an almost dreamlike state, she thought, *I am in true bliss*. The shade provided the perfect temperature: it was humid and tropical but not too hot. *If only Katie had not absconded with my sunglasses*. Fortunately, after some searching, she found Katie's sunglasses on her bed. Ugh—they were so dirty, they were almost opaque. But after cleaning the grimy lenses, she found them comfortable, and now it was time to enjoy this perfect moment of relaxation. *My moment in time*, she thought.

Wondering at the back of her sleepy mind why Katie had taken her glasses, Janeva mused that Katie's sunglasses were too precious because she had talked her father into buying expensive Maui Jim ones. Janeva's, on the other hand, were thirty-five-dollar Nike sports glasses purchased from Costco, so Katie had prudently taken her mother's glasses in case she might lose them overboard on the dinghy.

Now fully relaxed, with Katie's prestigious sunglasses on and a cold glass of iced tea in hand, Janeva settled down to enjoy the clear blue sky and salty ocean breeze, and she even saw some migrating butterflies to fully complete this moment of perfection.

But as soon as she was relaxed and had emptied her mind just like the yoga instructors always demanded, her brain decided to force upon her the extraordinary, almost outlandish, sequence of events that had conspired to destroy both sailing holidays.

Her brain reminded her of the chip. There had to be more to it than Deputy Sheriff Dugud implied. Sitting alone on the deck listening to the water lap against the pontoon hull, Janeva started to review what she'd learned about the chip. OK, coincidence, but what were the odds that one family taking two separate and independent sailing vacations to distant places would be witnesses to *yacht-club members'* deaths both times? And the chip? She had researched graphene chips and recorded into her iPhone that graphene wasn't even discovered until 2004 by Andre Geim and Kostya Novoselov at Manchester University when they were described as performing an offbeat experiment one Friday evening. It was, she had recorded, really a two-dimensional crystal lattice of pure carbon and in 2004 was certainly the thinnest and strongest substance known to science. Her information said it was more than forty times stronger than steel, and it was a semiconductor with electrical conductivity one thousand times better than silicon.

Everyone in America had at least one silicon chip now, she thought, so the deputy sheriff had returned the chip to Katie because it was just another computer chip and not apparently related in any way to the events under police investigation. Katie had found the chip at Chatterbox Falls and called it the Chatterbox chip. She would get over her fascination with it. No information seemed in any way to involve the chip, and in fact, the chip didn't contain any information other than the theoretical photo imager and the apparently meaningless bar code of zeroes and ones.

The more she pondered, the clearer it became that the Jag family connections with these deaths were chance happenings. Coincidence. As one of her favorite authors, Leonard Mlodinow, noted, random events can shape our lives. Then again, Thomas's office had been raided and searched, and even here, thousands of miles away, this boat had been searched, so was this stretching the coincidence.

OK, she surmised, *Thomas's business must be in some way related to the searches.* Why waste time searching if there weren't at least some connection with his business? As Thomas often noted, 3-D printing was changing the manufacturing world, and Thomas and his close associates were quietly perfecting their process and doing research into areas that he never discussed or revealed to Janeva. She wondered if Lorenzo's and Betty's seemingly unrelated deaths could in some way be associated with the 3-D printing firm. In fact, Janeva said to herself, the only connection with the deaths was that they had both occurred in association with the Jag family sailing vacations.

Enough, she told herself; *forget it. This is not a mystery! Enjoy this holiday away from Jag Tags and 3-D work.* Then the demon investigator inside her head asked her, what if they were being followed? What if they had searched their home? So much for quiet sleep. Janeva reached for her iPad and texted Tiffany, asking her to check on the house.

She heard a shout and noted that the dinghy was back. She reluctantly got up, caught the bowline, and heaved the dinghy up to the back of the catamaran, tying it off; she then assisted with the unloading.

"Where is Katie?" Janeva asked.

"She's behind us," Greg said with a sly smile and a gleam in his eye.

"What? Where is she?" she asked, concerned. They all ignored her and instead sat down at the table around Thomas's laptop.

"What's going on?" Janeva asked, baffled. "Where is Katie?"

Chapter 11

"We ran into Terri," Steph said casually.

"Who?" Janeva looked confused.

"You know Terri." She was baiting Janeva.

"Terri who?"

"You know, Terri Turnell, the membership director from the yacht club."

"She is *here?*" Janeva exclaimed. "Where did you find her?"

"At the Tierra! Tierra! Restaurant. It's great: overlooks a private beach, perfect for kids like Terri's to play in the sand as the adults enjoy yummy drinks, and Terri said the food is great too."

"So she is staying at the resort?"

"No, on a superyacht. She invited—"

"Demanded," Thomas interrupted with an eye roll.

"OK, demanded that we all come to the yacht tonight and join them in a memorial service for Betty."

After a moment to process the astonishing revelation that Terri was also in the BVIs, Janeva rallied with, "Well, that makes sense. Terri was probably Betty's closest friend, and I guess the membership director wasn't critical to the day-to-day management of the club, so they were together. Are we going?"

"Yes," Thomas growled.

"Really? You agreed? It's not like you to give up a night of your holidays to spend on a boat with people we don't know, remembering a woman you didn't know."

"I didn't say yes—Greg did."

"Greg!" Janeva was surprised. It was not like Greg to jump in like that.

Greg looked up at her with a sly smile. "I am a bit uncomfortable with Betty's death. There are many unanswered questions. I can't help wondering if she was trying to escape. Are we to understand that a seasick older woman who we now know had a fractured arm and whom we all saw had a significant laceration on her head actually swam to our boat?"

"She had a fractured arm? When did you find that out? Did you tell the police?" Janeva asked.

"Of course I did," Greg snapped. Janeva was taken aback. She was used to this from Thomas but not Greg; he was always so quiet and laid-back.

"But—" she ventured.

"Once they got the call from *Lady Cécilee*, they were happy to mark it down to accidental drowning." Greg groaned.

Thomas added "Makes sense. The last thing they want is that kind of bad press. Think about it, Janeva: an American woman gets murdered on a superyacht. It would be bad for tourism."

"I'm sure you are right. Why do you call it a superyacht?" Janeva asked.

"Come here and check it out," Steph said and moved to the other side of the table so Janeva could get in and see what was on the computer screen. What she saw was a gorgeous dark-blue yacht. The online specs said it was a 240-foot yacht and could accommodate twenty-two guests as well as a crew of twenty-three. According to the website, the yacht had six decks in total, with a range of guest areas, including a main saloon, a dining room on her main deck, a Jacuzzi with pool on the observation deck, a chart room or library, a fitness room, a dive room, and a swim platform. She was available for charter for the small fortune of $400,000 per week. This included the crew, a dive master, and a vast selection of dinghies, Jet Skis, and other water toys.

"Holy crap" was the first thing that came out of her mouth. "Oops—sorry. That was not my most intelligent response."

"Yup, and that's where we are going to spend our evening," said Thomas, who was completely unimpressed by huge powerboats. But if it had been a sailboat, wild horses couldn't have kept him away.

"Terri chartered that superyacht?" Janeva stammered. "I didn't think they were that wealthy, but—"

Steph chimed in. "You never know. Her husband, Chad, is in the oil business, so maybe they really are so rich that they don't know what to do with all their money."

"I was warned to keep away from him." Greg thoughtfully drummed his fingers. "He has a reputation for worming himself into business deals." After a pause, he added, "To charter a yacht like that, you'd need to be serious *M* money, probably *B* money?"

"OK, so we have a couple of mysteries to solve. First, where is Katie? Then, did Chad charter *Lady Cécilee*, and finally what really happened to Betty?" Janeva decided it was time to take control of the conversation before it digressed into *B* money versus *M* money—*B* as in billions and *M* as in millions.

"Relax, Janeva. Katie is fine. Do you think I would just go off and forget about her? She will be here in a moment," Thomas said with an eye roll. "As for tonight, we will not be solving any mysteries. We will make a quick appearance, then leave."

"We can't just rudely leave," Janeva exclaimed. "Betty was our club manager. None of us knew her well, but I care, and you can at least display some sensitivity and compassion."

"Janeva's right." Greg nodded in agreement to Thomas's scowl.

"Honey, is there any way you can think of that Betty might have sustained her head injury in the water?" Steph put her arm around Greg.

"I guess it's possible. I'm not a forensic pathologist, but when I examined the laceration, I felt that the skull was depressed, and that hints at a pretty significant injury. Let's assume she was knocked unconscious, fell overboard, and drowned despite her self-inflating life vest. Then pathology should confirm that there was water in her lungs. Of course, we know that some people die of respiratory arrest from laryngeal spasm when they hit cold water, but this is the Caribbean, and the water is warm, so it's my guess, based on what I saw, that the head injury would have done more than knock her unconscious. It might have killed her."

Before anyone could respond, a dinghy pulled up to their boat and stopped the grisly conversation.

"Hello! Permission to come aboard?" said a voice in a familiar British accent.

"Trent!" Janeva exclaimed, astonished. "What are you doing here? I just e-mailed you."

"My dear Janeva," he said, chuckling. "You're surprised." His round face broke out in a huge grin. "I missed you all, you see. It is boring at the club without the Jags and Writemans. That's why I kept asking you where you were going—because I wanted to come down and surprise you."

"You certainly did that." Katie was on the dinghy with Trent and his guide. The anchorage was full of similar white catamarans, and it wouldn't have been easy for him to find *Joie de Vivre*.

With Katie's help, Trent heaved his round figure up onto the pontoon and came up the stairs to join the group seated at the outdoor table. As usual, he was dressed in a suit, but this time it was a cream-colored linen suit with knee-length shorts instead of trousers. The one concession he had made for the heat was that he was not wearing a tie on his short-sleeve, button-up shirt. A stylish, cream-colored, brimmed straw hat completed his ensemble. Janeva looked down at her bikini top and colorful wrap-around sarong and felt a bit underdressed but then shrugged. She was on holiday, after all.

"Where are you staying, and where did you get the dinghy?" Janeva returned his hug.

"I'm staying at the luxury Scrub Island resort, naturally," he replied as he removed his linen suit jacket and carefully draped it over his arm. "They have many variations of boats you can charter. Now"—he looked at her critically—"you must go and get changed. You can't go to Betty's memorial in that outfit."

Janeva realized that he was correct; they all needed to change into something more appropriate. Fortunately, she had insisted that Katie bring at least one nice sundress. Katie didn't like dresses these days and had argued that they would spend all their time in their bathing suits, so why use up valuable luggage space with a dress?

Chapter 12

Exactly an hour later, the promised tender came to convey the group to the memorial service. The tender, a forty-foot powerboat, was painted dark blue to match the superyacht *Lady Cécilee*. The crew, wearing matching blue-and-white uniforms, professionally and efficiently collected the group and delivered them to the anchored yacht. Once aboard, they followed a crew member up to the main deck, where a distinguished gray-haired and bearded gentleman smiled and walked over to welcome them.

"Welcome aboard the *Lady Cécilee*, and thank you for coming. I'm Ford Douglas."

"Sir Ford," Terri said, coming up behind him. "Sir Ford, this is my good friend Janeva and her husband, Thomas, and their daughter, Katie," she correctly identified them. Her introduction surprised Janeva because Janeva felt that she hardly knew Terri and certainly would not have considered her a "good friend." And how did she know Katie? Janeva couldn't recall any instance where Terri and

Katie had ever met, but she thought that was, after all, the role of a membership director.

"Right," said Sir Ford, "and of course you know Terri and her husband, Chad, from your yacht club." Chad greeted them with a smile and said he'd never had the privilege of meeting the Jags before, but it was nice that members of the yacht club were here.

"But"—he made a show out of pointing and tapping his watch to get Sir Ford's attention—"please. I do apologize; I know this is a somber moment, but very soon, Sir Ford and I must take a short break and take a quick, prearranged conference call."

Thomas took over the introductions and said, "And these are our good friends: Trent Braise-Bottom III and Steph and Dr. Greg Writeman, who are also longtime yacht-club members and who knew Betty."

Trent grabbed Sir Ford's hand and said, "We are all so deeply sorry to hear of Betty's death. She was a pillar of our club, and she made it our comfortable second home."

"Thank you, Mr. Braise-Bottom. Are you by any chance a relation of Charles Braise-Bottom, Waverly Manor in Gloucester?" Sir Ford asked Trent.

"Trent, please." Trent smiled at Sir Ford. "And why, yes, he is my great-uncle."

"Well, well, now, we might have a lot to talk about," he said and pointed Trent toward some comfortable lounge chairs. "I'll join you shortly." Trent was in his element: he loved nothing better than to talk about his prestigious family tree. Chad and Sir Ford left the group to Terri and slipped into Sir Ford's.

"Janeva, thank God you are here," Terri said, grabbing Janeva's arm in a friendly girlfriend-like manner. "I need a friend to talk to," Terri cooed at her as if they were long-lost best friends.

"I'm so glad you're here; it's been dreadful," she continued, sighing dramatically as she directed Janeva away from the group toward the railing of the yacht. As the two walked away from the group, Janeva looked back over her shoulder to Steph. Catching her eye, Janeva gestured with her chin for Steph to join them, but to her surprise, Steph shook her head, pointed at the TV, and went to the bar. Janeva could see that CNBC was showing scenes from Hispaniola, and she saw the heading that included Haiti and the Dominican Republic. *Of course, a yacht this size would have satellite TV*, Janeva thought to herself.

Interrupting her thoughts, Terri started talking, this time in a stage whisper, and leaned out over the boat railing so that Janeva had to do the same to hear her. *My God*, Janeva thought, looking down, *even from the lower deck, there is no way Betty could have fallen from this height and then swum to our boat in a storm, even with a flotation life jacket.* Shaking herself, she realized that Terri had stopped talking and was waiting for her to reply, something she was unable to do because she hadn't been listening.

Instead, she said weakly, "I'm so sorry about Betty. I know you two were close friends. This must be just awful for you. And on your holidays—"

Tears filled Terri's eyes, and she interrupted Janeva. "Oh, it is. Betty invited us on this cruise, and now she is dead, and I'm so uncomfortable here now. It doesn't feel right. I feel like we should go, but the kids would be so disappointed, and Sir Ford insists that we stay."

"How did Betty know Sir Ford?" Janeva asked her gently.

"Oh, Betty and Sir Ford were longtime friends. They had known each other for much of their lives, and because Betty had no family, she wanted us here, as, you know, as her family. It is so sad. Now she is dead." Terri started to cry softly. Between sobs, she said, "I mean, she used to say that I was the daughter she never had, but I thought she just didn't have a daughter. I didn't realize that she had no family at all—that is, until this trip."

Rubbing her back and handing her a tissue, Janeva asked, "Have you gone on many holidays with Betty before?"

"No, this was our first. With the two kids, it's just easier to go out on our boat or to our ski cabin, you know?"

"I remember how difficult it was to travel with a small child, and it's such a long flight here," Janeva replied.

"That's true, but this time Sir Ford sent his private jet for all of us, and we even brought the nanny, so it was really very pleasant until"—she sobbed—"Betty's death."

"It must have been so hard for you," Janeva said again. "How did it happen?"

"Well, we don't know what happened. There was that terrible storm. She didn't turn up, so of course, we searched the boat. We were all so scared. How could she have fallen off? It just doesn't make sense. If she was drunk or confused, maybe. But she was very careful about alcohol. I just can't understand how she could have been swept overboard. Look, these railings are thick and solid. Of course, it was a nasty storm with high waves, but not so high to break over this deck—it's two stories up. It just doesn't seem possible."

Janeva asked, "Do you know why Betty was on the deck that night?"

"No, we were all staying indoors and out of the rain."

Before she could ask more questions, Sir Ford clapped to get everyone's attention and asked them to move to the stern of the boat, where they had set up for the memorial service.

Everyone dutifully moved back and found chairs set up in rows of three with an aisle down the middle. Janeva's group picked the port side and took their seats.

Sir Ford walked up to the front and gave a touching speech about how he met Betty and shared some funny stories. He told them he had known Betty for many years and said tearfully that she had been the love of his life. Betty was now his wife. This was their honeymoon, he said. They had been married only the week before in a private ceremony.

Gasps went up from the small audience. As Janeva looked over at the small group of guests whom they had just met, she was startled to see looks of outrage and anger. Sir Ford must have sensed or expected that response, because he continued in a conciliatory voice.

"I know you are surprised, and our wedding was planned to be a surprise. But I wanted and needed you to be here, for the honeymoon and celebration." He turned and looked directly at an attractive woman in her thirties and a handsome man sitting beside her. "I wanted you," he said, "to get to know Betty first before you knew her as your stepmother. She was"—sobbing, he stopped to regain his composure—"such a lovely and wonderful woman. I just knew that you would all fall in love with her as I have.

"We had planned to announce it and make a grand family celebration our final night of this trip." He looked pointedly at his daughter and son-in-law as if expecting a response. Getting only blank faces, he continued. "Now I would like to ask Terri, who was Betty's dearest friend and like a daughter to her, to say a few words; then please will you all join me in a toast to my wife, Betty?"

In a short but emotional speech, Terri confirmed that she had been a witness to the wedding and that her friend Betty had asked her to keep the secret until the planned time when she and Ford could make the announcement. "Words cannot describe how sad this celebration cruise has become. But," she continued, "let us at least toast the memory of our friend Betty." Champagne was distributed, and the staff walked around topping up champagne flutes and offering tasty appetizers.

Janeva glanced at the other young people present and was curious to know how they were connected to Sir Ford and Betty. She did not have to wait long because Sir Ford arrived and corralled the group to make introductions.

"You already know Terri and her husband, Chad, and their lovely young children, Colin and Bella." Katie charmingly crouched down and said hi to five-year-old Bella and three-year-old Colin. Colin gave her a cheeky grin and then joined his sister hiding behind their mother's legs, all the while staring up at Katie, intrigued. Janeva knew that in no time, Katie would be playing happily with the two children.

“This way,” said Sir Ford as he directed them toward the bar, where the handsome man was now back on his barstool with a large golden-colored drink in front of him. It was sans ice. Janeva guessed it was probably scotch because that was the only golden-brown alcohol she could think of that you drank without ice, especially in the tropic heat. He was intently watching a large TV screen. Two stools over, a fashionable woman sat lethargically flipping through a magazine.

“This is my son-in-law, Ashton Winston, and my beautiful daughter, Sylvia.” He gave Sylvia an indulgent smile, and the two gave the group a disinterested look. They politely and limply shook hands but made no effort to engage in conversation. Sir Ford, unfazed, said, “Now for the young people.” He looked around and, not seeing them, said, “Let’s take you on a tour of *Lady Cécilee* and track them down, shall we?”

As they started the tour, Sir Ford noted to Terri, “I’m a bit worried about Sylvia and Ashton; I had expected more of a reaction from them when I told them about the wedding. Would you be so kind as to check in with Sylvia and make sure she is OK?”

Janeva was sure she saw a brief look of distaste pass over Terri’s face, but Sir Ford was ushering them along the passageway into the yacht, and Terri turned away to go and join Sylvia and Ashton as requested.

The group dutifully followed him through a set of large sliding doors and emerged into a spacious salon tastefully finished better than many luxury homes. Designer furniture and perfectly placed artwork and statues complemented the space. As they walked through room after impeccably decorated room, Janeva started to worry about letting Katie out of her sight. Turning to Steph, she said, "I wonder where Katie's disappeared to."

"Under the circumstances, I know why you might be worried. I can't believe how amazing this yacht is," she replied in a whisper.

"Don't worry about the young lady," Sir Ford said. Clearly, his hearing was very good. "I set one of my most trusted crew to keep an eye on her and the other young children, so I'm sure all is well."

"Thank you, Sir Ford; that's a relief," Janeva replied.

They had toured the main salon, main dining room, library, den, office, and gourmet galley.

As someone who loved to cook, Janeva sighed and oohed and aahed as she caressed the Sub-Zero fridge and freezer, Viking six-burner range, commercial-sized double ovens, granite countertops, and a whole wall designated to hold a huge wine fridge.

"Wow, what I wouldn't give to have a kitchen like this," Janeva said to the group at large.

"Janeva's an excellent cook," Thomas replied, to Sir Ford's puzzled look.

"Oh yes, of course. My cook and kitchen staff seem to enjoy working here as well," he replied, looking at Janeva a little strangely.

Janeva smiled to herself as she realized that her precious and satisfying hobby was to Sir Ford a job for a paid chef. Now Sir Ford must be wondering why he was the host to a chef. She suppressed a laugh as she heard Steph whisper,

"I don't think it has ever occurred to him that a wife would cook, much less enjoy it."

They left the galley and headed down a window-lined hallway. "The next door to port is our VIP guest room." Ford hesitated and then explained, "We set it up for Betty as her office. Even when she was on holiday or in this case our honeymoon, she concentrated for a few hours every day on her business affairs, mostly yacht-club business. I even installed a new computer and printer for her personal use. As you can see, the staff has already completed packing up her personal belongings to send back to her home in Archipelago," Sir Ford said sadly. Janeva saw tears in his eyes.

"What about her family? Where are they?" Janeva asked, ignoring the outraged looks from Steph. Steph knew that Terri had told her Betty did not have any family.

"Sadly, she didn't have any family—no one at all. Unbelievable and unexpected as it seems, as her husband I am now legally required to assume management of her affairs until we can find her will. I suppose that I have power of attorney. In any case, I have initiated the appropriate arrangements. I expect that she'd want cremation, but of course, we spent our moments together discussing our plans for our new life and never even considered death." He wrung his hands. "I only hope that that is what she would have wanted. I wholeheartedly believe she would want her final resting place to be in Archipelago. She loved your town, sailing in the San Francisco Bay, and the yacht club was her passion. And we all knew that Betty had both business sense and lots of common sense and would almost certainly, in this hot Caribbean climate, insist that cremation was the best option." Again, he sighed and moved away from the door of Betty's room.

Janeva could see that Betty's room was empty and cleaned, as Ford had explained. Her possessions were packed in her suitcases for transport home. As the rest of the group stopped to look in the doorway of a beautifully lush room with a king-sized bed, Janeva held back and then said aloud, "Oh, look at this fabric," as she casually wandered into Betty's room.

"What fabric, Janeva?" Thomas queried. Janeva ignored him. She was not interested in the fabric. She needed to experience Betty's space. She hoped there might still be some clues. "Leave the fabric, Janeva. We are almost ready to leave," Thomas said from across the hall, in the nicest possible voice, but his teeth were bared when he said it, making it very clear that he did not want his wife snooping around.

Sir Ford unwittingly jumped into this marital debate. "Oh, you must meet the kids before you leave and see the entertainment deck."

Janeva had moved to the far side of the room, in front of a small desk that she imagined was where Betty worked on her laptop. Above the desk was a large window framed by tasteful patterned curtains. She reached across the desk to touch the material.

"Janeva, come on," Thomas said in a loud whisper as the group had all turned away to follow Sir Ford. Janeva noted, however, a single sheet of paper in the printer shelf. The printer was probably part of the basic office supplies, and whoever had emptied the room had removed the laptop but missed the printer. She reached down, slipped the paper off the printer ledge, and quickly dropped it into her shoulder bag; then she rushed to join the group.

Sir Ford ushered the group up an elegant stairway that framed an enormous painting.

"What a lovely piece," Trent said, admiring the painting as a whole and then squinting to read the signature.

Janeva looked at Trent in surprise. How did he know this stuff? He couldn't have read the signature; it looked indecipherable to her.

"You have a good eye." Sir Ford gave Trent an approving nod. "I had all the artwork specially commissioned."

The tour continued, but now Sir Ford included details of the artwork, light fixtures, chandelier, and other custom finishes. Janeva and Steph found it very interesting, though Janeva could see that the men, except Trent, were pretending to be interested and were probably eager to move along.

Fortunately, before Thomas could come up with a valid excuse to leave, the tour arrived at the top deck—or as Sir Ford called it, the entertainment deck. They walked past a gym stocked with weights, a wall of mirrors with a ballet bar, a treadmill, and stair climber, all positioned so you could either stare out the large windows at the fabulous Caribbean view or watch a large TV.

Leaving the icy-cool, air-conditioned gym area, they were "wowed" again as they walked through what could have been a nightclub: to starboard was a wet bar and to port a small dance floor equipped with disco ball and lights. Hip-hop music was blaring. Katie, who, much to Janeva's relief, had joined them, ran to the dance floor to do a cartwheel, followed by a back bend and other hip-hop moves she must have learned in her jazz-dance classes. Sir Ford reached around behind the bar and turned down the music; then, seeing the disappointed look on Katie's face, he pushed some other buttons, and to everyone's surprise, a clear glass wall slowly descended from the side and closed off the dance floor from the outside deck. He then turned the music back up and gestured to the adults to follow him through the glass door. As the door closed, it muffled the music, much to the relief of the group, some of whom thought it was more like noise than music.

"I had the dance area soundproofed, so the young kids can dance all night," Sir Ford explained.

They were now on the upper aft outdoor deck, where lounge chairs surrounded a shallow dip pool with a step up to a built-in hot tub. Here a small group of young adults, twentysomethings, were sprawled on the lounge chairs talking and laughing. As they approached, the young men stood awkwardly. Janeva both was impressed by their formal politeness and had the distinct impression that they couldn't wait for this event to end so they could change into bathing suits and zoom around on one of the Jet Skis or other water toys Janeva's group had already seen on their tour.

"This is my grandson, Finn," Sir Ford said proudly, and Janeva had to stifle a giggle. For a moment, she thought his name was Finn Ford, but then she realized that Ford was Sir Ford's first name and that Finn would have his father's last name. There was no doubt that Finn was his handsome father's son, with his chiseled jaw and spiky, dark-blond hair and penetrating hazel eyes. A feeling of relief washed over

Janeva as she looked over her shoulder to see Katie still happily dancing by herself on the dance floor. *I am not ready for when a handsome young man like this one would change her behavior*, she thought.

Sir Ford continued to introduce the group. "My granddaughter, Penelope."

Next, they met a stunning raven-haired girl named Natasha. She turned her big blue eyes toward the group and said she was Terri's and Chad's nanny here to look after their adorable children, Colin and Bella. Lastly, they were introduced to a tall and gangly, though attractive, young man named Brandon, Finn's friend. As they made their way back down through the yacht, Sir Ford explained that he always encouraged his grandchildren to bring a friend with them, so they didn't have to hang out with the old folks.

Chapter 13

To Thomas's great relief, it was finally time to leave. Sir Ford had arranged for the crew of *Lady Cécilee* to deliver the group back to their catamaran.

"What are we going to do now?" Katie asked.

"You will you be my guests for dinner at the hotel, of course," Trent said.

Seeing that Thomas was about to decline, he added, "The hotel has very fast Wi-Fi."

"Well, hmm. Right. OK then. I need to Skype the office and do some downloads that can't be done from the boat. The Wi-Fi is just too slow."

"And for Katie, it has a wonderful pool, with a waterfall and waterslide."

"Yeah," Katie said and gave Trent a thumbs-up.

"Wonderful. I will make a reservation at the Caravela restaurant. It is very elegant. Did you know that it was named for the wooden caravel ships from the fifteenth century, of which the *Pinta*, the fastest of Christopher Columbus's three ships, was one? But more important, the restaurant has an incredible view of Camanoe Pass, and we can see the sunset," Trent said enthusiastically.

"We're leaving tomorrow morning. Trent, what will you do?" Steph asked.

"Well, I guess I'll have to force myself to suffer through some snorkeling, swimming, sitting around the pool, and eating gourmet food," Trent said with his large, jolly laugh. "And Sir Ford invited me back to *Lady Cécilee* tomorrow morning to trace family histories," he added with a wink. Trent loved nothing more than English history.

***

The next morning Janeva slept in, dashing her unrealistic hopes of doing a morning yoga routine on the deck. The night before, they had decided to get an early start, so breakfast was scrambled eggs and toast as they sailed. Granola bars would have been a better choice, as they were experiencing a twenty-knot blow. The first batch of eggs was nearly blown off the plates as Janeva handed them outside, so they reefed the main and were now eating out of bowls instead. It was a great sail, and even reefed, *Joie de Vivre* lifted off. They watched the knot meter register seven, eight, nine, and finally ten knots. Surprisingly, the GPS and knot meter coincided, which meant they weren't in a current. A matching catamaran was keeping pace to port—a challenge that explained Thomas's and Greg's burst of activity on the boat. Thomas, now at the helm, was demanding the full main, and Greg was constantly cranking the sheets tighter or just giving a bit more slack as he kept the draft full and the telltales flying straight to achieve maximum speed. Despite the heavy load of food, water, and baggage, this was going to be a race.

Steph and Janeva were holding on. It was exciting but certainly not the usual catamaran smooth sail. Instead, they were close-hauled and pitching into the wind, and Thomas controlled the roll. Katie had wedged herself into a corner near the sliding-glass doorway. There, she was well positioned to both eavesdrop on the conversation and escape when the conversation got dull.

"Well, I didn't expect that on our vacation," Steph said with a sigh.

"What, Betty's death? Or spending the afternoon on a superyacht?" Greg asked from his perch above. He was grinding a winch, tightening the main as they tried to beat even closer to the wind.

"Both." She shook her head. "Betty's death is tragic. What will our yacht club do?"

"Hire a new manager, I guess?" Janeva agreed.

"Yes, you are right. It's just…" She trailed off.

Determined to brighten the mood, Janeva changed the subject. "This boat feels rather small compared to *Lady Cécilee*."

"True. We lack a cinema, pool, hot tub, dance floor, and twenty-five crew members, but we make up for it in fun. Is it beer o'clock yet?" Thomas asked.

"Dad, you know the power squadron rules: no alcohol ever while the boat is sailing," Katie said to provoke her father, who had insisted she read the manual.

"Ha-ha," her father jested back. "But believe it or not, we're not in Canada or America, and we need hydration. The sun is well over the yardarm."

"And it's never too early for beer in the Caribbean," Greg said. With a roll of her eyes and a shake of her head, Janeva provided the beer to the boys and handed out Coke Zeros for the rest. The evening before, during the "where should we go tomorrow?" debate, Janeva had convinced the group to go to Anegada Island. They were convinced by her description of the succulent under-the-stars lobster dinners that she had read were available on the island.

Janeva had an ulterior motive for wanting to go to Anegada Island. Trent's research had found out that Lorenzo had been at Anegada Island just before bringing his yacht up to Canada and Princess Louisa Inlet. Maybe it was just another coincidence, but here they were in the same area, and she wondered if just maybe in some way, Anegada was connected with the events that had occurred in Princess Louisa Inlet. She convinced herself that this was a win-win: they would get to see the island and sample the recommended food, and she could indulge her curiosity. *I mean*, she thought, *there is no harm in doing a little investigating.*

"Listen to this." Steph had opened a guidebook called *The Cruising Guide to the Virgin Islands* by Nancy and Simon Scott.

Katie groaned and said, "Noooo, I don't want to know about resorts and dining rooms. I want to explore the shoreline and snorkel some reefs. Do you know that there is a ton of scientific data that concludes that humans are on the verge of causing unprecedented damage to our oceans and the animals living in them? I want to see the coral and ocean before it's all gone, and I have to write a report for science class."

"Um, really? Where did that come from?"

"It's from the journal *Science*, if you really want to know. Right here in the Caribbean, they are starting seabed mining." She raised her eyebrows and widened her eyes. "Yes, for huge profit that will wreck the ecosystem and pollute the Caribbean."

"OK, but you know it's also important to understand the history and story of the island, if you want to observe and help. The best scientific observations are still meaningless without context."

Steph, engrossed in the guidebook, ignored this mother-daughter exchange and read, "'Anegada Island is comprised of coral and limestone. At its highest point, the island is twenty-eight feet above sea level. Created by the movement between the Atlantic and Caribbean plates, which meet to the northeast of the island, Anegada is only eleven miles long and fringed with mile after mile of white, sandy beaches. Horseshoe Reef, which extends ten miles to the southeast, has claimed over three hundred known wrecks and provides excellent scuba diving. This reef also provides a home for some of the largest fish in the area, as well as lobster and conch.'"

Steph looked up at Katie.

"See, you will have it all. You love to snorkel: you can study the reef and look for damage and possibly snorkel over a shipwreck."

Katie gave her mother a big grin, in one of those instant mood changes her parents were getting used to, and said, "OK, that sounds fun…but do I have to eat lobster?"

"I checked, and the menu has other options that I'm sure you will like, but I would really like you to try the lobster," her mother said in that tone known to all children that sounds like a request but is understood to be a command.

"OK, one bite."

Janeva smiled in response, knowing that if they provided garlic butter, she would love lobster.

Katie disappeared into a corner of the boat with her iPad to watch one of the shows she had downloaded, and Thomas and Greg were engrossed in getting maximum sail speed, leaving Janeva and Steph to themselves.

"Now that we are alone, I want to show you what I found on the printer in Betty's room. I did a quick read, and I think it has some information that might be of interest."

"Really?"

"It's a list, but I think there might be clues in it." Janeva flattened the crumpled sheet of handwritten paper on the table to read.

Chapter 14

<u>*To-do list and memo to myself*</u>

1. *Get legal advice re joint tenancy and estate law.*
2. *Learn more and get details on Ford's new financial venture.*
3. *Learn how to be a step-grandmother.*
4. *Activate the new ideas for youth activities and team building at the yacht club.*
5. *Do something special for Ford to show him how much I love him!*
6. *Ask for confidential help, i.e., a person not connected to the current executive, re yacht club membership issue.*
7. *The crew is splendid. Ford is loving. I've always been an optimist and idealist, so why, why, why do I sense hostility here?*

Janeva looked up and then finally broke the silence. "That's all of it. I'll bet this was written the same night we found Betty's body."

Steph nodded in agreement. "And she was worried. Hmm. It's another fragment of circumstantial information adding credence to Greg's concern that her head injury might not have been an accident," Steph said contemplatively. "I wonder what will happen now. I guess the local police will have to investigate."

"You know, I'm not sure that we should give this letter to the police," Janeva replied.

"What? Why not?"

"Let's review what we know. The police confirmed Betty as death by drowning. There will be no postmortem exam, physician, or coroner assessment, and then she is to be promptly cremated. And I'd have to explain how I got it."

"I guess you are right," Steph said. "We have no way to prove that Betty wrote the letter, and Ford is grieving enough; he needs to heal. And I have a feeling that the locals would rather it was an accident anyway. We should tell Thomas and Greg."

"I know, but Thomas is going to roar when he finds out I've been looking for clues."

"You're right about that. He hates you snooping around," Steph replied sympathetically. "I could say that I found the letter?"

Janeva shook her head and took a deep breath. "No." Janeva thought for a moment and continued. "It would be really interesting if we could find what she thought might be happening at the club."

"Too bad you didn't get her laptop," Steph teased.

Shaking her head and laughing, Janeva said, "I expect it will just show up…after all, it's been one unusual coincidence after another. Betty, Terri, then Trent. I mean, now every time we go somewhere, I expect to see someone I know from our yacht club that is thousands of miles away."

"It was nice of Trent to treat us all to dinner last night—"

"Look up, girls; we can just see Anegada!" Thomas called down.

The low island was barely visible—more like a shadow or cloud formation. No wonder it had sunk so many boats before GPS.

Chapter 15

The fantastic sail came to a slightly disappointing end as they arrived to find all the mooring buoys taken. To make matters worse, just as they entered the bay, they were smacked by a sudden squall—gusts of strong wind and a downpour of tropical rain. They had to drop anchor. Janeva retrieved the light rain shells she had packed for exactly this kind of weather. Handing Thomas his shell, she went forward to help, relaying messages between Thomas, who was operating the anchor windlass, and Greg, who was at the helm. Then the weather changed right after their perfect job of anchoring, getting the rode out five times the depth plus the vertical from the water surface to the bow winch, and confirming the grip on the bottom.

As is common in tropical climes, the rainstorm ended as quickly as it had begun, so by the time the anchor was set, the sky was again blue and the sun shining, and everything was drying. They dropped the paddleboard into the water for Katie; then Greg and Steph went off in the double kayak to explore. Thomas and Janeva stayed behind to catch up on their business e-mail.

"Trent wants to know where we are going next," Janeva said, relaying his e-mail.

"He should have told us he wanted to come with us," Thomas said with a smirk. "We could have booked a bigger boat."

"That would be the day. You know Trent: he isn't interested in sailing, but he does love staying in the luxury resorts."

"Harrumph. You're right, and he did treat us to a lovely dinner last night. Tell him we are staying here for one more night but will return to Marina Kay the day after tomorrow and will look forward to seeing him there."

"He will like that," Janeva said as she dutifully e-mailed this back to Trent, who must have been online because she immediately got a response back. "He wants to know where we are going after that."

"Probably over to Prickly Pear Island," Thomas said, and he paused in thought and picked up the cruising guide. After looking at the small charts printed in the book, he said, "Recommend to him the resort at Bitter End; the book says it's a luxury resort."

To keep their agreement with Catherine, as compensation for the use of the boat, the group had agreed to do an inventory of all that was in it and on it. The boat broker had told Catherine that most buyers decided on the description, and it was essential that his listing include the details right down to things like tool kits, manuals, PFDs, and galley supplies, and then the full, expert survey of the boat and engine. Catherine, of course, didn't like boating and had never been on the *Joie de Vivre*, and she was pleased that the Writeman and Jag families were going to compile the inventory.

So, with the boat empty except for the two of them, this was a good time to initiate the inventory, and Janeva turned on her small MacBook Air travel computer. She opened the inventory document file and noted that Thomas and Greg had already recorded the mechanical and sail inventory. She scrolled down the Excel spreadsheet, creating a tab called "Navigation Station." Then she lifted the navigation tabletop and started to document the burgees, magnifying glasses, small extra compass, barometer, navigation aids protractor, and dividers. She tried to name or describe the collection of other small bits and pieces in the table.

Finished with the nav table, she moved to the stern compartment lazaret and started to rummage around, pulling out and documenting flashlights and a first-aid kit. She found some other plastic boxes and opened one that held what looked like cell-phone parts, power plugs, and other parts to the router, she guessed by the logo. At the very bottom, almost hidden in a cubby, she found a small, waterproof box that held a smooth black box with no markings. It was about the size of a deck of cards but with rounded edges.

As she turned it around in her hands, she saw that on one end were two slots; one looked like the right size for a USB connection. *What do you call this, and what's it for?* she wondered. It looked like a power pack or backup charger, so that was what she would label it for the inventory. *Excellent*, she thought; her computer was running out of battery power, they were at anchor and without shore power, and certainly she didn't want to start the engine to generate power or use up the boat batteries if she didn't have to, so she connected it to her computer.

Almost instantly with the connection, a small yellow light lit up on the opposite end of the black box she was holding, and that confirmed it was doing its job of charging the computer.

"Mom, can you bring me my cover-up and a towel...pleeeassse?" Katie called to her, standing soaking wet on the back deck. She had been so absorbed in the inventory and charging box that she hadn't even heard Katie return and climb aboard.

Katie's clothes were in a heap in the corner of the settee. When she picked up the bundle to hand out to Katie, the necklace cross dropped onto the table. After handing Katie, the bundle, she picked up the cross to admire her daughter's handiwork. It was quite creative. She never said it, but she was proud of her daughter. Janeva thought to herself that she had never in her life made anything like the cross. Katie hadn't made a standard cross. It was a circular Canterbury cross with a square in the center, from which extended four sections, wider on the outside so that they looked like triangles. The tips of the sections were arcs of a single circle, giving the overall effect of a round wheel.

As she studied the cross, she was impressed by her daughter's artisanship. The center square was not made of plastic but instead held a tiny graphene chip. Katie's chip was the center square of the cross. The cross was the container for the chip. Something out of *Alice in Wonderland*, she thought; a chip of no use had grown a cross. Carefully, to not break the plastic, she pressed on the back of the chip and popped it out from the cross.

She held it up to the light and noted that it looked like it might also fit into the other port on the black box, so she impulsively inserted it into the port. It fit, and as it connected, the smooth black surface of the box lit up and flashed green computer code and random numbers. *Oh my God*, she thought, *the chip does something after all. Well, that supports Katie's repeated claim that the chip must have had some purpose.* That was it, however; nothing else happened, and she wasn't even sure that the laptop was being charged.

Before she could give it any more thought, she heard the rest of the group return to the boat, laughing and calling out, "Janeva, come and grab the bowline." So she extracted the chip and reinserted it into Katie's cross, clicked save so she'd have her inventory work recorded on the Excel spreadsheet, and shut down the computer. Then she rushed up to grab and cleat the bowline and assist the group back onto *Joie de Vivre*.

***

The next morning everyone was up early, eager to explore the island. Janeva couldn't wait, because she had a feeling—hoped at least—that somewhere on this small island, there might be a clue that would help explain Lorenzo's past and maybe even his murder. As planned, Steph had kayaked into port and arranged for a rental car, which turned out to be a well-used and rather beaten-up Jeep.

"Does it run?" Katie asked.

"It belongs in a junkyard," Thomas grumbled.

"It's not easy to get vehicles to a remote island like this, and they do the best with what they have," Greg said, admonishing the group. Now humbled, everyone piled in to explore the island.

"I'm being eaten alive!" Thomas complained.

"By what?" Greg asked from the front seat.

"Hundreds of mosquitoes. They are eating me alive. We all need to be coated with bug spray. This is Zika virus and dengue territory," Thomas said.

"Really?" Steph asked sarcastically as she negotiated the Jeep out onto the narrow road. She couldn't help reminding him that he was too old to get microcephaly.

"Yes."

"I don't hear Katie or Janeva complaining."

"It's just my seat."

This went on for a time until Steph, like a frustrated mother, said, “Fine. I am going to pull over so you and Janeva can change seats. Will that make you happy?”

“Yes” was the reply as he switched seats with his wife.

Katie, sitting in the middle back seat, had the important job of reminding Steph that even though this was an American Jeep with the steering wheel on the left, this was the BVIs, and you had to drive on the left as well. Greg had the map and navigated from the front seat until Thomas, looking over his shoulder, pointed out that he was looking at the map of Tortola, not Anegada. So the map was handed back to Janeva to guide them.

Laughing, Thomas said, “Now I’m finally enjoying myself. This could get fun. Janeva’s dyslexic and doesn’t know her right from her left.” Thomas, who wasn’t enthusiastic about spending a day sight-seeing when he could be on a boat, had clearly decided to entertain himself with sarcasm.

“That’s right! Mom doesn’t know her left from her right,” Katie chimed in. “I should be navigating.”

“You have the important job of making sure that Steph stays on the right—I mean left side of the road. Right, so instead of left and right, I will say ‘your side’ for Steph to turn her way and ‘Greg’s side’ to turn the other direction.” Janeva was not about to give up the map; she was doing a perfectly good job of navigating, after all.

“And that’s not confusing.” Thomas laughed. “So where are the flamingos?”

“Contrary to popular belief, it’s not my fault that the flamingos are nowhere to be seen,” Janeva said. Pointing, she added, "That is the midisland lagoon where the map says the flamingos are." As they drove on, Janeva said, "No flamingos, but look at the wild donkeys, cows, and large steers with scary-looking horns standing in the middle of the road and many, many roosters."

"But, Mom, those aren't exotic animals," Katie said, feeling the need to point this out, "not like flamingos. Even back home there are cows and roosters."

Ignoring her, Janeva continued as designated tour guide. "Now here is the settlement…um." Looking around, she continued, "Observe the quaint, run-down houses intermixed with neat, tidy, colorful cinder-block houses to your left—I mean right—ugh—Steph's side of the car. And now that you all missed that, look at the school; it must be lunch break. Katie, look at the tidy school uniforms. Some of those kids look like they are your age."

Katie groaned dramatically.

"Next stop: Loblolly Bay and Big Bamboo."

Everyone piled out of the Jeep to walk on the bright-blue concrete sidewalk to the beach and lagoon.

"*Wow*" was the collective exclamation as the group rounded the corner and the breathtaking view of ocean waves crashing onto the reef just outside the lagoon appeared. Even Thomas was impressed, and though he would never admit it, he was starting to enjoy himself.

After a quick libation on a bench and a photo op as the magnificent waves rolled and crashed into the lagoon reef, they were off again. *Enough sight-seeing*, Janeva thought. *I have to get them to the place Trent told me about before Thomas orders us back to the boat.*

"Next stop: Cow Wreck Bay for lunch," Janeva announced.

"Umm, I think we just missed the turn," Janeva said a while later, looking at the map and trying to read the street signs.

"I told you that you shouldn't have put Janeva in charge of the map," Thomas griped. "I'm hungry."

"It's OK; the island is only fifteen square miles, and I'm sure this road will get us there too," Steph said, countering him.

"The mosquitos are still biting me," Thomas whined, mimicking a child on a long car trip.

"Not again. OK, I'm pulling over," Steph said in a tone of rebuke.

At her direction, they changed seats again, and this time she directed Thomas to the front passenger seat, which was exactly where he wanted to sit.

"Nothing is biting me. Hmm. I think they must have filled up on Thomas," Greg reported as the Jeep bumped along.

"Turn left," Thomas and Greg suddenly cried out in chorus. Steph, ever obliging and up for an adventure, did as she was told and turned onto the narrow dirt road leading to the beach on the opposite side of the lee of the island, sheltered from the huge rolling waves from the open-ocean side. They had seen several huge yachts, including a fabulous sailboat anchored, and wanted to get a better look at them.

"Is there no suspension in this Jeep?" Greg asked.

"Don't you start," Steph chided good-naturedly. "What an incredible beach. It's like something from a postcard or what you see in movies," she said, sighing in pleasure.

The group walked down to the water, looking left and right. As far as the eye could see, gentle turquoise waves lapped palm-lined, soft-sand white beach. Even more remarkable was that they were alone.

"I could stay here all day," Steph said.

"But I'm hungry and thirsty," Katie cried in alarm.

Laughing, after taking photos and scrutinizing the length and make of the various superyachts, the group piled back into the Jeep.

"Katie, can you read the name on that yacht?"

"Maxx spelled with two *x*'s. Really, Mom, your eyes are so bad."

"It won't start," Steph said, which was unnecessary as everyone could hear the "rrrrr…rrrr" of the engine as she tried it over and over again until it eventually flooded. She let it rest, and still, it wouldn't start. Fortunately for the group, Greg knew something about engines. He popped the hood, and as Steph turned over the engine, he pulled on the accelerator; to everyone's great relief, the engine started.

"Thank God!" Steph exclaimed. "We're out in the middle of nowhere with no people around and no cell phone. I don't know what we would have done."

Later, Steph said, "I didn't think the road could get any worse, but I was wrong. Are you sure this is the right road, Janeva?" The Jeep rattled down the rutted, bumpy, single-lane dirt road.

"Yes." Janeva held up the map and pointed at it.

After studying the map, Greg agreed. "This is the road all right, because it's the only road on this part of the island. The real question is, what are we going to find when we get there?" he said over the general rattle of the Jeep.

Amazingly, the Jeep held together, and they made it to Cow Wreck Bay in time for lunch. The bright-yellow restaurant and beach bar stood out in striking contrast to the turquoise blue of the Caribbean Sea behind them. Rum punches were ordered, in keeping with their holiday routine.

Studying the pink beverages, Thomas said, "Either it's their own recipe, or she gave us the creative version. I think the bartender took the word 'punch' literally and added everything within reach."

"Don't stress, buddy," Greg said, taking a sip of the drink. "It has lots of rum in it, so it's drinkable even with all the grenadine." He toasted Thomas.

After a lunch of excellent shrimp and shark tacos, it was time to do some exploring, and the group walked down the endless, white, sandy beach, which, except for one other group, was deserted. Janeva looked around the lagoon, thinking. Trent had told her that Cow Wreck Bay was the last place Lorenzo had visited. His very next trip had been to Chatterbox Falls, a remote inlet of Princess Louisa Inlet in Canada, and that was where he was murdered. She thought he must have hired a crew to sail the yacht through the Panama Canal and up the Pacific Coast because Lorenzo had too many businesses to manage to be able to spend weeks moving his boat. So, she wondered, could a hired crew have used the yacht for some nefarious purpose? A secret journey?

She forced herself to stop imagining and developing mysteries that didn't exist. Anyway, she wanted to understand why he had come to Cow Wreck Bay. It was almost too remote to be a vacation spot or a getaway. What did he want? What was he looking for? *What am* I *looking for, and could it be underwater?* she asked herself.

"Anyone up for some snorkeling?" she asked the group.

"Absolutely" was the resounding reply. It was fun to snorkel in a real lagoon with lots of coral islands, but the visibility was poor; the water was just too cloudy with sand, probably a leftover from the storm. Thinking of the storm brought back the grim reminder of Betty's death. Janeva gave up on the snorkeling and headed for a beach chair to dry off. Then, as the first out of the water, she decided to treat the others to a nice, cold Corona and to pry around for clues without attracting Thomas's attention.

She waited at the bar for a server who never materialized, so she wandered around and found an aerial photo and placard explaining the history of Cow Wreck Beach:

> Visitors to Cow Wreck Beach may wonder how it got its name. In the late nineteenth century, before the age of plastic, cow bones were used to make buttons and various other items. A ship laden with cow bones was wrecked off Anegada's northwest coast, and for years afterward, cow bones were swept ashore. Here is an aerial picture of Cow Wreck Beach and the reefs surrounding its shores.

A quick look at the photo proved to Janeva that it was unlikely that Lorenzo had taken his boat to this side of the island. If he had, it must have stayed well offshore because of the cluster of coral reefs that looked on the aerial photo like dark, underwater mountains in the clear, turquoise water. Frustrated, Janeva peeked into the kitchen and saw the server/cook busy cooking. As she wondered how to get his attention, a man dressed like a cowboy, hat and all, sidled up to her and explained the trick of how to get a beer or drink.

"You just find your tab, over yonder in that there coil book"—he gestured with his thumb—"what you'll be wanting, then go and make it yourself. When you're ready to skedaddle, ring that there bell by the cash register, and someone will cheerfully take your money."

As he explained this to Janeva, she noticed a young couple giggling as they wrote what they were drinking in the book; then together, like attached twins, they went to a large white cooler and extracted two Mike's Hard Lemonades and, still entangled, went to the dartboard.

As Janeva looked at the thick coil notebook, she was struck by an idea: what if Lorenzo had a tab? The book was very thick. She flipped back through the pages quickly, and there it was, proof that Lorenzo had been there, kept a tab, and drunk rather a lot.

"Mom, everyone wants to know what you are doing." Katie's voice surprised her.

"Just getting some drinks for everyone."

"Oh, good. Can I have a Diet Coke too? I'm thirsty."

Janeva wasn't going to let this clue slip out of her fingers. She quickly tore the sheet of paper out of the coil binder, flipped to the front page, and wrote down:

Jag
4 Coronas
1 Diet Coke

Then she went into the bar fridge to find those beverages.

"Mom, what did you take out of the book?" her all-too-observant daughter asked her.

"Shh," Janeva said and showed her the crumpled page under the counter that she had taken out of the book.

"Mom," Katie whispered back, "Dad will kill you."

Looking for a distraction, Janeva noticed a flash of light at Katie's neck. *Could it be a reflection from the sun?* She wondered.

"What?" Katie demanded, seeing the strange look her mother was giving her.

"Nothing. Um, I was just wondering if you wore your 3-D necklace swimming," her mother said as she handed her the opened bottle of Coke.

"No, of course not! That would wreck it," her daughter replied, offended. "I put it with my flip-flops when I'm swimming." Katie looked down at the cross. Just as it flashed again.

Looking up at her mom with big eyes, she said, "You saw it too, didn't you?"

Her mother nodded. "Does it do that often?"

"No, not really, just sometimes. It's our secret, OK?"

"We should show your father," Janeva said.

"No. You can't do that! You promised me, and you know he doesn't want anything to do with the chip. He'll throw it away. It's our secret, remember?"

As her mother nodded in acquiescence, Katie gingerly slipped the cross under her T-shirt, and together they headed down to the beach chairs, where everyone was thrilled to accept a cold Corona.

Finally, it was time to go, because they had reservations for lobster that evening.

Fortunately and surprisingly, the Jeep started on the first try, and the group headed back to the dock in front of Neptune's Treasure Inn, where they had left their dinghy. Except for a few tense moments when they had to navigate around some cows that had taken up residence in the middle of the dirt road, it was an uneventful trip back. Greg, Steph, and Katie dropped Thomas and Janeva with all the collection of gear at the dock where the dinghy was cleated and went to return the Jeep.

After a quick swim to cool off, everyone showered, and then, golf shirts and sundresses donned and a thorough coating of bug spray applied, it was time to pile into the dinghy and head in for the lobster dinner. The hostess showed the group to a prime table right on the beach beside the water. They ordered drinks, and each, in turn, went to check out the big tin drums that they used for barbequing the lobsters.

***

As the earth spun east, the sun gave a final flash of sunset light, and it disappeared into the ocean edge. The stars came out, one by one, until the night sky was a mass of stars. Katie couldn't get over how the city of San Francisco, even across the bay from where she lived, was so bright that it blocked out all the stars. So this was a very special moment to savor as the group toasted to family and friends and tried to identify the different constellations.

Katie was fascinated by the magic of the mass of stars making a lighted roof for the earth. Laughing, her mother told her that she'd had an experience once, many years ago, with her grandfather, who told her that everyone believed that the material between the stars was ether, and that was what sustained the transmission of light. But Einstein had proved that light didn't need ether to travel, and now we knew there was no such thing as ether. Katie's brain jumped from the romance of starlight to science, and she replied that it was hard to believe that all those stars were traveling away from one another at thousands of miles an hour.

"And even if there isn't ether, the vast thousands of light years between each star is filled with dark matter and dark energy that we can't yet detect."

"OK, smarty-pants," said Greg, who they had not even known was listening, "what is dark matter?"

"Don't call me smarty-pants! Dark matter just happens to be what most of the universe is made of. And if you really want to know, I read that it's a form of meson. Dark matter doesn't react with anything except gravity, and it's invisible and doesn't reflect or absorb light. And it's made up of something that scientists call WIMPs, which are weakly interactive massive particles, or more likely axions, which are able to convert electricity into magnetism and are probably made up of pions, and pions are made up of quarks and antiquarks."

Possibly a bit embarrassed by their ignorance, Greg broke the silence by saying, “Wow. Very impressive. You must get really good marks at school.”

“I wish you’d tell my English teacher,” Katie said. “We were asked to write a poem based on our studies, and there’d be extra marks if it contained humor, so I wrote a fantastic poem and got an F. She said the rhyme and cadence were OK, but the poem didn’t make sense, and I had misspelled some words.”

Thomas said he wished he had seen the poem; then they were all trapped into reading it when Katie brought it up on her iPhone.

The Boson Will Win

Unbelievably small, and just a poor charm quark
Without his photon, he was still in the dark.
They’d accused him of treason,
Because he’d released a pi meson.
Now he had to escape
Or face horrible fate.

OK, no hesitation
I’ll just change gravitation
To make levitation
And use electromagnification
Then travel along
From the weak to the strong

But to his dismay
They put strings in his way

So, he lepton a quark
To spin a symmetry mark
Hoping that six families of three
Would help him to flee.

But the quark had vibration,
A fact of creation
And up became down, charm became light,
And that's when he noted antiquark taking flight.
Gluon to her now or time warp our fate
But if you touch her, it's—annihilate!

But now he was on the quantum array
Location speculation—can anyone say?
Whether wave or particle, fermion or meson
Just hold on to your spin and challenge all reason
Without the boson to scatter
No matter, no matter.

"Um, yes," Steph said, "that is some poem, but I don't know how I'd mark it either. I mean, I'm not really sure what it's saying."

"Well—" Katie started.

Greg interrupted "Look, our meal is coming," with relief that dinner had saved them from another science lecture.

Salad, Anegada conch fritters, pepper shrimp, and homemade dinner rolls were followed by huge lobster tails (each the size of a dinner plate), baked potatoes, broccoli with cheese sauce, and a bottle of wine. It was perfect on the beach under the stars. With no wind or waves, they all piled into the dinghy for a smooth ride back to the catamaran.

That ride to the catamaran was rudely interrupted by "Ahhhhhh!" Katie had screamed and thrown herself across the dinghy, almost knocking Janeva over and out of the dinghy into the cold, black water.

"It's huge! What is it?" Katie stammered, pointing at the floor of the dinghy.

Fortunately, Janeva, who always traveled prepared, had thought to bring a small flashlight with them. She pointed the small beam of light in the direction Katie was pointing.

"Ha, we have acquired an additional crew member. That's a very large cockroach," Greg said, laughing.

"Kill it! Kill it!" Katie cried.

"I'm trying," Greg said as he tried to stomp on it.

"Where is it?" Steph asked with her feet up on the pontoon.

"There."

"No, there."

"Janeva, keep the light on it," Thomas demanded unreasonably as he just missed the large bug.

"Got it!" Greg eventually yelled and fist pumped in the air.

"Sit down," Steph and Janeva cried as the boat rocked dramatically, swayed by his over-six-foot frame.

"You would think you just scored the final goal for the Stanley Cup or Super Bowl."

"Better," Greg said over the buzz of the motor. "We really don't want him or any of his friends joining our crew on the boat."

"I can't argue with that," Steph said.

***

That night Janeva didn't sleep well. Was it her dinner of yummy butter-dipped lobster, or an interaction of all the recent events? The effect was nightmares, disjointed and confusing dreams. When sleep finally came, it was morning, and Thomas and Greg were up and keen to sail. It was another windy, gorgeous Caribbean day, so Janeva curled up in the corner of the cockpit settee, covered herself with towels as a sunscreen, and fell asleep, this time nightmare free. As though being cleansed from her troubled dreams, she was awakened once or twice by the bow wave splash that delighted Katie.

After another splash, she called out, "Are you trying to get me wet?" But she knew full well that they were. It was a game.

A steady twenty-five-knot wind, broad reach, and they were planing with the knot meter recording up to seventeen knots at intervals. This was what catamaran sailors dreamed about.

"Nice," Thomas declared happily and quietly to anyone within hearing range.

To Katie's delight, they returned to Scrub Island Resort & Marina, this time snagging the perfect mooring buoy with a view of both the sandbar and out to the Caribbean Sea. Later, after a swim and snorkel, the group piled into the dinghy to hunt down Trent at the resort and to find some ice at Pusser's Marina Cay. They had expected to find Trent entrenched at the beach bar, but to their surprise, he wasn't there.

"Seeing as we are here anyway," Janeva said over her shoulder as she went up to the bar and ordered the Napoleon-inspired rum drink called Napoleon's Blood.

"I want something too," Katie announced as she and Steph followed Janeva to the bar. Katie and Steph won the best-drink prize by ordering lime margaritas—virgin for Katie, of course. The view was incredible; their table overlooked a private beach with a soft breeze and a picturesque view of the open-sided, palm-thatched palapas that circled the beach, children playing in the surf, couples walking hand in hand, and others just reading or sitting, enjoying the view from lawn chairs or benches.

"Those look like Terri's kids," Steph said, pointing.

"Couldn't be; they must have left by now," Greg said.

His wife gave him a look and said under her breath, "Like you would recognize them?"

Laughing, Thomas said, "She's got you there, buddy; leave it to the gals to know one kid from another." Thomas looked around. "So where is Trent? Where else would he be?" Thomas mused as they left the pub by way of the path that wove through various palm trees and a variety of tropical flowers and shrubs.

"I am amazed how different each island is and how they each have their own personality," Janeva announced to the group at large. They nodded but made no comment, so she went into the store to look for ice.

Not finding Trent or ice in the store, they piled back into the dinghy and went to explore Trellis Bay and Beef Island, located across from Scrub Island. *This is certainly the complete opposite of Scrub Island's luxury resort*, she thought. Instead of superyachts, resorts with pools, and five-star dining, here they found decrepit ships, roosters, and skinny cats scrounging for scrap—a true juxtaposition.

A sudden sharp starboard turn jolted Janeva out of her thoughts. Thomas, sitting on the port stern bench, had pulled the tiller to see a yacht that they all surmised might be one of the largest personal catamarans in the world. It was, they determined later, 150 feet; it had just arrived and was dropping anchor.

After they had provisioned in Trellis Bay Village, Thomas announced, "Someone needs to sit in the front." He pointed at Katie.

"Not me," Katie said. "I'm driving."

"Not this time; the boat's too full," he replied.

Clearly overloaded, the small dinghy contained four adults, one teenager, several large bags of ice, and the many other bags of food supplies that Janeva and Steph had purchased at the local store. Janeva, with a sigh, was persuaded to sit in the wet seat on the bow tube and to hold down the bags of food.

"Fine, I'll be the wave barrier on this trip so you all can stay dry, but you owe me."

"Why did you buy all that stuff? We just needed ice for drinks," Thomas retorted and gunned the dinghy to a splashing plane before Janeva could reply.

Later, and quietly, without any small talk, they loaded the provisions into the fridge and bench lockers. Storing provisions and remembering where everything was stored was an ongoing puzzle aboard any boat. They heard Greg ask, "Where to next?"

Thomas was absorbed in his laptop but looked up and said, "I told Trent we would go to Prickly Pear Island."

"Sounds great," Steph said, flicking through their guidebook. When she found the page, she read out, "It's a five-minute dinghy ride to the Bitter End, which features water sports and has a resort with restaurants. It's a unique nautical village with an emporium, an English pub, and lots of small shops."

And as if on cue, Trent pulled up in the dinghy he had rented from the resort.

"Hey, pal, where were you? We looked for you at the pub earlier," Greg said.

Janeva asked, "Did you have a good visit with Sir Ford yesterday?"

"Yes, most certainly."

"We thought we saw Terri's kids on the beach today at the pub," Steph said.

"Quite possible. They didn't know where they were going to go next when I left," Trent replied. "Sir Ford said he didn't want to stay on the yacht any longer—too painful, I guess—so he flew off on his helicopter earlier today."

They all nodded in understanding but also thought it must be nice to have a helipad.

"How was he doing?" Steph asked sympathetically.

"I think he is deeply distressed and grieving over Betty. He wanted to talk about her and revealed that they were lifelong friends."

"Hmm." Janeva hesitated, wondering how much Sir Ford had told Trent. "Did he say how they met?"

"He did: it's a sad story, really."

Thomas interrupted. "I'm going to take the paddleboard out," he announced. Janeva knew he hated gossip, didn't know about the letter, and certainly was opposed to inventing a mystery, so she wasn't surprised he preferred some paddleboard fun to Trent's monologue of gossip.

"What about me? I want to go too." Katie looked around. Her father was already on the paddleboard paddling away, and her gaze landed on Greg. "Greg, do you want to go out in the kayak?" Katie asked hopefully. Good-natured Greg happily agreed, so the two to them went off to catch up with Thomas on the paddleboard.

"So how did they meet?" Janeva asked, prompting Trent to continue.

"Well," he said, "when Betty's parents were living in the United States, they both went to the same private school for a time."

"How old were they?"

"They weren't children; sounded like they were about sixteen or seventeen years old. They were in love. Betty was Sir Ford's first love." Trent smiled. "Sir Ford said it was the kind of deep passion that we as humans are somehow genetically destined for—not sex so much as a biochemical change in the brain, something that never completely goes away. They were inseparable—that is, until Betty's family moved back to Canada."

Canada again, she thought, and it brought Lorenzo's death back to her memory. Determined not to relive that memory, Janeva got up for the pitcher of iced tea to top off their cold drinks. Then she encouraged Trent to continue.

"They tried to keep connected by writing, but they were teenagers. Ford didn't write as expressively as Betty, and as time went on, they both found other interests. The letters became more difficult, they had less to say, and finally, it was clear that they would probably not ever see each other again. They were sort of pen pals, and over time the letters stopped. Years later, in Ford's final year at Stanford, his father told him that now he had to start his 'real' education—learn how to run the family's large commercial holdings that he would someday inherit. Then, one day as he was walking from one lecture hall to the next, he looked up, and to his great astonishment, walking toward him was Betty."

Steph and Janeva exclaimed, "Wow," and Trent continued.

"Again, as if it were meant to be, the passion ignited, and they were inseparable. He said if Betty hadn't been so determined to pursue her studies, he would have failed out in his final year. Fortunately, they both graduated, and not wanting to lose her again and worried she would have to move back to Canada now that her school visa was done, he asked her to marry him."

"No!" both Steph and Janeva said together; then they looked at each other and laughed. "We're speaking in unison; we've been friends too long," Janeva said, smiling. "Did they get married?"

"Sadly, no. His parents had other plans for him, and they had nothing in common with this woman or her family. Her parents were academics, both professors, and without any significant financial resources, and she was a Canadian. Sir Ford's father had been very successful in the United

States increasing the family fortune, including large property holdings in England, and it was only proper that their son assumed the rank, title, and role expected as part of that society. Betty was not the sophisticated upper-status kind of woman they wanted for their son. Good business acumen includes planning for the potential grandchildren—land, title, and connections with business and politics were the kind of qualities a proper daughter-in-law should bring with her. Ford and Betty were still young, innocent of the world, dreamers, and living every moment, but his future was already being planned out by his parents. Those plans did not include Betty; in fact, they specifically excluded Betty.

"His father insisted that Ford accompany him on a business trip to Europe, and Ford hoped that this time away would give his mother time to develop affection for Betty. After all, this was almost the twenty-first century, and they wanted only the best possible life for their son, didn't they? While they were in Europe, his mother used her connections to manipulate a business colleague to offer Betty an irresistible job in Alberta, Canada. Alberta, she guessed, would be as far away from her darling son as she could manage. The job acceptance required that the person recruited be able to start immediately, and since Betty's university degree was specialized and good job opportunities were infrequent, Betty went directly to Edmonton, Alberta. Ford was traveling and did not have any fixed address, but his mother promised to give or forward any mail or messages from Betty to her son. But to Ford, it was as if Betty had just disappeared, abandoned him, changed her mind. He was devastated. All he heard was from his mother, who reported that Betty had changed her mind and left to be with someone else."

"Trent, this can't be true. It's like a soap opera, not real life," Steph exclaimed.

"Why would he make it up?" Trent asked and shrugged.

"Then what happened?"

"Well, you have to remember that this was before cell phones or Internet, and Sir Ford had no idea of what had happened to Betty. It seemed to him that she had just disappeared, without a word or a trace. His father kept him on a wild travel schedule, making it impossible for Betty to track him down, and his mother carefully managed all his correspondence and the many phone calls and letters from Betty. Then they played the traditional game of planned social events where he was asked, as a favor, to attend a ball as the companion of Evelyn, the daughter of a prominent business colleague. As planned, with one event after another, it appeared to her family as if he was courting her. Ford had not seen or heard from Betty for a year, and his father promised him a promotion and less travel if he married Evelyn. The real pressure was from his mother. Apparently, she was a force to be reckoned with, by Sir Ford's description. He actually compared her to Maggie Smith's Dowager Countess in *Downton Abbey*!"

As they had both been *Downton Abbey* fans, Janeva and Steph nodded, understanding completely.

"So," Trent continued, "Ford married Evelyn to keep his family happy and worked his way up through the company. The mother may have envisioned a dynasty, but

Evelyn had great difficulty having children. After several miscarriages, Sylvia was born.

"Ford was happy. He was busy building the family business and raising his daughter, and after his father died, he became Sir Ford. He still had to cope with his overbearing mother, but now he was in charge. Evelyn was sweet and not demanding, and as fitted their social position, they had a busy social life. It wasn't until years later, when his daughter was sent off to boarding school, that—"

"They sent her away!" Janeva exclaimed.

"It was the family tradition."

"Then what happened, Trent?" Steph asked.

"Well, with Sylvia away, Sir Ford found that he was lonely. He realized that his relationship with his wife was empty. Without Sylvia to talk about and entertain them, they had little in common. Ford was an only child, and after a lot of introspection, he realized that Betty had been not just his true love but also his best friend. He had money, and he hired a private investigator to try to find her."

"Wow, that's so sweet." Steph and Janeva sighed. "He must have found her."

"Obviously, and to his amazement, she was unmarried. Twelve years had passed, but Betty was still living and working in Alberta."

"How did the private investigator find her?" Janeva asked, relieved that they were finally getting to Betty's life. That was what she needed to learn about.

"I asked Sir Ford the same question, and he admitted that he didn't start to look for Betty until after his father had passed away and his mother had moved to a care facility. As he sorted his mother's belongings, he found the file about Betty in the bottom of her dresser drawer. Hidden away but kept for some reason—guilt perhaps. He could not believe what she and his father had conspired to do. There were all the loving letters Betty had sent him. Saved. Hidden away from him! He was beside himself with anger and frustration, but his mother was now in the advanced stages of dementia, his father had died some years earlier, and there seemed nothing he could do, no one he could tell or vent his rage to. Certainly, he could not confide to his wife. He was trapped in a lonely, empty marriage. Betty was still in Alberta, still with her maiden name, and the search was not difficult."

"Then what happened?" Steph asked.

"He wrote and phoned, then flew over to see her. The rest is history."

They looked at him blankly.

Shaking his head at their naïveté, he said, "Yes, Ford was a married man, but he'd been seeing Betty surreptitiously for some years. And yes, the common word for this kind of relationship is 'affair.' Betty was, as you would expect, very successful in her business career and had risen to a senior position in the oil industry. Like many Canadians, she became obsessed by the phenomenon of climate change and persuaded her company to establish a research arm. They then put her in charge of a group that in the end relocated to the Silicon Valley region, where there was exciting innovation. But after a few years with a team looking for ways to reduce CO2 proliferation and working fourteen-hour days, true to the Silicon Valley culture, she cashed in her stock, retired, and moved out of the city across the Bay to Archipelago to do something she loved more."

"Sailing, I bet," Steph said before Trent could.

Trent nodded, pouting. "You're stealing my story. Actually, Ford said she couldn't stand retirement. The yacht club was recruiting a new manager, and on a whim, she applied. Her management credentials were outstanding, and she got the job. Then, and very secretly, she and Sir Ford became an item again," Trent blurted out before they could steal any more of his story.

"I can't believe it. You mean that Betty and Ford were, like, having an affair? Now that boggles the mind. She was so proper and uptight," Steph said, amazed. "I thought we had enough mysteries, but this takes the cake!"

"I didn't tell you that Sir Ford's wife, Evelyn, had ovarian cancer, and though she initially responded to treatment, the disease recurred. After a few months in palliative care, she died last year. He had supported her through her final illness. She never knew about his association with Betty. His daughter, Sylvia, and Betty met for the first time on this trip," Trent said. "But for Sylvia, it was as though her mother's memory was being replaced by another woman."

"That must have been awkward," Steph said with sympathy.

"More than that. Sir Ford said it was a disaster. When Sylvia found out, she was furious."

"I guess that makes sense. She was still defending her mother. Kids—even adult kids—can be like that."

"Then Sylvia found out that her father's will had been rewritten to include Betty."

"Well, they were legally married," Steph said.

"It must have been a shock to Sylvia, but surely there is plenty of money to go around?" Janeva commented.

"You would think, looking at the yacht," Steph said in agreement. "Does Sylvia need the money?"

"I wondered that myself but couldn't come right out and ask. I did learn that she is a socialite, she volunteers at several nonprofits, and she has taken over as lady of the manor since her mother's death," Trent said.

"Darn, here comes Thomas back…Trent, when you were talking to Sir Ford, did you find any mutual connections?"

"Of course, several."

"Any chance you can contact them? I would love to learn more about Sir Ford and his family."

Before he could answer, Janeva had to jump up and catch the line Katie was throwing to her. With everyone back on the boat, Trent took his leave, saying he would meet them tomorrow at the Bitter End.

Chapter 16

Janeva pondered the relationship between Betty and Sir Ford's family. *Money and greed*, she thought, *rule the world. Any chance that Sylvia and Ashton could be in debt? I'm scheming again.* She looked out the porthole in her cabin. She could see out without even adjusting her pillow, and she dreamily watched the other boats in the anchorage, masthead lights rocking back and forth and reflecting on the calm water. In the distance, she could see the blinking aircraft light atop the hill. The surf rolling up on the sandbar made a white, glittering line in the distance, framing the anchorage. The sky was clear with an almost full moon and a scant whiff of clouds in the distance behind the masts. That, plus the salty sea water smell and the gentle lapping of waves, made a perfect picture, and she soon fell asleep.

***

"I love this coffee," Janeva announced to no one as she poured herself her cup of morning coffee. "How come the aroma from the coffee percolating is so much more fragrant than that of the French press coffee we make at home?" she asked, again to no one in particular. When no one answered, she took her coffee up to the bow to enjoy the beauty and tranquility, embraced by clear, blue Caribbean water, cloudless blue sky, and the warm, gentle breeze with its scent of tropical flowers.

Katie interrupted her moment of revelry. "Mom, what's for breakfast?" Janeva took a deep breath, resisted the urge to suggest she make herself something, and instead got up, smiling, sure it was this peaceful atmosphere that was making her a better mom. She made poached eggs on English muffins with cheese for all.

As Steph did the dishes, the boys and Katie unhitched and slipped off the mooring buoy. There was a gentle breeze, and with sails unfurled, they were off to Virgin Gorda and Prickly Pear Island.

"Another glorious sail; I could get used to this!" Greg said as he coiled a line.

It was so hot when they arrived that the first item of business was to jump off the stern swim platform and go for a swim. Climbing out of the water, up the stairs off the back pontoon of the catamaran, Thomas lifted the lazaret hatch and came up holding up his flippers and mask.

"Anyone up for a swim to shore?" he asked.

As everyone scrambled up to don flippers, masks, and snorkels, Janeva dried off as best she could, went inside, and sealed their wallets, cell phones, credit cards, and camera into her waterproof container. As she was last out, she grabbed the last set of fins, mask, and snorkel and then jumped in and swam to catch up with the others.

"What took you so long?" Thomas asked when Janeva joined them on the beach.

"I locked all our valuables—cell phones, iPads, laptops, and Steph's big camera with the zoom lenses—in the travel safe, and it took me a while because they were scattered all over the boat."

"You're being overcautious, and under the circumstances, I think that's a bit unnecessary." Then, seeing the look from his wife, he added, "Um, well, I know you are only trying to look after us," and he gave her a hug.

Realizing Thomas had not seen Betty's memo and could not appreciate that she might have felt threatened, Janeva replied lightly, "I know it's silly, but it only takes a moment, and it makes me feel better. It would be such a hassle to lose our IDs or electronics."

Thomas put his arm around her and, giving his wife a kiss, said, "OK, if it makes you happy. What would make me happy right now is a cocktail."

They joined the rest at the picturesque beach bar, ordered strawberry daiquiris, and sat under an open-sided dwelling with a thatched roof made of dried palm leaves that the locals called a palapa. As they sat looking dreamily out at the bay, a tall ship sailed past.

"Mom, look," Katie said, pointing to the ship. "It looks like a real pirate ship."

"It definitely could be right out of the *Pirates of the Caribbean* movie," Janeva said in agreement. As she looked around to the end of the Gorda Sound, it was easy to imagine the pirate towns at Bitter End with the English garrison watching over them from Leverick Bay.

***

The swim back to the boat was into the waves and more challenging, but that just improved their appetites. A local couple motored from boat to boat in the bay, marketing their homegrown vegetables, and persuaded Steph to purchase enough to refill their containers, so dinner was barbeque pork tenderloin, roasted potatoes, and a salad made up of locally grown greens and veggies.

As they ate, they watched the full globe of the sun set in the gap between the two islands. A blaze of orange and gold reflected mirrorlike on the light-azure backdrop.

"Of all the sunsets this trip, this one is the most spectacular," Janeva mused aloud.

"Until tomorrow's," Steph said, laughing, and held up her glass so they could toast.

"Can we watch the moonrise from the trampoline?" Katie asked.

Following her to the bow of the boat, they watched an incredibly stunning full moon rise over the hill of Prickly Pear Island. Comfortable in the warm night air and trampoline netting, they couldn't tear themselves away, and no one spoke; they all just sat watching the moon make its slow progress into the sky and trace a long moonglow path of light that reflected off the bow and raced all the way to the shore.

***

"Goats," Steph said with a groan the next morning. "If it's not roosters, it's goats that awaken me." She sighed. "I can't decide which is worse," she grumbled, as Greg handed her a cup of coffee.

"I woke to the sound of the generator being turned on to charge the batteries, but in my sleepy state, I thought it was the sound of the engines being fired up, so I hopped out of bed to see if we were leaving already," Janeva said as she sipped her coffee.

Steph laughed.

"I think we should take this boat instead of the dinghy today to meet up with Trent," Thomas said between mouthfuls of scrambled eggs and coffee.

"Why?" Janeva asked. "It might be hard to find dock space."

"True, but I want to top up our water tanks."

"I can't argue with that! I'll get organized inside."

"I'm so excited to see the village and stock up," Steph said, flipping through the guidebook.

"Didn't we just stock up yesterday?" Thomas asked.

Laughing, Greg replied, "They never miss an opportunity to shop."

Later, with the catamaran tied up to the dock at the Bitter End Yacht Club, Steph said, "Oh, it's so cute," as the group walked around the small village. "I love these nautical old-fashioned wood boardwalks."

Finding the Provisions Emporium, Steph, Katie, and Janeva did a quick restock while the boys went looking for Trent.

"I'll go back to the boat to stow the ice-cream bars in the freezer before they melt," Janeva said aloud but found she was talking to herself. Katie and Steph had disappeared inside a gift shop. They were on a mission to find the perfect baseball cap and some T-shirts or tank tops.

As Janeva walked to the boat balancing her bags of food, she had the strangest feeling of being watched. She did a quick 180-degree turn, but no one was behind her. She scanned the boats on either side; their cockpits were empty. *Thomas is right*, she thought. *I'm getting paranoid.* She could hear voices, but they were distant.

"Relax," she told herself and kept walking, now onto the dock, but the feeling didn't leave. Loading and boarding the boat was a bit of a challenge because the wind was blowing the boat off the dock, and there was a big gap separating the boat pontoon from the dock. Janeva put down all the bags, grabbed the mooring line, and tugged the boat in close to the dock. She grabbed the two closest bags, which fortunately were the ones with the ice cream and ice cubes, and then had to jump onto the boat with the two bags before the wind blew the boat away from the dock again. She scrambled up the stairs with her two heavy bags, dumped one of the bags of ice in the beer-and-soda cooler, and then fumbled in her pocket for the key to unlock the large sliding-glass door. She still felt like someone was watching her. After stowing the food in the freezer, she locked the boat and went to join the rest at the English pub for lunch.

***

"Janeva, finally you arrive!" boomed a jolly, unmistakable British voice, and then she was embraced by Trent. "Come, come; we are over here."

Janeva was a bit taken aback to see her group sitting with the crowd from the *Lady Cécilee*. What were they doing here? She had not seen their yacht in the bay. It seemed almost like too much of a coincidence that with the whole Caribbean to explore, they would run into the same group again. A part of her guilt kicked in, because she was just a bit ashamed that she had stolen the letter from Betty's printer, and now she had to look the owners in the face. *Ridiculous*, she assured herself—*a bit of paper that would have ended up in the garbage anyway if they had found it. Stop with the idiotic suspicions. We are two groups of tourists having an escape in the Caribbean paradise, and we are looking for the same pleasure, so obviously, we are going to cross paths.*

"Janeva, what took you so long?" asked Greg, handing Steph a rum punch.

"Where is my rum punch?" Janeva asked. Thomas, who was right behind Greg, immediately did a ninety-degree turn on the spot and headed back to the bar.

"Thanks, honey," she said to his retreating back. He turned and gave her a cheeky smile. "What's up with him?" Janeva asked Steph.

"What's up with who?"

"Thomas. Something has him very entertained," she replied.

Steph shrugged. "I have no idea. Katie and I found them here with Trent and this lot when we left the gift shop."

"Did you find anything good?"

"I found a great laminated map of the area and a straw hat for Greg. Katie picked out a *Gilligan's Island* hat for Thomas and found a T-shirt for herself and some bracelets for her school friends."

Moments later, Trent handed Janeva a rum punch. *Where had Thomas gone*? Janeva wondered as Trent put his arm around her, directing her toward the empty chair between Sylvia and Terri.

Looking up, Terri said, "Oh, Janeva, hi. It's so distressing; you must do something."

"Trent, what are you up to?" Janeva asked in a whisper as she tried to turn away and go back to where Steph and Katie were standing at the opposite end of the table.

"I know you can help them solve this disagreement," Trent said and plopped her into the chair. If she hadn't been so surprised by Trent's unusually forceful behavior, she might have been able to duck away from the chair, but as it was, she landed right in the middle of it. That is, in the middle of an argument between Sylvia and Terri over what to do with Betty's belongings. Sensing new prey, they both immediately started in on Janeva.

Sylvia, on her left, said, "Janeva, dear, you are a yacht-club member and knew Betty well. Don't you think Betty would have wanted her belongings to go directly to charity?"

Janeva stuttered and started to say that she didn't know Betty well but was unable to get a word out before Terri interrupted her.

Terri on her right said, "Of course, eventually, but not right away."

"When, then?"

"When? When the time is right—you know, after everything has been sorted."

Confused, Janeva stupidly waded in. "What about Betty's family? Or Sir Ford? I'm sure he will take care of everything."

"Sadly, Betty doesn't have any family," Terri replied, and Sylvia snorted rudely.

"No one at all?" They had all been informed earlier, but still, Janeva was amazed at this possibility.

"Her parents are dead. She was an only child and childless. As far as I know, there are no cousins or other relatives. Sir Ford is gone. He flew off in his helicopter, then to who knows where in his private jet after the memorial ceremony."

Turning to Sylvia, Janeva said, "So is this about her belongings on your yacht?"

"Yes." Her eyes flashed. "We have friends joining us tomorrow, and I need the room."

In a yacht that size, there is no space where you could store a few suitcases? For once Janeva controlled her sarcasm, probably because Thomas had moved and was now standing behind her, waiting for her to say something sarcastic.

So instead she said, "I understand…so what is your plan for the suitcases, Sylvia?"

"To give them to the locals on this island. She had some lovely designer things that you can't get here. I'm sure they will be thrilled."

"You can't do that!" Terri exclaimed with tears in her eyes. "The will hasn't even been read yet."

"Well, if you're worried that some of the clothing will be willed to you, then by all means, take what you want. Then I'll give the rest away," Sylvia said, sneering.

Janeva was really beginning to dislike Sylvia.

Terri leaned across Janeva and hissed, "No, that's not what I want, and you very well know it. As if any of Betty's stuff would fit me!"

Realizing this was going downhill, Janeva interjected quickly. She did not want a catfight to break out in this nice tropical bar. "Can't you just store them somewhere on the yacht for a few more days, and then Terri can take them with her when she leaves?"

"*No*!" was the simultaneous and vehement reply from both women.

Janeva was stunned and started to push her chair back to leave, looking down the table to where Sylvia's husband, Ashton, was sitting with Thomas, Trent, Greg, and Steph. They were laughing and enjoying themselves. What was she doing refereeing these two crazy women? After all, this was not her problem—or was it? *I am in possession of a letter that implies that Betty was frightened of someone on that yacht*, Janeva thought. Taking a deep breath, she ventured to ask, "Why not?"

"We leave tomorrow for a week in Antigua," Terri said. "One of Chad's business associates has invited us to stay with them at their compound, and I'm not going to drag Betty's bags and urn around the Caribbean with me."

"Well, she was your friend, and they are not staying on my yacht!" snapped Sylvia.

"I thought it was your father's," Terri snarled. "And even if you didn't get to know her, she was your stepmother. I'm afraid it is now your responsibility, your problem."

"As far as I know, she was a tramp. I do not know what my father saw in her. She was a disgrace to my mother and her memory."

"Grow up and join the twenty-first century. What did you expect your father to do, join a monastery after your mother died?"

"Of course not."

"Your father and Betty had been seeing each other for years," Terri said and then smiled with satisfaction as she watched Sylvia's face blanch.

"You're lying to me. My mother died only a year ago. My father would never have done that, and I don't even know where they met." Something in her voice implied that as far as she was concerned, Betty was one step below a grubby street urchin.

"Well, your perfect father and Betty were in a relationship for some years. I wonder to what extent this conflict is more about your father's new will and your changed inheritance rather than his relationship with Betty?"

"What a nasty comment. How could my father's relationship with Betty have in any way affected my inheritance? We were having a sensible discussion about what to do with Betty's belongings, and you have turned it into a rant about jealousy and greed. I am out of here. Good-bye."

Janeva was very interested in the possible implications of Terri's statement. She wondered again if Sylvia might have benefited from Betty's death. Before Sylvia could leave, Janeva blurted out the first thing that came to mind.

"OK, I'll take the bags." They both stopped glaring at each other and turned to look at her.

Sylvia said, "Thank you, Janeva. I'll have one of the crew collect them for you right away." Apparently, she wasn't going to give Janeva any opportunity to change her mind, and she marched off with a final dig at Terri. "At least some yacht-club members have class," she said in her upper-class accent as she carefully placed her large sun hat on her head and waltzed out.

"Wait, Sylvia, how do I get ahold of your dad? I will need to ask him…" She trailed off, realizing that Sylvia had no intention of replying. Janeva turned to Terri. She thought she saw a sly smirk on her face but could not be sure because it was so fleeting. Terri reached out, putting her hand on Janeva's arm.

"Thank you," she said with feeling. "We can't get off that yacht quickly enough; it's been horrible." With a dramatic sigh, she continued. "Actually, Chad is looking to see if we can spend our last two nights at the resort here. It has a pool and a private beach, and Chad is keen to take the kids out dinghy sailing."

"It looks like they have a great fleet," Janeva said in agreement. From where she sat, she could see several types of small sailboats, including Hobies, Lasers, 420, and Optimists. "What would you like me to do with Betty's bags when we get home?" Janeva asked.

"Take them to her house. The key is in her purse, and it's packed in her carry-on." She paused as if something had just come to her and then added, "Seeing as you will be at her house anyway, you should probably go through her desk and find her solicitor's name and notify him. In addition, of course, don't forget to let the yacht club know so they can arrange an eight bells ceremony for her. And," she added, "someone must sort and organize all her clothes and belongings. I guess it will all be auctioned off or given to the Salvation Army to provide for the needy."

"Terri, surely this is something her family and friends should do. I will ask at the club. There must be lots of members who knew her better than me." Janeva started to feel that she was being treated like Terri's employee.

"Of course," Terri said. "I told you she has no family or next of kin."

"Then where will her estate go? That is who should be doing this. In fact, you were probably the person closest to Betty. Are you sure you can't postpone your plans and return home to help settle Betty's affairs?"

"Well, you're right. I was probably her closest friend, but as I already explained, I am traveling for the next month. Obviously, some matters must be attended to immediately, but others, as the lawyers direct, can wait. Someone has to take charge and at least coordinate the matters, and I'm counting on you to do it," she said, pretending to ignore Janeva's concern. Then she stood up, waving. "Oh, there is Chad. Look, Janeva, he's smiling. That must mean we have rooms at the resort. Thanks again, Janeva; you're a real treasure."

And she was gone.

Janeva was about to join Thomas and the group at the other end of the table when two uniformed crew walked into the pub, one pulling a large roller bag behind him, the other with a matching carry-on bag over his shoulder and holding something in front of him. Of course, they walked right up to Janeva and inquired if she was Janeva Jag. At her nod, the roller bag was positioned beside her at the table, the carry-on was balanced on top, and to Janeva's distress, an urn holding Betty's ashes was carefully placed in front of her. So much for any feelings of guilt over the letter she'd taken from the printer. Now she was in charge of Betty and all of Betty's belongings, whether she wanted them or not. She was angry at Sir Ford. How could he just disappear like that? He should be the one dealing with this, not her. She barely even knew Betty. How did she get herself into this mess?

"Is that Betty?" she asked very quietly.

"Yes, madam," he said, and then together they both turned and walked off in unison.

Janeva tore her eyes away from the nondescript urn holding Betty's ashes and looked down the table, meeting Thomas's gaze. He took a deep breath and shook his head in a manner that clearly said, "What have you gotten yourself into now?"

"It's Betty and her stuff," Janeva said in a loud whisper because she couldn't bear to speak aloud. If their vacation had not been totally ruined already, this somehow just emphasized and aggravated every negative aspect of the journey.

"Dare I ask why you have them and what you—we—are going to do with them?"

"Umm, well, since you ask: the reason I was given is that Sylvia needs the space on *her* yacht, and Terri is traveling on to Antigua, so I was recruited to take them back with us."

"Please tell me you are joking," Thomas said, groaning. "You didn't agree?"

Janeva nodded, not trusting that she could say anything right.

"You do realize that now we have to check bags that don't belong to us and that we didn't pack, and we don't know what's in them, and we are responsible for her remains. I hope they also gave you the death and cremation certificate, or we may not get it through security. You had better arrange with the airline today. I expect you will need to find a different container for the ashes."

Steph, looking concerned, stood beside Janeva. Putting a hand on her arm, she said, "When my mom died, they put her remains in a ziplock bag inside the urn, and that's what I flew home with."

"Thank you," Janeva said, still looking at the urn. "I guess I'd better open it and look."

"Here—for courage," Steph said, handing Janeva a rum punch and sitting down on her other side, giving her a sympathetic look.

"I know what you are thinking, Steph, but I didn't ask for the bags. I, uh, well, I was…"

"Of course you didn't ask; you were manipulated by Terri. I'm sorry, Janeva. I know what she is like, and I should have come over to help you."

"What is she like?" Janeva asked, mystified, with a shake of her head.

"She is a master manipulator, she is always in charge, and I think she's eager to assume the reins of the yacht club."

"Really? She seemed to work so well with Betty, and I thought they were great friends."

"Possibly, from Betty's perspective. She always treated Terri like a daughter, but I don't think she saw what Terri was really like. No matter what Terri did, Betty thought she was perfect."

"I had no idea," Janeva said, shaking her head. "You must be right: she literally insisted that I notify Betty's solicitor, arrange the yacht-club eight bells ceremony, and—get this—sort and organize Betty's clothing and belongings. Terri couldn't help because she was going to be traveling for the next month."

"Ha! No doubt, those travel plans were just made so she wouldn't have to deal with all that. She wants to waltz in as the new club manager without dealing with Betty's legacy."

"Will she automatically become the next manager? Doesn't there have to be a selection committee or vote?" Janeva asked.

"Well, that's a good question. I'll have to check the bylaws, but the timing is perfect, as the executive committee was just voted in last month. Terri is membership director, so she is a likely candidate to become manager, at least until next year, when the new board is voted in."

"Do you think she wanted it that much?" Janeva asked.

"I do—it means authority, prestige, influence, and more money."

Not knowing what to say to this revelation, Janeva took a sip of her rum punch. Then finally, her mind started working again, and she asked, "Steph, how do you know so much about Terri?"

At this interesting moment, both Thomas and Greg arrived with Katie in tow.

"It's getting late, and we need to get going if we want to go to the Baths today," Thomas announced.

As soon as they got back on the boat, Thomas said, "If we leave now, we can just make it." He checked his watch and turned on the instruments, knot and depth meters, and GPS.

"Hmm," Greg said, looking over his shoulder at the electronic chart. "It will be close, and only if we have the wind with us."

"Hold on; I'm coming with you," Trent announced.

"What are you all standing around for?" Thomas asked, bellowing. "Chop, chop—we have a race to win."

"Race? What race?" Katie asked, looking confused.

Janeva shrugged, just as bewildered.

Giving an audible sigh and an eye roll, Thomas said, "It's a race against time. We need to get to the Baths."

"Why?" Steph and Janeva asked in tandem.

"Because it's illegal to anchor, and the bartender told us we needed to get there ASAP if we wanted to get a mooring buoy. So let's get a move on; I don't want to be circling around waiting for someone to leave."

"Right, O Captain," Trent said, saluting Thomas. "I'll cast off."

"Excellent! Now, where is the rest of my crew?" Looking around, he saw that Greg was busy getting the sails ready, and Katie was untying lines and pulling up the fenders.

Realizing that he was referring to the girls, Janeva poked her head out. "Girls are present and accounted for. We are securing the boat for speed, battening down the hatches, and—"

He cut her off. “Enough. Just plot the course and check the depth at the point to see how close we can get. Give me a heading, please.” Janeva went to the navigation station to look at the instruments, again frustrated that the boat did not have the instruments at the helm where you needed them. Then she dutifully relayed the heading and depth at the point.

They powered out of the mooring area and sped through the narrow passage between Mosquito Island and Anguilla Point on Virgin Gorda. Then they were in luck, because around Mountain Point, the wind was astern. With the main full out, they sailed faster than they could have motored and had a great run down to the Baths.

Chapter 17

"Mom, what are the Baths?" Katie asked as they neared the shore.

"Worried you will be forced to take a bath?" Steph teased, laughing. Then, flipping open her cruising guide, Steph, the self-designated tour guide, began to read: "'Located on the southwest tip of Virgin Gorda, the Baths are a most unusual formation of large granite boulders. Where the sea washes in between the huge rocks, large pools have been created where shafts of light play upon the water, creating a dramatic effect. The beach adjacent to the Baths is white and sandy, and the snorkeling excellent.'"

"Snorkeling beats taking a bath any time," responded Katie, and Janeva nodded. She decided not to mention the obvious point about soap, as they were on holiday, after all.

Instead, she said, "Good. I feel like snorkeling too."

Trent, who was not to be outdone, lifted his cell phone and said, "I found this on the bvitourism.com website." He read aloud: "The centerpiece of this dramatic area on Virgin Gorda's north shore is the Baths, a geological wonder comprised of awe-inspiring granite boulders, which form sheltered sea pools on the beach's edge. The protected area also includes Devil's Bay, which can be reached from the Baths by a series of ladders scaling the boulders."

"Wow, it does sound like a really interesting place," Janeva said.

The bartender's intel proved to be correct, because they secured the last mooring buoy. After launching the dinghy, they powered the short distance to the area marked off by rope and yellow buoys that identified a swimming area, which was forbidden to boats. Janeva leaned over the bow and hitched the dinghy onto the swimming boundary rope, where it was just one of several other dinghies all secured to the rope.

Then they all had to swim to shore, and it wasn't easy. Even though they were swimming with the waves, there was an unexpected swell and current that tugged and pushed against them. They finally all made it and scrambled up the shore.

Janeva, a strong swimmer, swam behind Katie, and as she had secured the dinghy, she was the last to the beach.

She crawled out of the swells and started after them. She saw the sign that read "Devil's Bay" with a small triangular opening between two massive boulders.

As she was just about to duck through the opening, she heard Thomas shout, "Janeva, don't wander off."

Thinking that the others knew the way and had already seen the enticing opening and decided against that route, she turned and followed them up past the beach bar and restrooms and then onto a winding, sandy trail up the hill, through the mangroves, cacti, and palm trees. Everything about the trail was exotic—unusual lizards with purple tails, colored tropical birds with huge black beaks, and huge bees that looked like beetles. Katie had earlier named them beetle bees.

Finally reaching the gift-shop balcony, she called out, "Wow, look at that incredible view. I'm going to take a photo." She focused her camera on a collage of pink, purple, yellow, and red bougainvilleas that formed the bottom of the ocean view that was framed by palm trees. As she turned to walk back, she asked the woman who ran the gift shop where the Baths were.

Returning to the group, Janeva announced, "We are in the wrong place! This isn't the Baths. They're back at the beach where we just came from."

Frustrated, they started back down the trail, with Thomas and Greg in the lead.

"Hurry," Thomas called. "We need to see them before the cruise boats arrive and crowd us out."

"Only Thomas could make a vacation sight-seeing destination into a race," Janeva grumbled to Steph as they trotted down the path.

Back at the bottom, they looked around in vain.

"Where are these Baths?" Thomas said, watching all the people milling around looking at souvenirs, crafts, and T-shirts in the colorful stalls on the beach. Vendors were busy hawking their goods in front of them, while groups hovered around drinking piña coladas at Mad Dogs bar behind them.

As Janeva pondered Thomas's question, her gaze was drawn to the triangular opening to Devil's Bay that she had seen earlier, and that was when she saw him. It was Jeff, the blond guy. Suddenly it clicked; he seemed to have been everywhere they had been.

"Thomas!" Janeva exclaimed, grabbing his arm. "Look." She pointed. "It's as if he's following us."

He gave his wife a quizzical look and then said sarcastically, "Really?"

"Yes. The first day at the beach bar, and then again, remember, they were at the beach the day after the storm after we left the police station. We raced them to Marina Cay…then I'm pretty sure I saw him at Bitter End Yacht Club this morning, and now he is here again," Janeva said rapidly.

"Come on, Janeva; your imagination is on overdrive. I'm sure they're just taking the same tourist journey around the islands that we are."

"Fine. You always think I'm exaggerating, but it seems more than a coincidence to me."

"OK, I'll bite. Let's catch up with him. We'll ask him why he is following us…" Thomas looked around at the group. "Well then, why are we standing around talking? What are you all waiting for?" he demanded and took off down the trail.

Shaking her head, Janeva started followed him toward the opening after Greg and Trent. Looking around for Steph and Katie, she found them negotiating at a makeshift gift shop that was set up with a portable table and a mangrove tree to hang towels and T-shirts on for display.

"Steph, Katie, over here!" Janeva yelled.

Not wanting to be left behind, the two turned and started toward Janeva.

"Hurry—we're going over there into that opening." Janeva pointed. They took turns squeezing through the small triangular entrance formed in the rocks. Greg had to crawl through the opening, like a gorilla with one hand on the ground, because he was too tall. The cave was made up of huge, smooth boulders with a glistening pond of turquoise-green salt water in the center.

"Well, where is he?" Thomas asked as he looked around the cave.

"I don't know. We took so long getting here," Janeva snapped back.

"Are you sure it's him? I just glimpsed the person, and I don't see his family. How could you tell it was him?" Greg asked.

"Oh, I'm sure," Janeva said. "I don't recognize faces very well, but I recognize the way people move or talk, their manners…" She paused and then added, "You know, because of my dyslexia, I—"

"She recognizes patterns," Thomas said, finishing for her, stopping the long explanation he knew was coming.

"So where to now?" They all looked around. Steph led by wading through the pool of water.

"The best bet is probably this railing rope," Thomas said.

"Looks like a trail this way," Greg agreed as he explored a gap in the rocks.

But their direction was determined when a group of exiting tourists came down in a line holding on to the rope.

Thomas grabbed the rope as soon as the last tourist had passed and shimmied up the rock. Everyone followed him to crawl through gaps, shimmy over rocks, climb up and down ladders, and make their way around different-shaped boulders and through spectacular cavern after cavern, each pocketed with shallow saltwater pools.

"I'm sure he is long gone," Steph said gently.

The group had just crawled up from a turquoise-boulder-lined pond and up a steep ladder to emerge into a palm-lined clearing.

"Look: he's over there," Greg said, his voice a hiss, and pointed off to the right. There was Jeff, picking his way carefully like he was looking for something or perhaps for a different trail on the other side of the clearing where the lush tropical foliage started.

"I think that resolves the issue," said Thomas. "If he were following us, why is he now ahead of us?"

"We can cut him off over there," Greg said, gesturing to where the trail continued.

Janeva started to follow Greg with the rest; then she instinctively checked to see where Katie was but couldn't see her. Alarmed, she reasoned that Katie had already gone around the corner before they stopped. As much as Janeva wanted to follow everyone else and confront Jeff, she couldn't let Katie go on ahead alone, so she continued down the path to catch up with her.

"There you are," Janeva exclaimed, glimpsing Katie up ahead of her, as she came around the next huge, round boulder on the left side of the trail. Then she saw a tall, dark man had Katie cornered.

"Keep moving," he told Katie in a hissing voice without turning.

Katie looked terrified. What could he have done to Katie in those few short seconds? Then she realized he was trying to grab her daughter. Adrenaline kicked in, and Janeva took a step back and jumped on the large man from behind, yelling, "*Run*, Katie, *run!*"

Katie didn't hesitate. She yanked her arm out of his grip and ran.

"Keep going," her mother yelled and then yelped in pain as he slammed her backward into the boulder. She tried to say, "Find your father," but her breath had been knocked out of her, and it came out as a whisper. As she slid down the smooth rock side of the boulder, breathless and stunned, she let go of the muscular man's T-shirt, freeing him to lunge after Katie again.

Katie was in the open and had the advantage. Using her gymnastics training, she sprang away from him and then ran a few steps and did a roundoff into a flying leap that propelled her up and onto a small boulder. Then she smoothly hopped up to the next boulder, looking like Spider-Man as she scrambled up and out of sight. The frustrated assailant was slowly and unsuccessfully attempting to crawl up the smooth boulders to follow her, cursing and yelling threats at the same time.

Janeva was still gasping for breath; she was bruised and in pain, but the terror drove her to escape. The man was chasing Katie, and Katie was climbing up and up until she neared the top. What could her daughter do? Where could she go? What if she fell? Desperate to help, Janeva grabbed some small rocks and started to throw them at the man. Throwing was not one of Janeva's skills, but the rocks were landing close enough to bother him, so she kept throwing until, against all odds, she hit him.

"Take that!" Janeva yelled. He turned and swore at her.

Janeva bent down to find more rocks to throw at him. Then she looked up. Where was Katie? In the second it had taken to bend down to pick up the next rock, Katie had disappeared.

"Katie, where are you?" Janeva yelled, her heart beating, panic rising. Had she fallen? "Katie! Katie!" Janeva turned and started to run down the trail to where she would have landed if she had fallen. Finally, she could see the area where Katie would be lying in a crumpled mess, but thankfully, it was empty of all but sand and small boulders. So where was Katie? As relief flooded Janeva that Katie had not fallen, she was grabbed and pinned against the rock with brute strength.

"So she got away," he hissed. His breath in her face was foul, laced with rum, garlic, spice, and stale cigarette smoke. Janeva gagged.

"I missed the kid, but you'll have to do," he growled as he pinned both of Janeva's arms behind her and held her wrists so tightly that Janeva was losing circulation to her hands.

Janeva screamed, squirmed, and kicked. She flung her full force away, but at five feet four and 120 pounds, she wasn't much of a match for a six-foot-tall muscular brute who easily pushed her to the ground and jammed one knee into her back. One of his hands pinched Janeva's wrists together painfully, and the other drove her head and face into the sand. Janeva couldn't breathe, much less scream. Her legs kicked frantically in some exaggerated but ineffectual swimming kick, and the exertion caused her to inhale sand; it was hard to breathe.

Stop panicking! her brain screamed. *Think. He can't plan to suffocate me, at least not on purpose. What use would I be to him if he did that? Where is Thomas?* As these thoughts ran through Janeva's head, she stopped struggling. As her body started to obey her brain, she found that one corner of her mouth was not under sand, and if she focused and breathed very carefully, she could get a small amount of sand-free air. He was sitting on her now, talking quietly to someone, and as Janeva could only hear one side of the conversation, she guessed he was on a cell phone.

"I lost her. No, *relax*, man! I got another one. Who cares; one's as good as the other to trade. Chris, I don't know. Some lady. Her mom, I think? Where? OK, in five."

He ended the call and mumbled under his breath. "Fuckin' ridiculous amount of effort…" He trailed off, swearing to himself.

He was so strong that he picked Janeva up and threw her over his shoulder as if she were a doll. She was dizzy, in pain, and short of breath, but she flailed and shook her legs to no effect. He carried her off down some invisible trail.

Janeva's mind was racing. *Where is Katie? Is Katie OK? What is going to happen to me? Where is Thomas?*

Then Janeva sensed something fly past her and smack loudly into a boulder. Janeva's abductor turned, looking this way and that. Rocks were flying at him. He dodged and almost spun Janeva's head into a boulder. Another stone, and Janeva realized that someone was throwing rocks at them from above. Her abductor started to run in a zigzag pattern to avoid the rocks and was slamming and scraping against the boulders. Janeva knew this was her best chance to escape.

Her captor crouched beside a boulder to miss being nailed with a rock. She was prepared and had her knees bent, so as soon as her feet touched the rock, she jammed her feet onto the boulder and pushed hard. That propelled them forward and headfirst into the boulder directly across. He threw his hands ahead to protect himself and dropped Janeva. She crawled away while he was still trying to protect himself from a barrage of rocks; then he started after her. There was no escape, so she grabbed a rock and threw it. It hit him right in the abdomen, and he bent over just as a small rock from above hit him on the head. He looked dazed.

"Run!" she heard Katie scream from above. They both ran.

They backtracked, weaving through the boulders and pools of water. Janeva was worried that they were lost, but fortunately, Katie had an excellent sense of direction, and they eventually managed to find the original trail. The cries from Thomas, Greg, Trent, and Steph calling their names helped. When they finally connected, everyone started talking at the same time.

"What happened to you?" Thomas asked as he held her close.

Before she could reply, he said, "We saw the blond guy, but he disappeared."

"Disappeared?" Janeva asked, disappointed.

"Probably local knowledge—they know the trails, and we don't."

"What happened to you two?" Steph asked, looking at them critically. They were both filthy. Janeva was covered in sand and Katie with dirt she had picked up from the boulders.

"I got him with a rock," Katie said.

"Got who? Why?" Thomas asked Katie.

"Let me look at you," Greg said; he saw that she was injured.

"The *guy* who tried to grab me and then carried Mom off over his shoulder."

"What?" Thomas yelled. "You were attacked? Oh my God, not again. Janeva, I can't let you out of my sight for even one minute."

"We survived, but"—she started to sob—"it was a close call. Get the police now. The brute attacked Katie and smashed me onto the ground, then tried to kidnap me. Katie saved me."

"That's it," Thomas announced. "Everyone, back to the boat. Now!" He put his arms around Katie and Janeva in a protective manner. "Greg, lead; Janeva, Katie, and Steph next; then I'll protect the rear."

The swim back to the dinghy was easy, but trying to get into the dinghy was not. The dinghy didn't have a swim ladder; it required upper-body strength to reach up twelve inches, grab the starboard handle, which had only room for one hand, and then single-handedly pull up and over the round, inflatable tube. Then if they could kick hard enough, they could propel themselves over and into the dinghy headfirst. After some pushing and pulling, all were aboard.

Before Janeva could voice objections, Thomas interceded "Janeva, I know you've just survived a crisis, but we have another urgent matter. We can't stay here; it's too exposed. It's getting late, and the mooring buoys clearly state that there is no overnight mooring." Greg yanked the start cord. "We'll have to spend the night at Spanish Town.

***

The next morning Janeva's eyes opened to a gentle breeze coming in from the two open portholes in her cabin. In all her life, she had never been physically attacked. Her body hurt. She was stiff and sore. It hurt to move, even in bed. While she contemplated getting up, she thought back to yesterday's horrifying events and watched the moving square of reflected sunlight from the waves and sun on the cabin ceiling for a time. Then she moved slightly to look straight up through the ceiling hatch, where the mast with its red main halyard swung gently. At the very top of the mast was the wind finder and then the perfect Caribbean blue sky. Why she wondered, did she have to experience the best and the worst back to back? A perfect location, rocking in the swell under a beautiful blue sky, and enjoying it with her loving daughter and husband should be an equation for paradise—but then someone died, the office and the boat had been searched, and finally, she and her daughter were attacked. Heaven became hell became heaven, all in two days. *Why?*

she wondered. *Are we being targeted? Am I missing something?* When she tried to move, everything hurt.

It was not easy, but Janeva finally pulled her aching body out of bed, stood up with effort, and made her way to the head. With a strong anti-inflammatory, she would cope with the pain and enjoy another perfect Caribbean day.

***

"Where to today?" Greg asked as he readied the boat for departure.

"I'm starting to worry that Janeva might be right about us being followed or targeted in some way, so let's not plan a destination but go where the wind takes us," Thomas said.

"I'll second that. I can't fathom how that Jeff guy keeps turning up at the same time and the same place as us," Greg said in agreement.

The bow mesh that joined the port and starboard pontoons was like a trampoline, and Katie and Steph had found that it was the perfect place to sit during a smooth sail. Thomas, who had promised to go where the wind took them, instead sailed close-reached, enjoying blasting maximum spray up through the trampoline mesh. Katie squealed in surprise and joy each time a wave soaked her.

Though they hardly even adjusted their sails, the wind took them directly to Norman Island, where they coasted smoothly into the large, protected harbor known as "the Bight." They snagged a mooring buoy, dropped the dinghy, and took Trent to shore. Trent was now on a new island and without his belongings. He had spent the previous night on the settee of *Joie de Vivre*, and even though it converted to a spacious double berth, he missed his privacy and was eager to see if he could get a room in one of the cottages that lined the beach.

"Thomas, can you order me a healing drink as therapy for yesterday's criminal attack?" Janeva said teasingly and then, easily distracted, noticed the gift shop. "Oh, hold on; I want to go to the gift shop first." Clearly, her aspirin had relieved a lot of her pain.

"Good idea; I'll go with you," Steph said, and Katie hopped up to follow as well. Katie seemed to have taken the attack in stride.

"Should I be concerned about the emotional impact on her from the attack and now her newfound interest in shopping?" Janeva whispered to Steph as they walked down the beach.

"Kids are resilient, and she seems fine, but it's always a good idea to trust your mother's instincts. If you get worried, talk to her, and you know Greg is good at that kind of talk."

"Thanks. You're right. I will."

"This is the best selection so far," Steph said as she held up a cute T-shirt that said "I 8 the bounty" with a pirate image.

After picking a wide selection of souvenirs and gifts for friends back home, they joined Thomas, Greg, and Trent at a picnic table on the beach.

"Did you find a room, Trent?" Steph asked him.

"Ah yes, a lovely room just down the beach, and"—he pointed in the direction of the cottage—"here come my belongings from the other hotel." He jumped up and went down the beach to collect his bags from the hotel employee.

"Wow, that was quick," Janeva said in surprise.

"Note the amount of cash that has just changed hands," Thomas said with a laugh.

As the adults sipped tropical beverages, Katie played on hammocks and then kicked soccer balls on the beach with some other children, until the tropical afternoon rain started. Then the group of children from the beach ran under the cover of the bar and started playing a giant game of Jenga. The usual Jenga game is played with small pieces on a table, and the loser moves the piece that causes the tower to collapse. However, here the blocks were like building bricks, twelve-by-four-inch beach wood, and were stacked in the middle of the dance floor. The tower could grow to the height of the tallest player before toppling with a clatter to the ground.

"It's too wet to go back to the boat now," Steph said as she looked out at the water and at the beautiful setting sun that turned the rain into gold, orange, and pink rays. It was as if they were sitting in a prism.

"And I'm hungry," Katie announced, breaking the spell that had the adults mesmerized.

"Me too," Janeva agreed.

"Let's get a table and order," Steph said.

They sat in silence, enjoying the moment before the waiter came to discuss the menu. Then Greg disturbed the moment by raising the topic that they'd all tried to ignore. "I know we decided not to report this to the police because we've already spoiled our vacation with police business that was not helpful, and we couldn't identify or prove any aspect of the event. And," he said with emphasis, "we left the scene.

Now we will never find out what motivated the attack on Katie. From what Janeva overheard, it certainly sounded like a planned attack. Did we walk into a trap? If it was a trap, then who set it up? It's been easy to pat Janeva on the back and reassure her that we aren't involved in some sort of a mystery, but now Janeva and Katie have actually survived an attack!" He took a deep breath. "I now regret that we didn't demand a police investigation."

No one knew how to respond. Instead, they all nodded or looked down at the table. They knew Greg was right, and they had missed an opportunity to get to the bottom of the mystery.

It was getting dark, so the group quietly made their way back to the boat. They said good-bye to Trent, who said his beach cottage was picturesque, so he would probably stay on for a few more days to relax and do some reading on the beach. Then he'd take the water taxi to Beef Island to catch his flight home.

"See you at the yacht club next week. Cheerio." Trent gave hugs to the girls and shook hands with Thomas and Greg.

"Where is our boat?" Steph asked from the bow of the dinghy.

"How come we didn't leave an anchor light on?" Katie asked. "You said we always had to have our masthead light on when we were at anchor. That's the rule."

"Well, in an anchorage, an anchor light isn't considered critical, but I agree. You are correct. We should have had our anchor light on," Thomas replied.

"Because we didn't know that it was going to rain and that we were going be ashore until after dinner," Janeva answered.

"Unfortunately, we weren't the only ones who neglected to put on lights," Greg pointed out as they looked at many bobbing, dark boats.

"There it is." Katie pointed.

"Katie, we are very fortunate to have your young eagle eyes with us," Steph said sweetly to a gloating Katie.

Back on the boat, Thomas, Katie, and Greg stretched out on the trampoline for some stargazing, and Janeva decided it was time to go through Betty's bags. She carefully emptied each bag onto her bed, checking all the pockets. Soon she had a nice pile of crumpled Kleenex, mint wrappers, and coins, but to her disappointment, no new clues or other letters.

"Looking for clues?" Steph asked as she handed her a cup of steaming black tea and picked up one of Betty's light sweaters to fold.

Sighing, Janeva said, "I didn't find anything, and I've been through every pocket."

"Did you check her wallet?" Steph asked in her gentle manner.

"I did. Just the usual stuff, credit cards and such. I was so sure I would find more information in her luggage."

"No cash?"

"No. My guess is that the crew member who packed up her stuff took it," Janeva suggested. "Perhaps the murderer found what they were looking for."

"We don't actually know that it was murder. We keep making that assumption because of the head injury, and you can't examine the cremated dust, so we'll never know," Steph countered.

"You're probably right, because I can't find anything of interest here," Janeva said, as she flipped through a stack of loyalty cards, medical insurance, a small photo of Betty and Sir Ford, ticket stubs, and various store and restaurant receipts.

"You know I would help with Betty's belongings, but we are continuing on to Haiti," Steph said.

"Oh sure, I get it; you are going to abandon us just to go and save lives," Janeva said, teasing her friend.

The next morning Janeva woke up to a grumpy group of boaters. She looked around at the subdued group. "What's going on?" she asked.

"The Internet is down," Katie said dramatically. "I can't Instagram."

"Grrrr," Thomas said, steam practically emanating off him as he furiously typed at his keyboard.

"Thomas, what's wrong?" Janeva dared to ask.

"Someone is trying to hack into our system."

"What! Why would someone want to hack into this boat's router?" Katie asked.

"Not the boat. My company cloud. I shut down the boat router because the hackers were trying to access through my computer," Thomas snarled. Then, looking at his computer, he said, "Damn it."

Janeva made more coffee and went out to the deck to do her morning yoga routine. There was no cheering up the Internet addicted.

Fortunately, and to everyone's relief, Thomas was able to stop the hack and get the boat Internet up and running. A flurry of e-mail checking and, in Katie's case, texting followed.

"OK, who is coming shopping with me in the village?" asked Steph.

"What village?" Thomas asked sarcastically. Clearly, he was still grumpy.

"You know what I mean: the gift shop and small grocery store."

"I'll drive," Katie replied enthusiastically. She had become the designated dinghy driver, and except for her desire to soak and laugh at the person who was unlucky enough to end up sitting in the bow, she had become an excellent dinghy operator on this trip.

"No, you're not. You have homework to do. You haven't done any of the required reading and—"

"But, Mom, we are on holiday," came the pleading reply.

"Come on, listen to your mother and just get it done. Then you won't have to have it hanging over you, and you can enjoy the rest of the holiday," Thomas said.

"I'll stay here today with Katie, and we'll clean up and look after the boat," Janeva said to him quietly. "The rest of you go. I've got lots to do."

Pleased that she had managed to get Thomas off the boat and away from his computer, Janeva busied herself in the cabin cleaning and then finishing the inventory for Catherine. Inventory required detail, and Janeva was good at detail. She removed cushions, opened hatch covers and lazarets, and checked and stored the bottles of fizzy water. *How charming*, she thought. *Our clean water is stored beside the engine oil and spare impellers for the dinghy's four-stroke diesel engine.*

She thought back to years ago when she hardly knew the difference between a wind turbine and an internal combustion engine. Now she could bluff her way with all the other yachties. She thought with some pleasure about the fact that even though it was only a four-stroke engine, it was a lot more fuel efficient than a gas engine, and it did not pollute as much.

"Look, it's all done." Katie was waving a math worksheet under her mom's nose and a few more handwritten sheets.

"What's that?" her mom asked.

The exaggerated teenager sigh was accompanied with an eye roll. "My science report."

"Do you want me to check your spelling and grammar?"

"No. You're dyslexic, and I'm a better speller than you. Anyway, we do that in class, and I don't have the rubric. I want to go snorkeling."

Seeing the skeptical look on her mother's face, she quickly added, "It's for my biology report. I'm going to use the waterproof camera to take photos."

"I thought you were studying cells in biology."

"For my report, I need to get photos of the coral reefs and the fish that inhabit them—"

"Well, just stay close to the boat where I can see you," Janeva interrupted; she knew her daughter could be loquacious when it came to science experiments. Then she made her way to the stern so that she could keep an eye on her daughter.

Katie oiled herself up with sunscreen, put on the fins and snorkel, and then uncoiled the nylon line and threw it off the back of the boat, just in case there was a current, so that she would be able to grab the line and not get pulled too far away from the boat. It was one of the safeguards her dad had demanded. She slid into the bathtub-warm water, adjusted her snorkel and mask, and gently propelled herself with large black fins. The fish were everywhere, and they were brightly colored. She saw huge colonies of tiny yellow-and-black fish that exploded back into their coral home when she moved. Hundreds, maybe thousands of them, and they all moved to the same spot at the same instant. *How do they communicate?* She wondered. Quiet and motionless, she just watched them, and they watched her. How beautiful. How marvelous. Underwater photos were never as good as you expected, so she concentrated on trying to get perfect photos.

Suddenly she was in the shade, and then something grabbed her vest and started to drag her out of the water. She was being pulled up waist first and then feet first. *Oh my God. I'll drown!* She panicked. Head underwater and feet now straight up, she instinctively started to kick and wiggle around, and then suddenly she was free. Her fins had fallen off, and whatever had grabbed her had lost its grip on her wet, oiled legs. She got her head above water and gasped for air.

The lifesaving gasp of air exposed her head, and a man in an inflatable dinghy grabbed her hair with one hand as he tried to grab her arm with the other. She couldn't break free. She tried to scream, but her throat filled with water.

If it had not been absolutely quiet and peaceful, Janeva might never have noticed, but a sudden wave action and the sound of the splash caused her to look up. She saw her daughter being pulled into a dinghy by her hair.

It was a reflex. She acted fast, grabbing the emergency knife that Thomas always insisted be accessible; with it between her teeth, she dived into the water and swam to where Katie was fighting and flailing. Katie pushed away but was yanked back, and she slid under the dinghy but was yanked back again by her hair. They hadn't seen or heard Janeva, and she whipped the knife up and attempted to stab at one of the attackers. Katie was screaming. The knife thrust was useless because Janeva couldn't reach up high enough to stab anyone, and every thrust caused her to spin back in reaction.

Katie's next scream was piercing with physical pain as one attacker lifted her out of the water by her hair, while the other was twisting her left wrist. Janeva, still not noticed by the attackers, tried to lock her legs under the dinghy and with her right hand stab the dinghy or anything that she could hit. The dinghy material was too strong for her to penetrate. She used the knife tip like a climber's crampon on the top lip of the dinghy and started to pull herself onto the boat. This caught their attention, and one assailant jumped on her. Suddenly, with the added weight and force of the assailant, the knife penetrated and burst through the fabric, and the dinghy fired out an explosion of compressed air, flipping the boat up onto its other side and spinning both Katie and Janeva back from the boat. The assailants suddenly had to hold on to try to control the jet of the collapsing dinghy. Katie was in pain but, still wearing her floatation vest, was able to swim back to the boat, crying and shaking. When finally they made it, they saw two men swimming to their boat from the abandoned, deflated dinghy.

"Mom, call for help now," Katie cried, "before they get here."

Looking at the swimmers as her mother frantically searched for the cell phone that came with the boat, Katie exclaimed, "Hurry! They are getting close—Mom, I'm scared!"

Frantically Janeva dialed 911, the emergency number. It didn't work. She wondered if it was 911 here or 999 like in the UK—they were in the British Virgin Islands, after all. Desperate, Katie got the compressed air horn and started to honk, honk, honk over and over again. Janeva fired off two flares. Surely someone would notice and come to help.

***

Word got around the small beach resort that there was a problem or crisis in the port basin. The police boat and several dinghies from shore or off other anchored boats started in their direction.

Seeing the approaching dinghies and police boat, the attackers turned to shore and made their escape. Seeing the flares, Thomas, Greg, and Steph had rapidly returned. No one else had witnessed the attack on Katie, but the deflated, partly submerged dinghy was easily found, so the police insisted that Thomas, Janeva, and Katie come back to the village police station to file their report. As they stood in the small, cramped station waiting area, Thomas wondered if these two policemen had the skills or the technology required to perform an investigation. *Give a big guy a uniform and gun so he looks tough and hope for the best*, he thought. The policeman was calm and polite and took their statement, clearly surprised that the young girl had been attacked right in the yacht basin in midday. A sexual attack? What else could it be? Why, he asked repeatedly, had this apparently planned kidnapping occurred if it wasn't for rape?

"Look," Thomas told him, "why don't you try to find the attackers and ask them? They will know the answer to your questions. My daughter was attacked, and all you can do is ask questions. This is a criminal event."

"And," asked the policeman, "please explain why you think some men might want to kidnap your daughter. We haven't had a rape or sex crime here in many years, but we have had some rich Europeans and Americans visiting for reasons other than R and R, and so we do take an interest in activities like money laundering and movement of restricted material from Venezuela and Columbia. So tell me, what you are really doing in my country?"

"What are you talking about?" Thomas snarled. "We are here on vacation. I want to speak to your superior. We need help now. We have a problem, and instead of investigating, you are threatening me."

Giving Thomas a cold stare, the police officer said, "You are right: we are just simple island policemen. But I did learn a wee bit of police work during my training in the UK with the Yard after I got my degree at Cambridge. As for those crooks that got away, you are correct: this is an island,

and it is not so easy to escape. Also, just to let you know, even though we don't have sophisticated technology like you Americans, our ancient CCTV camera did record those men very early this morning, because they stole the inflatable dinghy from the marina. Moreover, while you were waiting, our unsatisfactory technology has done a search on each of your group, and we are surprised to find that just a year ago, you all were involved in a murder case.

"So, let me summarize. A young daughter of a man known to have been associated with a rich man of questionable character was by coincidence aboard the yacht of said man the very night he was murdered. Now, if I understand you correctly, you are back again on a yacht owned by that same murdered man. Why, I wonder, would someone try to kidnap your daughter? Thanks for the flares and the horns. Now I have an investigation to conduct. And while we were talking, I managed to get a search warrant for your boat, so let's all return to your boat together."

***

"That's it—we are done here! We're going home tomorrow. I refuse to spend one more day here with a group of bandits trying to kidnap my daughter!" Thomas ranted later after the police had searched the boat and everyone's belongings. Janeva's and Steph's eyes met, and they smothered grins because they were scheduled to leave the next day anyway.

As evening fell, Janeva and Steph prepared their final meal aboard. Earlier that day Janeva had made a marinade of coconut rum and classic Jamaican jerk seasoning for the chicken. Thomas and Greg were on barbeque duty.

"Um, what happened to our chicken?" Janeva asked, looking at it.

"I think they were distracted drinking their new favorite beverage," Steph answered. That new beverage was a dark and stormy.

"Nope, we're sure it was all that coconut rum caramelized on the charcoal briquettes making it flare up" was the response, but the end result was a delectable chicken blackened on the outside and tender and juicy inside. To use up the remainder of the supplies, Steph made yummy penne al vodka with spaghetti noodles, and Greg created a great salad with all the leftover veggies, including olives with Greek salad dressing.

Chapter 18

Back at the dock, the group gathered its bags and took the short taxi ride into Road Town, where the fast ferry departed to St. Thomas. Their search for a good place for breakfast failed, so they gave up and had an early lunch at Pusser's. It was only ten thirty. *Who says hamburger, fries, and beer aren't good for breakfast?* Janeva thought.

Later, on the ferry, Steph played Risk and Battleship with Katie on her iPad, and to Katie's great delight, Steph lost every game.

Laughing, Janeva said, "I could have told you that would happen. That is why I don't play these games with Katie or Thomas. Last time we played Risk, the board game took over four hours, and by the end I was desperate to surrender, begging, 'Please, please take over my last remaining country; I just want to go to bed.' But no, they made me stay up and lose properly."

"Next time tell me before I play." Steph laughed in good humor.

Customs at the ferry dock was a long process made worse by the fact that somehow, they ended up in the slow line. The tired group eventually made it to the airport, where they went through customs for the second time.

"Why do we need to go through customs twice?" Steph asked.

"Saint Thomas is a duty-free zone, so it's possible to make purchases on your way to the airport," Thomas replied.

"Whatever the reason, they take security and customs seriously." Janeva noticed, much to her amazement, that many travelers seemed to have forgotten the rules during their visits to the islands. "Look over there; that lady is trying to bring fruit through security, and that guy has all those small bottles of rum," Janeva said, venting to no one in particular.

Then she caught her breath. "Thomas, it's him," she whispered as she pulled on Thomas's arm and used her elbow in an unsuccessful attempt to point out the blond man standing ahead of them in the security lineup.

"Why are you grabbing my arm?" Thomas asked. "And whispering? I can't hear you in this cacophony."

"Thomas," she whispered back. "It's Jeff, the blond guy—you know, the one we saw at the Baths, with his wife and daughter, and we raced him—how come he keeps turning up like he's following us?"

"Where?"

Just then, Jeff walked through security, so all that Thomas could see was the back of his blond head.

"You missed him," Janeva said, disappointed.

"We will look when we get inside, but I hope you're wrong about this, Janeva," Thomas said and put his arm around her and pulled Katie closer as if to protect them.

Eventually, the group made it through security and into the boarding area. The first order of business was to get some food for the flight.

"There, do you see him now?" Thomas asked his wife as they stood in line for food.

"No, not yet," she whispered back.

Then the dreaded announcement came: "Your flight is delayed."

After a short interval, Thomas went to the counter to investigate. Katie and Janeva watched him talk to both the senior attendant at the check-in counter and then the pilot. Much to Greg's and Steph's entertainment, Janeva and Katie translated his body language for them. It went like this:

"Oh no; he is shaking his head and smiling," Katie said.

"What does that mean?" Greg asked.

"It's not good."

"But not too bad. The smile says he still thinks it might all work out," Janeva added.

But as they watched him, Katie and Janeva groaned.

"What?" Steph asked.

Katie said, "Look at his hands."

"They're on the sides of his head—not a good sign," Janeva said. Then a few moments later, she added, "Now they are rubbing his temples; that's bad."

"Here he comes. Brace for bad news."

As a stern-faced Thomas approached them, Janeva asked, "Are we stuck here for long?"

"No, the flight will start boarding any time now."

"So that's good news, right? Why the long face?" Janeva asked.

"Damn it. Because when I was standing there talking to the attendant, I saw him."

"Him? So you believe me now?"

"Who?" Greg, Katie, and Steph asked.

"Jeff, the blond guy who just always seems to turn up wherever we are," Janeva explained.

"Actually, that's not so unusual," Steph said. "You know, it is a Sunday. He and his family have probably been here for a week like us, and—"

"Thomas, did you see his family?" Janeva said, interrupting.

"No. Did you?"

"No."

"Relax. He may not be on your flight." Steph tried again to calm them down.

"She is right on both counts," Greg agreed.

But at that moment, just as Thomas was starting to calm down, Jeff walked up to the check-in counter where Thomas had just been and presented his boarding pass and passport to the attendant.

Groaning, Janeva said sadly, "It looks like he's on our flight! How is this possible? How could he know when we were leaving?"

"I don't know, but I'm not giving them an opportunity to grab Katie a third time. Maybe we have just been lucky. Janeva, you see if there are seats on any other airline leaving today to anywhere in the States, and I'll call United and try to get us on the Chicago flight."

As Janeva made a show of going from one airline kiosk to the next, Thomas got on the phone and booked them on the last three seats on the first flight going out the next day, and then he booked the last room at the Best Western.

"We aren't leaving here until we see him get on the plane. Until then we will act as if we are planning to get on our flight. OK!" Thomas said.

***

Greg and Steph's flight was called, so it was natural that Janeva, Thomas, and Katie held back from boarding to say good-bye to their friends and wish them success in Haiti. With extra hugs and waves, they watched their two friends walk across the tarmac and board their plane. Greg and Steph had planned to deliver medical supplies and help earthquake victims, but the situation was infinitely worse now because of the hurricane, and they were entering a cholera zone. Emergency medical aid is always associated with some risk to the well-meaning providers, but Greg and Steph were embarking on a mission that would expose them to a life-threatening contagious disease.

As they waved to Greg and Steph, both Thomas and Janeva took turns watching their United flight load, and they both saw Jeff waiting at the boarding area.

"Let's go catch our flight now," Thomas almost yelled, and Janeva quickly turned to Katie and whispered, "Just go with it."

Very confused, Katie just looked at her rather bewildering parents and wondered if she would ever understand adults. As Thomas turned to pick up his knapsack, he touched a hand that was also picking up his knapsack.

"What?" Thomas said, surprised, but the person had melted into the crowd. "Did you see someone try to take my bag?" he demanded of his wife and daughter, who both said they hadn't seen anything.

"Why would someone want your knapsack, Dad?" Katie asked.

"For my laptop," he said with a growl. "Hurry—they are calling our names."

"But, Dad, I thought we weren't going to take this flight," Katie said, confused.

"We're not; we just need it to look like we are! Now hurry up."

They walked up to the gate and presented their documents, and as they did, Thomas saw Jeff, who had been very, very slowly walking across the tarmac, start to climb the stairs to the plane. The documents were checked, and they were walking out the doorway of the boarding area when Thomas suddenly stopped in his tracks, half in and half out of the door, and said, "No, we can't take this flight." He turned on his heels and with open arms swept his family back inside.

"We are taking a different flight," he announced to the startled women.

"But we can't wait for you to—"

"No matter; I will figure it out."

The gate attendant shook her head with a look that said, "Really, now I've seen everything," and gave the all clear into her walkie-talkie. They watched as the plane's door closed and the stairway was wheeled away.

With a sigh of relief, Thomas asked, "So how do we get back out? Do we just go back through security?"

"No. To leave the boarding area, you need United personnel to escort you, and they are all busy loading the next flight, so you must wait."

After a frustrating search and wait, an official from the airline escorted them out, and they made their escape from the airport. Their hotel room was great and looked out over a palm tree–rimmed sandy beach and the turquoise water to which they were now accustomed. After a refreshing swim, they treated themselves to rum punches and used the hotel's strong Wi-Fi signal to cancel and reschedule many meetings and other commitments for Monday and Tuesday. Janeva finally started to recover from the frustrating day. At dinner, with a nice bottle of wine and baby back ribs, Janeva finally broached the subject that had been bothering her.

"Thomas, why was someone trying to steal your knapsack?"

"Ugh, hmm. Well, er—would you like some more wine?"

"What's up?"

"Nothing. I just want you to have a nice evening."

"No, you are equivocating."

"What does that mean?" Katie asked.

"He is trying to evade the question."

"Ohhh."

"Out with it."

"Well, keep it to yourself, but events have gone too far, and you have a right to know that my company developed an innovative technology that has caught the attention of our military. The company has a top-secret contract to produce and deliver a test model. At least we thought it was top secret until this trip, because between my office being ransacked, our boat being searched, and attempts to seize both my wife and daughter, it looks like it's not so top secret after all. Clearly, someone else is interested, and that's why I had so many confidential communications with some folks in the Pentagon."

"What is it?" Katie asked eagerly.

"Sorry, honey, I can't say anything else now. I took an oath of secrecy. You should know, however, that at any one time, the American military has hundreds of new technological items under research and testing. I do not have to tell you that humans have learned more since the year 2000 than in all the previous six thousand years. Survival means keeping technologically ahead of all the rest of the world. Now let's go to bed. I'm exhausted."

They climbed into soft beds and enjoyed a good sleep in the air-conditioned room.

***

The Uber car they took from the San Francisco airport pulled up late Tuesday afternoon. It was two days after their initial planned arrival, and Janeva anxiously surveyed the outside of their home. The front yard and shrubs that bordered the fence separating their yard from their neighbors' looked tidy and well maintained. *That is a good sign*, she thought.

"Katie," Janeva called as she gathered her bag from the Uber driver. Katie had started down the walk toward the front door. "Let your father go in first, OK?"

She gave her mother a look. "Just in case—remember the boat and the Baths."

Katie nodded knowingly, and the driver gave Janeva a quizzical look as he handed her the final bag. Janeva smiled. Yes, that did sound strange; what did boats and baths have to do with each other?

"All clear," Thomas said, and they followed him inside.

Janeva sighed. The house was tidy and as clean as she had left it—a bit stuffy, but she resolved that by opening the sliding door to the patio.

"I'm hungry. Do we have anything to eat?" Katie asked, looking in the fridge.

"No, but I'll go to the food store now. It's only two in the afternoon here, but it's seven in the evening our bodies' time. We will have an early dinner and then to bed. Tomorrow it's back to school and work for all of us."

Chapter 19

The rest of the week flew by for Janeva, as it was a short week, and she had to catch up on the two unexpected days of work she had missed due to the canceled flight. It was Saturday morning before she had a chance to even look at Betty's bags that they had brought home with them. The bags were still sitting by the front door exactly where Janeva had deposited them after taking them out of the Uber car.

"Well, Janeva?" Thomas asked, steaming coffee in hand, as he stared at the paisley roller bag and matching carry-on.

"I suppose I need to take them to her house."

"Why else did we drag them across the country? Do you even know where Betty lives?"

"Yes, it's on her driver's license, and there is a set of keys in the carry-on bag."

"Then I guess you'd better get on with it."

"Will you come with me?" she asked in a pleading tone.

"Oh no, you got yourself into this. The last thing I want to do on my Saturday is spend the afternoon going through Betty's house looking for nonexistent clues."

"What makes you think I'm going to do that?"

"Because I know you, and I know that if I'm there, you won't enjoy yourself, so I'm going to the boat; it needs a good wash."

"But I don't want to go by myself, and Steph is in Haiti, and Katie already said she won't come, and she is going to Alex's house to study."

"Ha-ha." Thomas laughed. "She knows you too."

"I know; she is getting too clever by half," Janeva said, pouting.

"Hmm. Why don't you ask Sara?" Sara was Alex's mom and a good friend and fellow yacht-club member.

"Good idea. Sure, why not? I'll send her a text."

Sara said she would love to join her, so Janeva texted back that she would pick her up in an hour when she dropped Katie off at her house.

"Thank you for coming with me," Janeva said to Sara as they drove to Betty's house. The GPS showed that it was across town on one of the many interconnected small islands, part of the archipelago after which both the town and yacht club were named.

"Turn left in two hundred feet," said the GPS.

"No problem," Sara said. "I haven't seen you since the women's committee lunch, the one where Steph was speaking about their plans in Haiti. How was your trip?"

Now that was a loaded question, Janeva thought.

As they drove, Janeva told her the story of the storm and Betty's body washing up, the memorial service, and Terri asking her to bring Betty's luggage home.

"I'm so sorry. What an awful trip for you," Sara said sadly.

They pulled into the driveway of an elegant, white, single-level, 1950s-built home. Janeva dug into her purse to retrieve the keys she had taken out of Betty's purse in her carry-on bag.

"It feels strange to just walk into her house," Sara said as she peered into one of the small, rectangular windows that ran on either side of the front door.

"I know. Ring the doorbell," Janeva said with a shrug. "I know what you mean." Together they waited and then knocked for good measure.

"Should we walk around the back just to make sure no one is home before we go in?"

"Good idea," Janeva replied. The backyard was large and beautifully landscaped. They tried to look into the windows, but the blinds or curtains had all been pulled.

"I guess that's our answer: the house was closed up for her holiday."

Returning to the front door, Janeva tried the keys until she found the one that opened the door, and then she paused. "What if she has an alarm?"

"I didn't see any alarm signs on the windows, and I don't see a control panel," Sara replied, looking again through the long, narrow window beside the door. Janeva pushed the door open, bracing herself to hear the squeal of the alarm and composing what she would say to the police when they arrived. Fortunately, Sara was correct, and no alarm sounded, so they proceeded into the bamboo-floored entryway.

"What now?" Sara asked.

"I want to look around, see if we can find her will or…something, anything." Seeing Sara's confusion, she continued, "I feel like she must have some family or at least friends that I should contact."

"I agree. It is just too sad to think that she had no one. Some air and light in here will help," Sara said as she pulled open the large curtains and opened the large sliding-glass door off the kitchen. She did the same for the other curtains, and soon a warm breeze and sunlight were streaming in through sliding-glass doors that opened from the kitchen, dining area, and living room into a rear patio and outside. The patio had a fire pit, a built-in barbeque, and what looked to be a table and chairs carefully covered. Janeva turned and looked back into the kitchen. It had been recently updated with granite countertops and stainless-steel appliances, with a large center island and breakfast bar that she was sure must have originally been a wall and pass-through, as that was common in the mid-1950s. The living room maintained the 1950s look and charm, with a large, rectangular fireplace partially separating the dining room from the living room.

"Look at this furniture!" Janeva exclaimed. "It's got to be circa 1960."

Sara smiled. "You're right—I feel like I'm in a museum."

Passing through the living room, they walked down the hallway, with the front entrance on their right, to find three bedrooms, two on either side of a full bathroom. One of the bedrooms was transformed into an office, and the other was a guest bedroom. Across the hall from the two bedrooms and behind the living room was the large master bedroom. What made it striking was that the living room's vaulted ceiling continued through and into the bedroom. The wall across from the king-sized bed showcased modern, knobless, built-in drawers and storage cupboards that stood full height and had a black, high-gloss finish. The triangular space above the wall of drawers and hanging closet was filled in with glass, letting in light that reflected off the glossy wood ceiling and solid center beam that ran the distance of the house from the master bedroom through the living room and formal dining room. It also gave the room privacy and quiet.

Drawing the curtains to the left of the bed revealed a wall of floor-to-ceiling windows and a sliding-glass door that led out to the deck and fire pit. To the right of the bed, a door led to a large master en-suite bathroom with his-and-hers sinks, a separate large shower, and a stand-alone jet tub. The toilet had its own small room with a louvered door and small window above the toilet. Across from the bathroom was a large walk-in closet that even had a small counter in the center for folding and laying out clothing.

"This house is perfect," Janeva said with a sigh as she looked around. "Really, it's my dream home."

"Maybe you could buy it," Sara suggested. "It's closer to both the club and downtown than your house is."

Sighing, Janeva said, "That's what I was just dreaming about. The location is excellent; it is closer to everything. I wonder what it will list for."

"You know, it really depends on her will. Who do you think her beneficiaries are?"

"I was going to ask you. You knew her better than I did," Janeva said over her shoulder as she pulled open various black drawers.

"What are you looking for, Janeva? Wouldn't her will be in her office?"

"I was wondering if she had a wall safe. But I don't see anything here." Janeva finished opening and looking in all the drawers and closets until she was satisfied that there was nothing of interest to be found in them. "Let's look through the office."

The office was the first bedroom beside the front entrance; Sara and Janeva stood in the doorway taking in the room. The bamboo floor was visible around the edges of the luxurious Ralph Lauren area rug. The room held only an elegant table-style desk with a rich walnut finish and slender curved legs that added to the grace of this lovely piece of furniture. A linen, button-tufted wing chair sat at an inviting angle to the only window in the room. Janeva walked over to the window, pulled the silk gold curtain aside, and used the bronze-colored tasseled tiebacks to tie them back. A climbing white rose bush framed the window.

"Wow," she exclaimed as she took a moment to admire the picturesque view of the manicured front lawn, dreamily visualizing herself working from this home office.

"Why don't I take a look through the filing cabinet and see if I can find her will or at least her lawyer's name," Sara said, snapping Janeva out of her daydream. The matching two-drawer filing cabinet sat below the desk on hidden rolling casters. Sara rolled it out and opened it to reveal two drawers chock-full of files.

"Good idea," Janeva said as she turned and ran her hand over the desk. "This desk is so very refined that I feel the urge to write handwritten letters instead."

As she looked at the desk, it occurred to her that the handsome desk looked so good because it lacked a computer. Every desk Janeva ever saw now had a computer, and then it dawned on her that when she searched Betty's bags in the BVIs, there had been no laptop, and the memo she had found was handwritten. There had not been a laptop on the desk of her room on Sir Ford's yacht either. There must have been a laptop or desktop computer, though as she reflected on the desk, she dismissed the latter possibility. A laptop, then.

What had happened to Betty's laptop in the BVIs? Who had taken Betty's laptop, and why? Surely anyone packing up her possessions would have included her laptop, but it was neither on the boat, nor with her possessions, nor in her own office. Did the computer contain important information that someone wanted to erase? Why would anyone want someone else's computer? *Well,* she thought, *it might be worth something to a deckhand, but if her jewelry wasn't stolen, why the laptop?*

Aloud she said to Sara, "There is no computer or laptop. If we're going to find out anything useful about Betty, it would be nice to be able to look at her computer files, but we are out of luck there." Janeva headed to the kitchen, and Sara checked the master bedroom.

"Found it," called Sara. "Here's a Microsoft Surface that was on her bedside table under a pile of books and magazines."

Janeva powered up the main screen, which demanded a password.

"Damn," Janeva said, grumbling, and started to open and rifle through the three drawers under the desk.

"What are you looking for?"

"Her password. I need it to get into her computer files. Hopefully, she hid a list of her passwords in a book like I do."

"Good point. I have one of those too."

"So where do you put yours when you go on holidays?" Janeva asked.

"Oh, I don't. I just leave it on my desk, but it's in a row of other similar books, and I figure a thief would just take my computer and go."

"That makes sense," Janeva said, walking over to the neat bookshelf that lined the far wall of the office. "I put mine on the bookshelf to hide it, just like you," she said as she started to pull out books and flip through them.

Sara started to flip through Betty's print files. "Is there anything else I should be looking for other than her will or the name of her solicitor and—" Sara stopped talking midsentence.

"What? Did you find something?"

Sara gave her a sly grin that quickly broke into a huge smile. "I found her password list."

"That's awesome; where was it?"

"Crazy. She had filed it—get this—in a file called 'passwords.'"

"Of course she did." Janeva laughed. Taking the password list from her, she returned to the Surface computer.

She moved her finger down the list of passwords and codes that only Betty knew. Fortunately, they were listed under headings, so Janeva picked the username and password for "computer," and to her great delight, the password was accepted. Then she repeated the whole process to get into Betty's Gmail account.

"You're in. That is wonderful! Find anything?"

"I'm starved! Let's get some lunch first."

"Good idea. I saw a cute café on our way here. I think it's only a few blocks away, but let's drive to be safe." Janeva grabbed the Surface and a stack of files that Sara selected, and they headed out to the restaurant.

Chapter 20

"We should have walked," Janeva grumbled as they drove around in circles looking for a parking spot. They finally found one by stalking pedestrians until one kindly got into a parked car and drove off. "We are practically back at Betty's house."

"The food looks good," Sara remarked, looking around as they stood in line waiting their turn to order from the menu written on a blackboard above the counter.

"The trick will be finding a table."

They were in luck. By the time they made it to the front of the line and placed their order, a table for two beside the large window had opened. Janeva put the metal number on the edge of the table for easy viewing. She was just opening the Surface when the food arrived.

"They are fast too," she said as she sorted the files along one side of the table.

Janeva had ordered a green salad with warm goat cheese and dried cranberries; Sara had ordered a warm panini.

"I'm drooling over your sandwich, but if I even look at bread, I gain weight. After our sailing trip to the British Virgin Islands, with all the rum-punch drinks and potato chips, I think I gained at least ten pounds."

When the plates were cleared and coffees refilled, Janeva searched Betty's document files. "Travel" had the details of her flight and itinerary to the BVIs; she had made some notes about Ford's family, Sylvia, Ashton, and grandchildren Finn and Penelope. Under "Archipelago" was a number of yacht club–related files, including one titled "Confidential." *Now, that is interesting*, Janeva thought. *Why would Betty have any yacht-club files on her personal computer instead of on the club computer? Obviously, they were matters of doubtful integrity or information she could not or should not share, or...*

Interrupting her, Janeva's phone chirped the "you have a text" sound. She picked it up; it was Katie, and their exchange went like this:

Hungry
Where are you?
Home
Where is your dad?
Boat
Have some cheese and crackers
K when r u coming home
I'm not done yet
What r u doing
Lunch with Sara

What about my lunch? I'm hungry
OK home in 15 min

Chapter 21

A pleasant surprise greeted Janeva when she met Thomas for a quick dinner in the club lounge: Greg and Steph were sitting with him. *What are they doing back so soon?* Janeva wondered. *Weren't they supposed to be in Haiti for at least another month?*

"Steph, Greg, what are you doing home so soon?" Janeva exclaimed as she hugged each in turn. They had a window seat, and she hesitated before sitting down to admire the beautiful red-and-orange sunset.

"How was the meeting?" Steph asked, recalling that Janeva had reluctantly attended a women's committee meeting.

Janeva repeated her question. "What are you doing back so soon?"

"The hurricane. Everything is much worse than we thought. We just were not prepared for the devastation and suffering. Haiti was chaos. We delivered our supplies as best as we could but found that even though we could contribute as health carers, we could help better by returning here. I guess you've been following the news."

Janeva's eyes went wide as she put the pieces together. "Yes, we saw the news on TV about Hurricane Matthew, and I wondered how it would affect you and your mission. How is it going?"

"It's a long, sad story. It's not under control, and the suffering and health problems are overwhelming, almost unbelievable. I'm frustrated that we aren't there. But, to change the topic, I have to admit I never thought of you as a women's committee person."

Thomas filled up her wineglass and told her they had ordered appetizers to share.

"I know! But somehow now I'm the marketing chair, and that means I have to attend women's committee meetings."

"The women's committee—at least Janeva can't get into trouble with that group," Thomas said sarcastically, and he and Greg nodded to each other in a conspiratorial manner.

"Don't they just arrange fashion shows and luncheons?" Greg asked, trying to look innocent.

Janeva rolled her eyes. "I'll have you know the women's committee raises a lot of money for this club and other important causes, including your work in Haiti, for example. Also, they do all the decorating that makes Christmas and other holidays festive around here, and they sponsor an impressive array of speakers and sailing education for our junior sailors and intermediate racers."

"I surrender," Greg said, raising his hands to match the words.

"Sorry…I've learned a lot in the last few days. I didn't mean to lecture," Janeva said with a shy smile.

"Touché," said Thomas, "and just to really make your day, I have something to show you. It's top secret, though, so you will have to wait until after dinner. I'll show you in our boat after we've eaten." He smiled and then added an evil laugh.

Janeva looked at Thomas; he just raised an eyebrow and gave her hand a squeeze under the table. "Can you tell us what it was like after the hurricane? Were you at risk for cholera?" she asked Steph and Greg.

"No," Greg said, "we could protect ourselves from the infections, but the reports that the devastation is unprecedented are not exaggerated. The storm lasted four days and nights, but people are still living in caves where they fled to escape. It's still their only sanctuary, weeks after the storm."

"I don't get it; I thought they rebuilt after the earthquake, so they must have a pretty good emergency system now," Janeva said.

"You are correct on one count; their emergency protocol is vastly improved and can be credited for saving hundreds and hundreds of lives during the hurricane. But as for rebuilding, it's not that easy; their homes were decimated, flattened to the point where there is nothing to salvage. Bridges were washed out, making it impossible to get help to many villages. Schools and hospitals are overflowing even as villagers try to cobble together some shelter from the detritus; then the rain drove them back into any overcrowded, unsanitary shelter they could find."

Steph jumped in with grimmer descriptions of daily survival. “There is no food; villagers old and young alike scavenge the hillsides for even the smallest scrap of food from flattened, drenched, and rotting crops. They are starving, exposed, sick, and suffering—”

“So, what gives? Isn’t that exactly the type of situation you two love? How come you are here and not back there helping?” Thomas asked with a shake of his head. Clearly, this was unusual behavior from his longtime friends.

With a laugh, Greg answered, “Cholera.”

“That’s an awful sickness causing nausea and diarrhea, right?” Janeva asked.

“Correct. Since its outbreak in 2010 after the earthquake, more than seven hundred thousand Haitians have been afflicted. Before the hurricane, it had already killed nine thousand people on their small island. It was an urgent and pressing situation even before this latest disaster. Treating cholera is now our primary action in Haiti.” He turned to his wife and put his arm around her with a smile. “Steph here has been leading the charge to provide clean drinking water.”

“That still doesn’t explain what you are doing back here,” Thomas noted.

“We are arranging funding and transportation for massive quantities of the two-dose cholera vaccine; plus, we need to restock our oral rehydration packages and antibiotics to treat current cholera cases. Because of the massive scale and dire need, we felt we could facilitate funding and organize supplies faster in person; but if all goes as planned, we anticipate returning by the end of the month.”

"Man, that country doesn't get any breaks, does it?" Janeva said with a sad shake of her head. "Corrupt dictators, earthquakes, cholera epidemics, Zika virus, now a category 4 hurricane."

Unsure what to say next, they were saved by the arrival of the meals. As they ate, Thomas and Janeva brought Greg and Steph up to date with club goings-on, and after a pleasant meal, they signed their chits, as was the custom. Then they eagerly went down to Thomas and Janeva's sailboat.

Thomas was taking his time unlocking the boat. "Thomas, don't tease us," Janeva admonished. That was a mistake. He turned and pointed to the moon.

"Look: it's a waxing gibbous moon. Isn't it lovely?"

"Come on, buddy, I know you don't care about the shape of the moon. What is a waxing gibbous moon anyway?" Greg chided.

"The opposite of a waning gibbous moon," Janeva replied, laughing.

"Janeva," Greg growled.

Still laughing, she added, "It's when you see more than half the moon, but it's not a full moon yet. See?" She pointed up to the moon. "Do you want to know the difference between a waning and waxing moon?"

"No, and I don't care! I want to see what Thomas has to show us."

Thomas had tired of teasing and had unlocked the boat. Because they were plugged into shore power, he was able to flick on the lights, and the group joined him, sitting on the settee around the table.

"Now, this is for your eyes only, and you need to swear secrecy."

"And if we tell, then you'll have to kill us?" Greg said, teasing.

"Exactly," Thomas agreed. "Well, actually, this is serious, and I need you to all sign this nondisclosure agreement, even Janeva."

After they quietly signed, Thomas reached into his knapsack and pulled out a thin, rolled sheet of almost-clear plastic. He unrolled it, placing its rolled edges down, and put his cell phone on it. They all leaned in to look.

"Uh, OK, it's a cell-phone place mat," Steph reported. "Am I missing something?"

Thomas smiled and flicked the switch on the side of his phone to take it off the muted setting (the yacht-club rules forbade talking on cell phones inside the clubhouse). Next, he pulled out a small drone and put it on the mat, and with a few clicks of his phone, the mat lit up. Holding his phone, he moved his finger on the phone screen, which moved the small, flying drone into the air. Drones were not unique or mysterious anymore to any of them, but what happened next caught them all by surprise. The drone started to fly around the inside of the boat and laser scanned the interior. They were mesmerized by the multiple green beams of light that became a large circle as it surveyed the ceiling, walls, and table and documented it all on the plastic membrane place mat he had unrolled earlier. As they watched, he changed the setting so that they saw themselves in three dimensions. Suddenly they all realized that a quiet, tiny, hard-to-see drone was watching and recording their activity in an augmented virtual-reality hologram.

"Holy shit," Greg muttered.

They all stared at the 3-D rendering of the interior of the boat and saw themselves looking at the mat.

"This is the beta version, and we are still perfecting the pad by including a solar panel so it can self-charge during daylight," Thomas explained. "In fact, charged, you could charge your phone, tablet, or laptop on it, and you can imagine why the military is so interested in it."

"Oh my God. Of course they are! Can you imagine? They could send this small drone anywhere and get a detailed image of not only the terrain or room dimensions but also who is there. What do you call it?" Steph asked.

"For those of you who love acronyms, it's called 'SLARD' for Stealth Laser-Augmented Reconnaissance Drone, of course."

"I like it. Do you need an investor?" Greg asked.

Thomas reached over and slapped Greg on the back. "You and Steph will be my first call. However, on a serious note, this is top secret, and I got consent to show you all because of our intimate connection with the events that happened to us in the Caribbean. You were each approved to be included as associates since it was increasingly difficult to keep the truth of this invention secret after all the events in the BVIs.

"So, my reason for showing you this is to discourage Janeva's ongoing investigation into the cause of Betty's death. The authorities do consider her death an accident. But our impression that we were being followed by Jeff, the blond man, might have been more than paranoia. I now speculate that he and the attempted kidnapping of Katie were related to attempts to get my laptop to obtain details of the manufacture of SLARD."

"How do you know that?" Janeva asked.

"Because the CIA has been in contact with me." Looking at his watch, he said, "Sorry, I hate to cut this short, but it's time for us to pick Katie up."

Chapter 22

"Do I have to go to the boat?" Katie whined to her mother, who was curling her hair.

"Yes, your father could use your help installing the new faucet for the head."

"But, Mom, it will be boring, and the boat doesn't have Wi-Fi, so I can't even Instagram or download stuff."

"I'm sure you can survive without Wi-Fi for a short time."

"*But* I can't even listen to good music because I can't stream Spotify!" She said this as if living without Spotify were a pain worse than death.

Janeva sighed. "Why don't you download some music onto your phone and play it through the speakers?"

"It won't work. Dad doesn't like my music. He will make me play Jimmy Buffet or Jack Johnson. Can't you go instead?"

Janeva was amused because this was the typical Katie on a Saturday morning, and she quietly said, "No, I promised I would meet the office staff to finalize some marketing material and the monthly newsletter."

"Um, Mom, your hair is burning," Katie said, pointing.

"Damn it!" She pulled the curler from her smoking hair. Katie had distracted her.

"Phew—it smells," Katie said, waving her hand in front of her, but then laughing at the burned ends of her mother's hair.

"I'm glad I cheered you up. Now go and get ready. You are distracting me, and I can't afford to burn any more of my hair."

She scampered off giggling happily, and Janeva looked sadly at the burned section of hair. It wouldn't have been so bad if she didn't have a hair appointment the following week, when she would have to fess up to her longtime stylist that she had burned her hair. He would, of course, ask how, and then she would have to confess. She restyled her hair, moving her part to the opposite side and covering the burned hair. *Maybe no one will notice*, she thought as she called to the family that it was time to head down to the yacht club.

***

Thomas and Katie went immediately down the dock with a wheelbarrow of tools, prepared to work on the boat. Katie had cheered up because she and Thomas had spent the car ride teasing Janeva about her hair fiasco and congratulating themselves for managing to keep her away from the delicate work they would be doing on the boat. Clearly, anyone who couldn't manage a hair dryer would be a clumsy obstruction in the cramped boat head, and for sure she couldn't be trusted with power tools. They giggled, and Janeva realized that Katie was looking forward to working on the boat with her dad—her initial reluctance was just another unexplainable teenage moment.

She wandered upstairs to the fireside lounge and was surprised to find that the lounge was full. It had never occurred to her that so many members came for Saturday lunch. The Jags usually used the more casual downstairs café, so the noon-hour fireside lounge congestion was unexpected._As Janeva stood wondering what to do, she remembered the large monthly payments Betty had been receiving that Sara had discovered in her banking files last weekend in Betty's house.

What am I missing? Janeva asked herself. *Who benefits from Betty's death? Wouldn't Betty's money and estate go to Sir Ford now that he was her husband? Sir Ford clearly didn't need her money, so if she was murdered for money, then he is out. What am I missing? I wonder if Sir Ford was sending her money. How can I find out?*

She heard Trent's booming and cultured voice call out, "Janeva, how are you?" and he motioned her to join him at his table.

"Trent, um," Janeva said. Her surprise didn't come from the fact that Trent had materialized, but more because he had put a glass of sauvignon blanc in front of her like he was expecting a companion. "So, Trent," she said, "catch me up to date. What has happened in your life since we all got back from the Caribbean? What are you up to?"

"I missed you," he said, sounding a bit hurt.

"Trent," Janeva scolded.

"OK, OK." He smiled, taking a big sip of his beer. "Try the wine; it's new and very nice, crisp. I tasted grapefruit and apple in it."

Trent was on the house committee, the committee that oversaw the food-and-beverage part of the club, and she had no doubt that he had been instrumental in choosing the wine. She did as he suggested and had to agree it was a lovely wine. Nodding to him in acknowledgment, she said accusingly, "It's lovely, but this isn't a social visit; it's an ambush."

"You know me too well, Janeva." Trent laughed. "I know you are busy, and I would be happy to help you by dropping Betty's bags off at her house for you."

"Thanks for the offer, but I already did it."

"Oh, um…" He looked away, shuffled, and then looked straight and coolly into her eyes. "Well, the fact is that I'm pressured by Ford and his family to try to accelerate closure of Betty's estate. Ford cannot emotionally deal with it; he is in a different country that has very different estate law, and unexpectedly some fairly urgent business deals are now delayed, maybe blocked until Betty's role in the estate is legally clarified. I was hoping you might be able to help me help them."

"Why me?" Janeva asked, astonished, as this was certainly not what she had expected.

"I really don't know whom else to talk to," he said. "Terri is away, there's no family, you were entrusted with her possessions, and really, Ford is right; someone must choreograph this and bring closure to Betty's death."

"Good news," she said. "You don't need my help. Sara and I found Betty's Surface laptop, and when I opened the document file, I found the name of her lawyer. We have arranged to meet, but now I am off the hook! You can meet with her lawyer and resolve all the estate issues. His name is"—she searched her contact list—"yes, here it is. Mr. William Chow." Then she said, "I can't imagine that it makes much difference, since Ford is the obvious source of wealth, and even if Betty were to inherit, that's no longer an issue. So I'd expect that the estate is a nothing more than a couple of lawyers signing a form, and Ford can get on with his business life."

"Oh, I hope she had it all arranged, and it doesn't need to go into probate," said Trent. "That could take a year." He hesitated. "It sounded like he wanted to get this done quickly—something to do with a business deal."

"I know you are just trying to help a new friend, and I'm sure this is difficult for Sir Ford," Janeva replied, "but let the lawyers to sort out. Connect Chow to Ford's lawyer, and we are both out of it."

***

Janeva headed down to the boat. Katie and Thomas were sitting up on the deck enjoying a Coke Zero. They proudly showed her the new-and-improved head sink faucet. Janeva nodded, said all the appropriate words, and made a great performance about trying it out. Then, as was always the case, she set about cleaning up the drilling dust, small plastic parts bags, boxes, and tools they had left behind.

Fortunately, it didn't take long, and soon she joined them on deck with a bowl of nuts and pretzels for snacks.

When Thomas asked, "Anything new up in the club?" she told him about the meeting with Trent and her free glass of white wine.

Thomas laughed. "Finally that's all over, and for your information, we released the SLARD to the military. It's in their hands now. Oh, and yes, I did tell them and the CIA about Jeff following us in the BVIs. So there is no more mystery."

"But—" Janeva started.

Putting his hand up in a stop motion, Thomas continued. "We need to leave now; Greg and Steph have invited us to dinner. And I said yes to Katie going to a movie tonight with Alex. We can drop her off on the way to dinner and pick her up after the movie on our way home."

Chapter 23

Janeva loved Greg and Steph's gorgeous penthouse suite with its panoramic view of San Francisco Bay and Golden Gate Bridge.

"Welcome," Greg said as he opened the door and ushered them in.

Taking Janeva's arm, Steph said, "Come inside. Let's all move out of the entryway and have a glass of champagne. I've been waiting for you to open the bottle." Janeva and Thomas dutifully followed.

The wine was excellent, as was the food. Greg and Steph employed a housekeeper who was a fantastic cook, and their wine cellar was outstanding.

They told Janeva and Thomas the latest about their efforts to arrange supplies for Haiti as they stood around the kitchen island enjoying champagne accompanied by a tomato, basil, and ricotta tart that was divine, if a bit messy because of the melt-in-your-mouth puff-pastry base. Then

Greg directed the group to the elegantly appointed dining area; a round glass table was set with china and crystal glassware that twinkled with the candlelight. An absolutely breathtaking collage of twinkling colors from the city lights and the Golden Gate Bridge shone through the large floor-to-ceiling windows set behind the table.

Steph had asked her cook to make Janeva's favorite kale salad, paired with Greg's famous barbequed baby back ribs and buttery orzo pasta to soak up the ribs' sweet secret marinade. No one knew exactly what was in his special sauce except that it had a large quantity of Mount Gay rum. Greg decanted a velvety-smooth Opus One red wine, and they toasted to friends and to summer boating. After the meal, they moved out to the large outdoor deck and curled up on the two overstuffed love seats placed on either side of a gas fire pit. It gave off a surprising amount of heat, but Janeva still took advantage of the soft throws draping the back of the love seat and wrapped one around her shoulders as she snuggled into Thomas. Greg came out carrying a tray with a port for Thomas and tea for Janeva.

Steph walked out the large sliding-glass door with a tray of bite-size, homemade dark-chocolate truffles on small, white paper napkins. After handing them around, she settled herself on the opposite love seat next to Greg and asked, "So, Janeva, what did you discover when you went to Betty's house?"

"Not much," she said, sighing. "But I did find Betty's laptop. I haven't studied it carefully. I mean, it's not really my business, but on the other hand, we're all suspicious of her death, and I hope that her files might just have some clues. I found the name of her lawyer, and Trent is looking after that aspect. I also found some financial information, tax returns and stuff that I really don't understand."

"So did she have a revenue stream other than from her job as yacht-club GM?"

"Yes," Janeva replied, "and quite a lot. If I understand her tax and financials, our yacht-club manager was extremely well-off. She certainly didn't have to work."

"Hmm. Interesting. I wonder where she made her money," Thomas mused.

Greg asked, "Really? I mean, do you think there might be enough wealth involved to represent a risk to her life?"

"Well now, if we take that route," Steph said, "when I was sitting watching the Haiti coverage on the TV, I overheard Sylvia and her husband, Ashton, talking about some big business deal they were doing with Sir Ford and Chad."

"I remember, even as we arrived at the memorial service, they had to leave to take an urgent business-related conference call," Janeva agreed.

"Interesting. I wonder what kind of business it was?" Thomas broke in.

"Actually," Steph responded, "Greg and I talked to Ashton at the bar for a bit, and he told us all about some oil project near Vancouver, in Canada. He said he was organizing the financing, and if we were interested, we could get in on the ground floor."

"Really? That's strange; you had just met him."

"We thought so too. So later, when we had good Wi-Fi, we googled him," Greg said. "We decided that it's a good thing he married Sir Ford's daughter because it looks like he lost a bucketload of money in the financial crash. As far as we could see, all the companies he had invested in went bankrupt—lots of crazy tech start-ups with no revenues, just huge debts."

"Hmm. All right," Janeva said. "I'll move him up to suspect number one and Sir Ford's daughter to suspect number two."

Thomas laughed. "Janeva, you are not a private investigator."

"Ignore him, Janeva. What else did you learn about Betty?" Steph asked.

"As far as I can tell, she was never married before. Sir Ford was the love of her life. We found her birth certificate. Rothman is—was—her maiden name. Other than what Trent told us in the BVIs, we don't know much about her life, like what she did prior to taking over the club." As she said that, Janeva decided to search a bit more into Betty's life. Where exactly had she worked? What was her life like before the yacht club?

"I'll take a wager those deposits you found in her bank account were from a trust fund set up for her by Sir Ford," Thomas said.

"You're probably right. He was that smitten with her," Janeva said.

Thomas laughed. "That's it—no more *Downton Abbey*."

"What? Why? I love that show."

"Because you're using words like *smitten*. Who talks like that?"

Everyone laughed, and Janeva said, “Touché.”

It was time to pick up Katie, so they said their good-nights.

***

Sunday morning, Thomas was up before Janeva, as was the usual routine. He had made a pot of French press coffee and was reading the news on his iPad on the outdoor sofa under the wisteria-laden pergola. Turning on the *Best of Mozart* as she passed through the kitchen, Janeva joined him, and he thoughtfully handed her a cup of steaming coffee. Janeva took a sip and then moved into the sun to do some yoga. After several sun salutations, she relaxed and opened her laptop to see what was new on Google News.

Katie wandered out onto the deck a short time later, announcing that she was hungry. Thomas and Janeva exchanged a look that said, “What else is new?” Katie was in a growth spurt and seemed to always be hungry. Janeva refilled her coffee cup and went inside to preheat the oven for the tea biscuits—another Sunday-morning tradition. She mixed flour, baking powder, and salt together and then cut in the butter. Finally, she carefully stirred in water to the right consistency and spooned the sticky, white dough out onto the cookie sheet to cook. Then she filled the Vitamix blender with fresh spinach, kale, apple, ginger, lime, banana, and water, with a handful of frozen pineapple on top. She pushed the top down on the blender and blended until it was smooth. Voilà—three green smoothies to go with the steaming, tender tea biscuits and homemade raspberry jam.

After doing the dishes, Janeva spent the rest of the morning working in the garden, deadheading flowers and pulling up weeds. It was the perfect task for reviewing the events of the past weeks. Moving forward, Janeva had promised Sara, the treasurer, that she would review the yacht-club finance files, though it wasn't clear to Janeva how she could help. It made sense that, as a dyslexic, she was not a numbers person. But Sara had said she wanted another pair of eyes, so Janeva wiped the dirt off her hands and sent a quick e-mail off to Sara to arrange a meeting at the club early the next week.

She looked up from her computer to see a Maserati pull into the driveway. After the Caribbean adventure, Trent now seemed to consider himself a close friend, even a part of the Jag family, because here he was—uninvited, displaying his new car to his new best friends. The Maserati was sleek and dark silver. Always the gentleman, he hopped out of the car and beckoned Janeva and Thomas to come for a spin, one at a time. Janeva got the first ride and lowered herself into the plush, leather bucket seat.

"Trent, your new car is gorgeous."

Trent focused on the road and said, "I should have bought a McLaren hybrid. I fell in love with the McLaren when a friend took me to see Stirling Moss and Mario Andretti race at a Can-Am, but, well, I guess I just couldn't resist the roar of the engine. Just listen to it, Janeva." Trent revved the engine for her to fully appreciate the sound. "Did you know it goes zero to sixty in four point seven seconds and has a top speed of one hundred eighty-five miles per hour? With a four-hundred-fifty-four-horsepower engine and…"

Janeva couldn't help it; she started to softly sing the words from Life's Been Good by Joe Walsh's.

Ignoring her, Trent continued with his monologue, and Janeva refrained from asking when and where he would drive at 185 miles an hour. *By the way*, she thought, *doesn't all technology use automatic transmission? What is with this paddle clutch?* However, she held back and couldn't help but smile fondly as she stole a look over at short, round Trent wearing a tweed driver's hat, his chubby arms gesticulating wildly as he gleefully raved about his new toy.

***

"I bet if you whipped up some snacks for us, honey, it would put me in just the right mood to study some of these financial reports that you got from Betty's Surface," Thomas said with a wink, and Janeva dutifully went to the kitchen. It was only the beginning of the third period, and it would be dinnertime soon. So, she mused, she might as well make a meal for everyone. Trent, after showing off his new car, had just stayed and was watching the game with Thomas. Greg and Steph were also expected.

Burgers and quick-rise hamburger buns would be just the thing.

***

"What's that heavenly smell?" Greg asked as he walked through the door.

"Janeva's made burgers for us," Thomas said, standing and greeting his friend. "Should I fire up the barbeque?"

"That will be great," Janeva said as she slid the buns into the oven to cook. "Where is Steph?"

"I'm here," she said, walking in at that moment, brandishing a lovely bottle of chilled white wine. Janeva smiled at her and went to find the corkscrew.

"Where are your plates?" Trent asked. He was especially helpful when food was involved.

Fifteen minutes later, she pulled the buns out of the oven and set them to cool.

"I just love the smell of fresh-cooked bread." Steph sighed as she poured each a glass of crisp white wine.

Thomas was outside barbequing the burgers. Janeva sighed and took a sip of her wine. "To a perfect moment in time." Holding up her glass, she said to Steph, "To good friends," and they toasted.

"Who wants cheese on their burgers?" Thomas asked, peeking his head in the door. "I do, I do!" came the chorus from everyone, and Janeva handed Thomas the plate with sliced cheddar cheese on it.

"Where is Katie?" Janeva asked.

"I'm right here" came the indignant response, as the teenager in question appeared from the hallway. "You know, I can hear you from my room."

"What have you been up to?" her mother asked.

"Homework," she answered.

Why is it that sometimes she talks my ear off, and other times I can barely get more than one word out of her? Janeva wondered. "How much more do you have to do?"

"I'm finished! I was texting."

Janeva refrained from asking how she could be doing homework and texting at the same time.

Thomas came in with the burgers. Janeva tossed the Caesar salad, shaved fresh Parmesan on top, pulled out the cold potato salad, and everyone dug in. Afterward, Thomas turned the next game on, and everyone migrated back to the family room. An hour later, after Thomas concluded that the reason his team was losing was because he was watching them, he reluctantly agreed to examine the financials.

"Our club general manager was a rich woman," Thomas said, looking up from the Surface laptop.

"Really? I can't believe it. She didn't seem or act like she was rich," Steph said, much to Janeva's private amusement, as Steph was also very wealthy and did not act like it.

"Well, unless I'm suddenly afflicted with Alzheimer's or dementia and can't appreciate standard financial statements, our friend Betty was very prosperous," Thomas said as he continued to study her financials.

Before Janeva could ask where she had made her money or what she was invested in that paid such good dividends, Trent exclaimed, "Good work; that is the kind of information I was asked to get for Ashton."

"What? I thought you said Sir Ford asked you to help him get the essential information he needed to resolve the estate. Where did Ashton come in?" Janeva asked.

"No, no, you've got it wrong, Janeva. Please, you must understand that Ford is not functioning well just now. He is in bereavement, so his son-in-law, Ashton, is acting for him. Ashton will need more than just these financials."

"Why?" Janeva asked, still unsure.

"Because Ashton thinks that Betty had access to some very sensitive business-related information that must not get into the wrong hands. I do think that our best move would be to get Betty's Surface laptop with all its information couriered ASAP to Ashton. Then we'd be out of it."

"Hmm," said Thomas. "I don't think so. Things have gone too far for that. Lawyers are involved. I must insist that this Surface computer, as with the rest of Betty's possessions, be delivered into the hands of that lawyer Chow tomorrow." With that, he closed the little computer, and Greg announced it was time to head for home. Steph gave Janeva a hug and extolled the dinner. Trent nodded to imply that he agreed with the lawyer decision, thanked Thomas and Janeva, and left with the Writemans.

***

Later after cleanup, when Thomas was reading in bed and Katie was already asleep, Janeva realized that this was her last chance to surf Betty's document file, since the computer was being handed over tomorrow. She opened a file titled "Ask Terri," which read:

> Probably correct club business, but when earlier today I needed some information from Terri, I went to her office, but she was down the hall using the head. There was a handwritten note on her desk that disturbed me, so I took an iPhone photo because I wanted to discuss it privately with her later.
>
> > *Chad, here's the list of contributors that I promised.*
> > *<u>Don't forget to emphasize the big dividends!</u>*

1. *Anchor, Nathon 50K*
2. *Haringon, Sherry 290K*
3. *Calloway, Roy 250K*
4. *Posner, John 130K*
5. *Fraser, Lisa 150K*
6. ~~*Braise-Bottom, Wiffy 120K*~~ *died*
7. *Scott, Jack 50K*
8. *Walter, Sean 400K*
9. *Peters, Christopher 620K*

Janeva mused over the list of names and realized they were all club members. She supposed that "K" referred to thousands. Donations to charity were tax deductible, and donations to the women's committee charitable events were noted in the annual report, so why this special file designation of "Ask Terri"?

Chapter 24

The next day at 9:50 a.m., Janeva entered the café and looked around. How would she recognize the lawyer? The café she had chosen was very popular in the area as a "work outside the office" place, so many tables were occupied by single people working on laptops or reviewing documents. As was her lifetime habit, she had arrived ten minutes early. This custom, she believed, improved her ability to focus and be in the moment by enabling her to get a coffee and settle herself before a meeting.

As she waited, she reviewed the list of names that she had read the night before. It was not like Betty to keep frivolous information, so there must be some reason. Also, the list included the now-dead Wiffy, and she realized this might have a more sinister meaning. Should she ask one of them? What kind of a question could she ask? She didn't even know what she was looking for. What did the amounts refer to? No, that wasn't the right question, she mentally scolded herself. She felt she was on to something; something important was on the edge of her consciousness.

The creative moment was lost because at that moment her latte was placed in front of her, and a tall, sophisticated, gray-haired gentleman wearing a tweed suit and balancing round glasses on his long, angular nose walked up to her and asked if she was Janeva Jag. At her nod, he said, "Thank you for agreeing to meet with me, Mrs. Jag."

"Janeva, please," she insisted. "Mrs. Jag was my mother-in-law," she added with a smile.

"OK, Janeva." He directed her over to the table where he had been sitting, opened a large file of papers, and methodically started to flip through them.

"Here we go," he eventually announced. "First, let me thank you for finding and contacting me. As you know, I'm overseeing Betty Rothman's estate. You do not know me, so I want to show you this file." He opened a manila legal-sized folder and flipped through various documents, naming them as he went. "The legal trustee agreement and her will. This should be enough to confirm who I am and my legal obligation to the late Betty Rothman. Also, please know that the law firm, of which I am a partner, can arrange for us to have this meeting in a local legal office boardroom if you prefer, but for now, you requested this informal meeting here in this café."

"I don't think we need a formal meeting," Janeva said. "In fact, I probably can't even help you very much. I didn't really know Betty that well."

"After I got your message, I did contact Sir Ford as you suggested," Chow replied, "and he indicated that you were my best lead to find Terri Turnell. I need to contact her."

"The last I heard, Terri and her family were in the Southern Caribbean." Janeva smiled. "Terri mentioned something about traveling with an associate of her husband, Chad." Seeing the disappointment on the lawyer's face, she added, "I'm sorry; I guess that's not very helpful. If you like, I will ask for Terri's contact information at the yacht club and see if anyone has spoken to her recently or knows where they are or where they plan on going."

"Thank you; that would be most helpful. When could you get her information for me?"

Opening the calendar app on her phone, she said, "I'll make some phone calls, but really, I just can't spend any more time at the club for a few days. I have a business to run."

"I do understand, but apparently, we need Terri's signature to start the distribution of Betty's estate."

"Why?" Janeva asked, confused.

"I require her signature; Terri was her trustee."

"And it has to happen now?" Janeva asked.

As if reading her mind, the lawyer replied, "You see, it's a substantial amount of money, and Sir Ford, well, he has indicated that time is of the essence, and it's important to him that Betty's will be executed as she desired."

Janeva thought, *He thinks that I am actually a good friend of Terri's.* Then she remembered that Terri had made a show of being good friends in front of Sir Ford on his yacht at Betty's memorial.

Seeing her confused look, Chow said he simply wasn't at liberty to reveal any confidential information, but he added that he was sure that Sir Ford would enlighten her when next they met.

"OK. I'll make some calls this afternoon and see what I can find."

"Excellent." He opened a gold business-card case, extracted an expensive-looking blue-and-white embossed business card, handed it to her, and added, "Please feel free to contact me at this number, or…" He flipped the card over and, extracting a pen from his briefcase, wrote the name of his hotel on the back.

He then gathered up his papers and held out his hand for Janeva to shake. "I look forward to hearing from you. I fly out late tomorrow, and if it is at all possible, I would like to hear from you before I leave."

***

But after the meeting with the lawyer that morning, she had more questions. *Coincidence upon coincidence upon coincidence*, she thought. *Katie and I were attacked, Betty's death is suspicious, there's urgency about clearing up Betty's estate, there are yacht clubbers in a secret file, and*, she reasoned, *none of that could have had anything to do with Thomas's top-secret SLARD project.* Nothing fit.

She accomplished nothing at work that afternoon because she couldn't resist the urge to do Google searches of Betty, Sir Ford, and Mr. William Chow; Sylvia and Ashton; their children, Penelope and Finn; and finally, Terri and Chad. Lots of gossip but not much substance. She did, however, learn that Betty had worked in the Alberta oil industry prior to moving to the Bay Area.

Chapter 25

Another afternoon away from work—she had promised to meet Sara at the yacht club. She wondered if she would ever get caught up. Her to-do list was so long now that the items referenced sublists—almost like her to-do list items were breeding and having little to-do lists of their own. She mused that the unintended consequences of her family vacation would result in her working weekends for probably the next two months.

At Sara's request, she had agreed to join her to go over the club finances. Sara had a master's degree in economics and had plenty of experience working with QuickBooks for various charities, but mostly she was a stay-at-home mom. Janeva was the only person on the club executive committee who also had business experience, and in truth, they were friends and knew they could work together. It was because of this meeting with Sara that Janeva had not mentioned to Chow that she had Betty's Surface laptop. She hoped Sara would be able to explain the list she had found, so she brought the computer with her to meet with Sara at the club.

Sara had uncovered an accounting error—a small error, but it carried on month after month and, as they searched, year after year. It was a challenge to balance the books, and Janeva spent the time reviewing club files and comparing them to Betty's Surface laptop documents. Betty had been writing a history of the club, and as Janeva flipped through the material, something was bothering her.

Finally, she asked, "Sara, does anything else jump out at you?"

"What are you looking for?" Sara asked.

"I don't know—any unusual charges authorized by Betty or Terri, or any unusual spending or costs?"

"Well, that's exactly what auditors are for," Sara said as she flipped through the most recent board-meeting minutes, income and expense statement, statement of financial position, and check detail report. She put aside the minutes and financial-position report and focused on the expense statement and check report, running her finger down the column and matching up expenses to checks. Looking over her shoulder, Janeva pointed to a line item.

She asked, "What is this?"

"Oh." Sara nodded and then checked back in the binders to older reports. Pointing to the line item in question, she said, "That's the storage shipping container for the medical equipment for the Haiti charity."

"What?" Janeva asked, confused.

She laughed. "They're your friends, Janeva. You know, Steph and her husband, Greg! You were at the luncheon where she spoke about it."

"Yes, I know, but, umm…that container was in Florida, and now it's in Haiti."

"Really? Betty must have just forgotten to cancel the contract before she left. I will take care of it after our meeting. I have the receipt file right here," Sara said, patting a stack of files on the desk.

"Can I see?" Janeva said, and she started to scan the stack of receipts that Sara produced. She found the one that matched the cost. Handing it to Sara, she asked, "Are you sure this storage shipping container is or was for Stephanie and Greg's medical charity? Could it have been for anything else?"

"Definitely not. We talked about it at the meetings. Paying for the container storage was part of our contribution. It is in the minutes. Do you want me to find them?"

Looking over Sara's shoulder at the invoice, Janeva added, "These invoices are for a container right here in the Bay Area, and the container that Steph and Greg filled was always in Florida. Could there have been two containers? Maybe to store all our decorations, signs, and vases for luncheons?"

Shaking her head, Sara said, "All that stuff is kept right here at the club. We have our own storage area in the basement. I can show it to you."

"And what is this charge?" Janeva pointed to the invoice. "Look here: each month there is an electrical and a storage charge. Why would a container need electricity, and so much of it?"

"Light? Air conditioning for medications, perhaps?" Sara held out her hand to look at the invoice. "You're right; I hadn't paid much thought to the electrical charge, but it's a substantial amount."

Did Betty know? Janeva asked herself. What could be in that container, and why did it need electricity?

"Sara," Janeva said, "this container business has reminded me to discuss another possible financial matter that I thought was a bit unusual, and the only connection is money. Betty had a list of names of yacht-club members, and each name was associated with a K that I believe meant one thousand dollars. It doesn't make sense to me, but the title of the list was 'Ask Terri,' and as she isn't here to ask, I was wondering if this made sense to you. I don't want us to miss something obvious."

After studying the list carefully, Sara replied definitively, "No, I've been all through the club book in detail, and I have no idea what that's about."

Janeva wondered to herself whether Thomas was right. Was she just being paranoid? "Well, OK. I don't think there's much more I can do here, so unless you need me, I think I'll take a look at this container on my drive home; its address is on the invoice. Let's connect tomorrow by phone to review what we've done here and how to proceed."

***

A few days before, on a whim, she had decided that the sequence and seriousness of the events were too important to ignore, so she had sent an e-mail chain-of-events tabulation to Deputy Sheriff Dugud. Not unexpectedly, she had not heard back from Dugud. Now, heading to the address on the invoice—which, according to Google Maps, was about a thirty-minute drive—she found she had a voice mail from Dugud. He had left her a message when she was in her meeting with Sara, but since cell-phone use was forbidden in the club, Janeva had missed his call.

She pulled over to return his call but went directly to his voice mail, so she told him she was on her way to inspect a yacht-club container at the rail-and-marine port and would be happy to stop in at the station afterward or arrange an appointment later in the week. She would check out the storage container at the old loading dock first. She thought that if Dugud was interested, then maybe someone on the list of names resonated in some way.

"Damn it," she said aloud as she remembered that Chow had pressed her to get the information quickly, and she'd missed his deadline. No one at the club seemed to know how to reach Terri. The front-desk receptionist had tried to call Terri's cell phone, but there was no answer and no voice-messaging option. That, Janeva thought, was a bit strange, since Terri was usually closely attached in person or by phone to the club. Interesting that no one seemed to know much about Terri's past, her personal life, or her family. As she drove, she wondered what Terri's husband, Chad, did for a living. He wasn't a member of the club.

Janeva arrived at the address stamped on the invoice, but that was no help finding the container. She looked out at a sea of large metal shipping containers, most a dusty gray, some even rusty red or faded blue. As she walked around a section filled with containers that looked abandoned, the impression was of a container graveyard. Walking through the rows, she lamented not having worn Keds; her feet were getting very dirty, and small rocks kept getting caught in her flip-flops.

Eventually, after squeezing herself around the yard's overhead crane, she found a container with the same number as noted on the invoice, but unlike the other forty-foot, rust-colored containers surrounding it, this one was black and, under a thick layer of dust, looked newer. Some containers were huge boxes that opened from the top; some, like railway freight cars, opened from the front. This one opened at the end. There were large doors at one end of the container. They were locked, and as she searched the area, she noted there weren't any other doors or windows.

She also noted that the container was attached to power, and when she stepped back, it looked like there might be ventilation pipes protruding out of the roof. She wondered why an empty container might need power and ventilation, especially when the containers were designed to be stacked one atop the other for shipping, and unless it was the top container, packing would flatten the ventilation ducts.

She went in search of an office to see if she could get some help. It wasn't, she noted, a junkyard, because the roadways between the rows of containers were clean and not littered, so someone was caring for the loading space. Eventually, after more wandering around the seemingly endless rows of shipping containers, she finally found the office. Not surprisingly, it was close to where she had parked her car. The container port was adjacent to a waterway where the container ships moored, and despite the decrepit look of the yard, a large crane was actively lifting containers onto a large oceangoing freighter tied to the dock. Who would have thought a century ago that there would be ships that could hold a ten-story building and have the deck space for a Super Bowl game?

Inside the office, an older, grizzled, dusty man sat at a cluttered desk. He was glaring at his computer screen as if it were an object from outer space, put on this earth with the singular purpose of making his life difficult. Looking up, he gave Janeva a lopsided smile.

"What can I do for ya?" he asked.

Janeva held out the invoice. He took it, glanced at it, and then turned back to his computer, ignoring her. Slightly baffled by his response, Janeva held out her hand and introduced herself.

"Hi. I'm Janeva Jag from the yacht club, and I'm hoping you can help me open our container."

He waved huge, thick, dirt-stained hands. "No" was all he said.

"But...," she said, floundering, "we are paying for it; please arrange for me to get in."

"Sorry, I can't help you. If it is your possession, then you should have the keys to the locks. I don't have access to the container, and I only deal with the employees. If you want to do business with the facility, here's the web address. I can't help you," he said flatly.

Janeva reached into her purse and pulled out her yacht-club membership card. She held up the invoice.

"This container is rented by the yacht club, I am in charge of paying the storage, and I have full rights to access it," she declared as forcefully as she could. "Our contract stipulates that you also have the keys to all the containers, so if you want our business, let me in now or cancel our account, and I will have our lawyers arrange for you to return our unused rent." She realized that if she were really in charge of the club, she would have the club key or code to unlock the door, but of course, she did not.

"Hmm. Let me see now. I'll make a call and see if there's anything I can do." She heard him on the phone; without hanging up, he turned around and told her that he could arrange to let her into the container tomorrow, or if she wanted to wait, he could have it opened in about a half hour. She decided to wait, so he hung up and returned to the counter where she was standing. He took the invoice, wandered over to a gray file cabinet, and motioned to her to sit down.

"Make yourself comfortable." He busied himself at the sink beside the file cabinet, came around the counter, and handed her a cup of fresh coffee.

"Sorry," he said gruffly, "I don't get many visitors here."

She took a sip to be polite. It was strong and bitter coffee, not softened by the spoonful of powdered pretend milk he'd stirred into it. After fifty minutes, Janeva was about to give up and leave when the phone rang. He spoke briefly into the phone and then turned back to her and said, "OK, take this flashlight, and you can go to the container now; it's open."

She made her way back to the container and was surprised that the door was open and the container unattended. It was totally dark, so she flicked on her flashlight as she entered. Suddenly she was grabbed from behind, her legs yanked back, and her body slammed facedown onto the floor. She screamed as her wrists were bound behind her back and her forehead was banged again and again into the floor. Her ears were ringing, and she could feel the blood streaming down her face. The weight and pain of a knee rammed into her back, and a voice shouted at her, saying, “Shut up! Shut up! Shut up, or I’ll really hurt you!” Then as she turned her head, her nose was clamped, and when she took a breath, a mass of cloth was forced into her mouth.

“Now,” her attacker said in a calm, quiet voice, “there’s no one around to hear you or help you, so listen carefully; then I’ll untie you and let you go.” The attacker held a cell phone to her right ear and removed the gag.

A deep man’s voice came out of the phone and said, “Listen very carefully, Janeva Jag, if you want to protect your daughter, Katie. The only thing you will say when I finish is that you understand.” Then the voice went on. “Number one, do not ever try to trace me. Now tell my associate where your own cell phone is and instruct him on how to phone your husband. When he has your husband on the line, I will give you a message, and you will repeat it to him. Do not tell him where you are or the conditions of this call, but do tell him that your daughter, Katie, was picked up from school today by one of my associates, and if you ever want to see her alive again, you will do exactly as I say. Now, let’s get your husband, Thomas, on the line.”

Thomas and Janeva had an unwritten rule that they never contacted each other during working hours unless it was an emergency, so Thomas answered his cell phone, prepared to hear about some domestic crisis.

"Thomas, they have Katie! If I tell you where I am, they will hurt her! I am instructed to convey their message to you." Janeva was breathless and almost panicked as she screamed into her phone that was held to her ear.

"Whoa, whoa. Calm down, Janeva; what are you talking about?"

"Thomas," she said again, "if we don't cooperate, she'll be hurt or worse." She started to cry. It was all she could do to talk, and she could taste the blood dripping down her face into her mouth.

Her captor, taking her phone back, growled into it, "Don't talk—just listen now!"

Thomas screamed, "Who are you?"

"Listen," he growled. Then suddenly Janeva's arms were forcefully extended high over her head, and she screamed in pain.

"Ask me one more question, and you will really hear a scream; a third question, and you won't hear anything, because it will be Katie who you are torturing. Get it? Now shut up and listen!" Janeva's hands were relaxed, but she was still crying in pain.

"If you want to ever see your daughter, Katie, again, listen very carefully and say nothing. You have a graphene chip that belongs to my employer, and he wants it back. Put the chip into an envelope and leave the envelope on the front desk of your yacht club addressed to 'Container key—confidential.' Tell no one. You have exactly ninety minutes."

Janeva watched as her phone was placed on the floor and smashed by the heel of his shoe; then she heard her attacker say, "OK," presumably into his phone. Another nose squeeze and the rag gag was whipped off the floor and shoved painfully into her mouth. Then with the squeal of the metal door being shut, the container went quiet. It was dark, virtually black. She could not see and couldn't easily turn her head. She was in pain and terrified. Her back hurt, her head hurt, and her brain throbbed. Then suddenly the whole container moved. It tilted and lifted. She slid first to her right and then faster to her left as the tilt corrected and overcorrected. She felt herself slam into the wall. Her hands were being scraped raw as she tried to control her sliding. She skidded uncontrolled down at the far wall but was slammed into a mass of electrical equipment and a wall of electric cords, cables, and computers.

The container tipped the other direction, and the door flung open. She saw that the container was an office filled with electronics. Then, unexpectedly, it tilted door-side up, the door slammed shut, and she slid painfully across the container into the back wall.

Sliding and scraping across the floor, hands still tied, she rolled atop a coil of electric cords and, fumbling, was just able to grasp a cable. She held on to save herself from the agonizing scrape across the floor when the container tilted sharply in the other direction, and she looked down as the door flung wide open again. She was slowly slipping, facing down as the cable stretched toward the open door. She was easily a container height above ground, and she realized that the container was being lifted up in the air. She was looking straight down; then her weight yanked the cord taut and spun her arms over her head, and the cord pulled out of its socket.

She tumbled down the floor and soared out the door like a bomb. She hit the ground feet first and rolled.

Chapter 26

As usual, Max had prepared for this moment. He had looked forward to it. His job was often dreary. Max liked to think of himself as an anti-narcissist. He never directly associated with special and important people, he did not envy anyone else, and he did not want to be admired. In fact, he avoided social contact. He found personal interactions tedious, so he isolated himself using a mass of computers to run his empire. A few individuals—he called them very smart survivors—knew him, but otherwise, he thought himself invisible. Those survivors, some at the end of a computer, others always at the end of a mobile phone, managed his business empire. He had made them rich. Like him, they loved the game; they didn't ask questions, and they knew how to deal with competitors. *Rule number one*, he repeated to himself: *protect yourself and always attack first.*

But now he had a chance for some real hands-on fun, and that was getting into the crane and lifting the container onto the container ship. He had wanted to maneuver a huge container onto a ship for more than a year, and this, right now, was his opportunity. He directed the interrogation of Janeva from his vantage place in the crane cabin.

"Now," he said into his phone, "let go of that woman and get out of the container. Do it now, and destroy your phone!" Max threw his own phone in a wide arc into the sea, the perfect disposal place for a burner cell phone. Just as he had planned, if ever the container was discovered, the four people connected by three phones were totally untraceable.

No one knew he was there. No one saw him, and as was his lifetime practice, he was only an invisible voice giving orders at the end of a phone—unseen, his veiled presence was secure. Everyone he dealt with knew that you never had a second chance to disobey his request.

He had practiced using the crane lift but had never lifted a huge container high enough to swing it around and gently position it into a space between rows of containers high up aboard a freighter. Turn the ignition key, hold down the start button, and the crane roared into life. Now, gently easing the joystick, he slid the lifting hook to the top center of the container, grabbed it, and started to lift it straight up. Precision in all things was his style, and this was a measure of his care. The container was nestled between two others, so the lift had to be straight. Loaded containers are filled and balanced, but this was an office, unbalanced. One side, heavy with computers and electronics, tipped. It slammed the top of the neighboring container; a flick of the joystick righted it, but, when it overcorrected, it tipped in the other direction and swung in an arc, just missing the crane.

Then, for almost the first time, things hadn't gone as Max had planned. The container swung erratically toward the container ship, its door flung open, and he saw the woman fall or jump out. Now juggling a huge container in the air and seeing his captive sprawled unconscious or dead on the ground, Max became aware of a police car entering the compound. *Time to get out*, Max thought to himself, and he scampered out of the crane control booth, down the rear stairs, and unseen onto the dock, where he strolled to his Harley. *Good plan, minor slipup—no one saw me arrive, and no one saw me leave.* He had enjoyed running the crane, and he enjoyed driving his Harley just as much.

As he headed back to the center of town, he decided it was time to take stock. He prided himself on being in control. The Jag computer-chip situation was one small aspect of his conglomeration, and he had delegated their observation to another unsuspecting but fully reliable servant. His employees were well rewarded, most appreciating that their own survival was at stake, and he'd received regular reports about the Jag family activities for months. But he still didn't have that damn chip.

Just another anonymous cyclist in his solid and full-face black motorcycle helmet, he relished roaring through traffic. He did not lose any sleep wondering what else those guys who carried out his orders might be doing to feather their own nests. It was his strategy, his plan, and he gave the orders. How his orders and plans were followed was not his concern. But the damn chip was becoming an obsession. Those dumb Jag idiots and random happenings had frustrated his goal to get the chip back, and time was up. He needed the chip now. As of a few minutes ago, even the Jags now knew that he required the chip and was determined to get it. *Play the game my way, or just maybe your daughter, Katie…hmm,* he pondered. *I wonder if Janeva survived the fall?*

No matter. He had their darling daughter, and Thomas wasn't going to let anything happen to her. *I wonder, will he just hand it over, or will she need to feel some pain so he can hear her plea for help?* Was torture the word he was searching for? Oh well, she was just an unimportant kid anyway.

***

"*Janeva*, look at me," he yelled at her in alarm.

"Save Katie," Janeva said weakly.

"Katie? Yes, I will" was the last thing she had heard before she slipped back into unconsciousness. When she came to a short time later, she was vaguely aware that she was lying on the ground, and her head was being moved. Everything was double, and she was going to vomit.

"Can she walk?" came a voice.

"Can you walk?" he asked her.

"I think so, with your help."

"I've called the ambulance. Just stay still. You'll be OK now."

"No, no," she said as her awareness started to return, "get my husband, Thomas. I need to see Katie!" She tried to get up but collapsed back in pain. "My ankle," she said, wincing, and inhaled a sharp breath to suppress her nausea. "I think it's broken."

"OK, let's hope that's the worst of your injuries. You're lucky to be alive. You probably fell fifteen feet with your hands bound behind your back. Your face is covered in blood, your hands and wrists are scraped raw, and you were unconscious when we got here." Then her fuzzy brain clued her in.

"Deputy Sheriff Dugud! Thank God you are here. How did you know? What are you doing here?" she asked.

"Saving you," the officer said.

"Please, it's Katie we need to save," Janeva cried, exasperated; then she realized that Katie's life depended on her not revealing the kidnapping. "No, no," she croaked, still suffering from the damage imposed by the rag gag shoved down her throat, "just find Thomas. Katie is not part of this. Please, we must get Thomas. Fast. Now. Please help!"

"You're going to the hospital. You are in no condition to assist me or to direct our actions. Now just do as you are told. The ambulance will arrive soon." Dugud instructed his backup officer, who had now appeared, to accompany Janeva to the hospital and to take a full record of the events. A second backup officer had responded and was instructed to search the container and crane and find the crane operator. Then Dugud started to leave.

"No, no, please don't interfere. This is not a police matter. It is all my fault. Just get my husband. We don't want your help. Please stay out of it. Stay away. Let me go. Please."

Dugud instructed the other officer to loan Janeva a cell phone to call her husband or whomever she wanted; then he left, quietly and without siren or lights. This was his own search. The more Janeva declared that it wasn't about her daughter, the more it reinforced his idea that the real crisis might in some way be centered on Katie.

He heard his officer console Janeva and tell her, "Of course you are not under arrest. We are here to look after you and to help you, and we have determined that you've had a head injury and need hospitalization." An interesting thing about letting someone use a police cell phone is that every conversation is recorded and every recipient GPS located. Janeva called Thomas.

***

Success in Thomas's international business endeavors depended on constant communication, and he was programmed to respond twenty-four/seven to his cell phone. He kept it close, but suddenly, out of an otherwise calm, ordinary day, he was facing the worst crisis of his whole life, and this was not the time to answer his business phone. The survival of his wife and daughter depended on his moves in the next ninety minutes. He was driving home as fast as possible to search for the chip. The phone didn't give up, and his glance confirmed that it was an unknown number that could be ignored.

But it rang yet again, so he grabbed it and shouted, "I'm busy; I'll call you back; leave me alone." He was about to click off when he heard the muffled voice of Janeva. "Please listen, Thomas, please listen; I'm OK with the police, but you *need* to save Katie."

And he understood her veiled message that she was fine, but Katie was in grave danger. He swung into action. He knew that Katie had the chip! He could not remember if Katie had worn the chip to school that morning. He knew that on PE days, she didn't wear it because she had to take it off, and she was worried it might be lost or stolen.

Finally home, he searched Katie's room. Like most teenagers' rooms, it was a mess of disorganization. He turned in a circle in the one small space that was free of clutter and admitted to himself that finding anything could be hopeless. Clothes littered the floor, and the desk was covered with books and other random things he presumed were for a science experiment. Every surface was covered with clutter. How did she live like this? He was amazed that even her bed was full of crumpled blankets, pillows, and stuffed animals—so many stuffed animals.

He stood in despair. There was no way he would find one small necklace in this mess. *Think.* Where would she keep it? Where was it when they were in the Caribbean? He looked around. Would it be in a drawer? A closet? Where would you keep a cross necklace that contained a chip? Then he remembered that Katie had hidden the necklace chip on her favorite stuffed animal in the BVIs. His eye was drawn to the messy bed. *Yes*, he thought, *in her bed*, and he started rummaging through the heap of blankets and stuffed animals until, amazingly, there it was, carefully tucked into a corner: her favorite sleeping bunny, the one she had had since she was a child, and it wore a cross necklace.

With enormous relief, he extracted the chip from the 3-D cross that Katie had designed and constructed herself at his office so many weeks before. He grabbed an envelope from his own desk down the hall, inserted the chip, and labeled it as instructed, "Container key—confidential." He broke every speed limit and drove like a maniac to the yacht club. No one was at the desk.

Then the reception clerk called out from the office, "Can I help you, Mr. Jag?"

"Uh, mmm, no, I don't think so. I'm just leaving an envelope here for someone."

"Oh, Thomas, good to see you," said a voice he recognized. "I need to talk to you." It was Trent.

"What?" Thomas demanded, turning to look at his startled friend.

"I was wondering if Janeva ever managed to find Terri. She called me, and I understand that there was something important. That's all, just asking and wanting to say hello." Thomas was obviously distressed and angry, so Trent blurted out, "What is upsetting you?"

Thomas glared at Trent and then lost it. "Shut up. So you're the guy collecting the envelope. Stop this crap. Give me my daughter. Now!"

"Hold on. I'm sorry; I don't know what you are talking about. What envelope? Where is Katie?"

Thomas turned back to the reception desk, but the envelope was gone.

Chapter 27

"What!" cried Thomas. "Where is it? Who took it?"

"Thomas, what are you talking about?" Trent demanded.

The receptionist, startled by Thomas's yelling, returned to the front desk from the back office, where she had been making photocopies. She remarked that lots of members walked by the front desk in both directions, some to get to their boats, others to the dining room and restroom.

"Quick—now check the CCTV," said Thomas.

"Sorry," said the receptionist, "we don't have closed-circuit TV monitors. This is a respectable club. We don't monitor our members."

"Then you took it!" shouted Thomas.

"Mr. Jag, calm down, please," said the receptionist. "I didn't see any envelope and certainly didn't pick one up."

Thomas was starting to panic. Katie's life was at stake. "That's it, Trent," he said with a growl. "Come clean—where's Katie?"

"Thomas, please listen. I still don't know what you're talking about," Trent said, shuddering with surprise and a bit of fear at Thomas's aggressive tone.

"Then why are you here?" demanded Thomas.

"Well, I am usually here at this time every day, in case you hadn't noticed," he challenged back and turned to leave.

"Please, you two, I don't want to call security, but you mustn't make a scene. Go out to the parking lot if you must argue. Or I will call for assistance." The receptionist's demand was enough to stop the confrontation.

In desperation, Thomas tried one more time. "I left a critical envelope right here on this counter, and it's gone! One of you must have taken it." Then his cell phone rang another unknown number. Now desperate for anything, he turned and ran the short distance out of the front door of the yacht club as he answered.

"Thomas Jag." It was an electronic voice that said, "Do not speak to anyone. Do not explain to anyone. Calmly walk to your car. Go alone and await instructions. Go now."

Thomas prided himself on his ability to remain calm in times of stress, but he was sweating and breathing fast. He made it to the car, cradled his phone, and sat. *Don't panic*, he told himself. *Just stay calm, and it will soon be over.* Nothing happened. The phone did not ring. He sat and waited the longest five minutes of his life. Then it rang. The same electronic voice spoke to him in an audio message.

"This message is not traceable, so do not try. Very carefully watch the attached video from your daughter; then hang up. We are analyzing the chip that you delivered and will contact you soon about how to pick up your daughter."

As he scrolled down to the video, he thought, *Pick up my daughter—they make it sound like she is at a friend's. No, I need to rescue her, save her.* The video opened, and there was his beautiful daughter, Katie. She was as relaxed as anyone could be in a hospital bed while a uniformed nurse wearing a mask was taking blood from her left antecubital arm vein.

"Hi, Dad," Katie said. "Don't worry about me. I'm fine. The nurse told me this is just a precaution. They need my blood to see if I'm sick. She told me I could infect my whole class, so I have to stay here until they know. Dad," she whined, "you know I hate needles, so please, pleeeease come and get me soon."

"Where are you?" Thomas yelled at his phone as if the video could reply.

"The nurse said she would tell you where I am so you can come and pick me up; please come soon. Pleeeaasse."

The video ended, and the automated-sounding voice said, "The blood test is a basic DNA and histocompatibility analysis. Be aware that we never waste good organs; it's, shall we say, a lucrative business, and we have multiple recipients awaiting a new kidney. So if your information isn't perfect or if we ever learn that you or your wife, Janeva, have in any way tried to expose us, we will not hesitate to harvest a kidney. Katie can enjoy a normal, happy life with one kidney, but life is a bit more of a challenge with no kidneys or liver or heart. We even have a diabetic who is desperate enough to try a donor match of islets of Langerhans. As I said, we never waste good tissue, and, well, a beautiful, intelligent thirteen-year-old is about as good as it gets as a tissue donor." There was a pause, and then the electronic voice said, "Do not try to trace this call, and stay where you are, alone, in your car, and await my next call."

His earlier panic and sweat had now given way to cold, helpless fear, and he sat alone, gripped by a mental paralysis. His brain just repeating over and over, *Thomas Jag, what have you done? How could I have sacrificed my own daughter? I love Katie more than anything. My own beautiful daughter. I failed Katie; I failed Janeva. Oh God, how did I get into this mess?* Then the phone rang. It was yet another different number but the same electronic voice that spoke.

"Mr. Jag," the voice said, "do you not care about your daughter's life? We trusted you; the chip you gave us was empty, a blank. Yes, it was an excellent decoy chip. Mr. Jag, I think that was a one-kidney mistake on your part. So let us start over, shall we? Mr. Jag, I'm giving you one final chance; beautiful Katie has two kidneys, doesn't she?"

"But that's our only chip. That's the one she found," Thomas said, aware that his voice was almost a pleading squeak. "Believe me; that is the chip. We could not identify any information; the police couldn't extract any information. It was always blank—it *is* blank. Search my house, search my office—that is the one and only chip we found!"

The electronic voice snapped back, "Shut up and listen. Your time is running out to resolve this mess that you made; you have one hour. Go see your wife, Janeva. You will find her in a private room in Central Bay Hospital. Take a taxi or Uber, but do not drive yourself to the hospital. Speak to no one except your wife. Do not in any way, by gesture or note or voice, communicate with anyone, and instruct Janeva to follow the same rules. In exactly one hour, stand outside the front ER door and await instructions and the next video."

***

Dugud's junior officer wondered if his job was in peril. He was new to the force, keen and enthusiastic, and he had what seemed like a simple job: take down the facts of the event so that the force could initiate a proper investigation. But this woman wouldn't reveal anything. She had shut up in the ambulance, he was excluded from the medical exam and X-ray, and now finally the nurse had left him alone with her in the hospital room, and still, she was mute.

"Madam," he said, "please tell me what's going on. Why were you in a giant container swinging from a crane in an industrial shipping port?" No answer. So he tried saying, "Mrs. Jag, can you hear me? Do you understand what I'm saying?" Still no answer. Then, "Lady, you are a witness and maybe involved in a serious crime. I must know what happened. Deputy Sheriff Dugud is risking his reputation to help you, so you help us!" Still, Janeva said nothing, and he waited, unsure what to do and wondering if maybe she had been concussed. However, she had passed her mental assessment Glasgow Coma Scale in the ER.

As he stood over her in her hospital bed, the RN quietly entered and reported that the patient's husband was here to see her.

"Would that be OK?" *That's it*, thought the officer: *Her husband will ask questions; I'll get him to help me.*

"Invite him in," he said to the nurse.

Janeva was relieved to see Thomas and couldn't help noticing that this was not the usual crisp business-dressed husband she knew. Thomas was disheveled, and when he took her hand, he was shaking.

"Oh God," he said, "you're all right. I was so worried. Thank God you're safe. I need to speak to you urgently about another problem."

"Yes, great," said the police officer, who was at Thomas's side. "Please ask your wife to help me understand what happened and how she was involved with the shipping container."

"Please leave now," said Thomas. "I'm sorry, but we have a life-or-death matter to discuss, and it's private. Please, you must leave us alone. Time is of the essence now."

Ignoring Thomas's plea, the officer continued, "Mr. Jag, I won't take long. I must get this information. If you just help me, we can get this done."

"No, no. You do not understand. We must be alone. And we have only minutes to resolve a crisis. You've got to leave us alone now," Thomas almost shouted, and the astonished police officer noted that he was close to tears. The officer realized he had no authority to force either the husband or the wife to discuss or confess anything. They were not the criminals; they were the victims.

"OK. I will stand outside your door and give you ten minutes together."

As the police officer was leaving the hospital room, Greg burst in and blurted out, "What happened? I was just making rounds, and I saw Janeva's name. Can I help?"

"Greg!"

Greg started to speak, but Thomas interrupted him. "Later! I don't want to get you mixed up in this mess," Thomas said; then he quietly added, "You need to go. Please leave."

"Hold on, buddy." Greg walked deeper into the room. Clearly, he wasn't going to leave. "We are best friends. Nobody knows I am here in your room, and only a handful of coworkers even know I'm back in the country. I took an oath to never disclose anything patients tell me—so for God's sake, let me help." Then he added, "I'm not leaving this room; you look like you're in shock." He pulled out his flashlight to look into his eyes, and Thomas realized he was beaten.

"Fine then," Thomas said. "They're going to kill Katie and may already be cutting her up for organs. They said if I told anyone, it would be fatal for our little girl. And now it might already be too late because I didn't pay the right ransom."

"What?" Janeva had turned white. Greg quickly crossed over to her and elevated her feet, worried that she might faint.

Worried about his wife now as well, Thomas rapidly told Janeva and Greg what had happened and concluded by saying, "It's possible that some criminal, discredited surgeon might at this very moment be performing a nephrectomy on Katie." He was distraught.

Janeva, desperate to save Katie, tried to focus on all the events related to the chip. In desperation, she grasped at anything to do with the chip and told Thomas and Greg about the initial flash that Katie reported and the second flash that she had seen. She also told them about slipping the chip into the power bank portable charger that she had found on *Joie de Vivre*, and the surprising sudden flash and computer code. It hadn't charged up the computer, so she'd disconnected it. "But," she finished, "I can't remember more; I'm dopey from pain-relieving drugs, and my head hurts; it's a deep, throbbing headache from my fall."

"What can we do?" Greg said to Thomas.

"Think. Tell me anything you can remember," he said to Janeva. Nothing helped. Almost in desperation, he asked, "What happened to the computer that was connected to the power bank charger?"

"Um, I don't know. I never checked. I just turned it off to save power, and we didn't use it again."

"Is there any possibility that you might have downloaded the chip contents onto the computer?" Thomas asked hopefully. Then he added, "My God, it may be our only hope! I'm going home to get that laptop and search it."

As if he was being watched, he had hardly exited the hospital when his phone rang. It was the same metallic, disguised voice that said, "You have only thirty minutes left…things don't look so good for your daughter, now do they?"

"No, don't do anything," Thomas almost yelled into his phone. "We figured it out. The chip contents—whatever that was—were accidentally downloaded into our travel laptop. I'm getting that laptop now, and you can have it and everything on it. Just take it. I am sure it has what you want. Give me twenty minutes to retrieve it from my home and tell me where to meet. Please do not hurt my daughter. Twenty minutes, and I'll have what you want."

The phone connection went dead. No response. Thomas jumped into his car and headed for home. He raced home and was opening the front door when he heard his home-phone landline ringing. Time was critical, but what if it was the disguised voice with more instructions? He picked up the phone.

"Say nothing; just listen. It's me, Deputy Sheriff Dugud. Dr. Writeman has filled me in. We will rescue your daughter. It doesn't matter whether you want help or not—there is no way they will allow your daughter to survive. We are your only hope. You need my help and the coordinated help of my force. You are involved in a much bigger criminal affair than you realize. The criminal syndicate involved is unconcerned about your daughter's life, your wife's life, or your life. So from this moment on, we are working together."

"But—" Thomas interrupted.

"Now," Dugud went on to say, "get the laptop and await instructions. I am working on a system to trace your movements. Do not release the laptop until you are with your daughter. They are desperate for the information on that computer and know they are more likely to get it if you believe she is still alive and well. Under no circumstances let them get the information they want until we are in place."

The travel laptop, unused since their return from the BVIs, was still squeezed into the bookshelf where it had been shoved upon their return. Thomas grabbed it and ran to his car; then he stopped. He didn't know what to do next. Where to go? What to do? So he got into the car and sat. Just as he was wondering if he should go back in to get the power cord, his phone rang.

He grabbed his cell phone on the first ring and listened. It was the same disguised voice. "Did you get it?" it said.

"Yes, yes, I have it. What do you want me to do?"

"Now," the voice said, "go to the East Port Commercial Shipyard and await instructions. If you want to see your daughter, do not under any circumstances tell anyone. Don't think for a minute that you are alone. I know your every move and location." Again, the phone just went dead.

As he started to back out of his driveway, he was blocked by a car that drove in behind him. Further panicked by this obstruction, Thomas yelled, "Get out of my way!" Greg got out of the car, leaned into Thomas's front window, and said calmly, "Thomas, buddy, we are in this together." Then in an even softer voice, he said, "When you get your instructions, just drive. I will follow behind. Pal, we *will* get through this, and we *will* save Katie. Take care and don't lose me in traffic."

***

It was very quiet on the outskirts of the city when Katie found herself being escorted not out of a city hospital but out of a mobile home. The interior had been decorated to look like a hospital room. Her nice, calming, and efficient nurse was nowhere to be found, and two men, both with face-disguising masks, were pushing her into a car.

Earlier she had been reassured that she'd been conveyed to a hospital at the request of her mother, and as a dutiful daughter, she'd cooperated, but suddenly she now realized she was in trouble. Her heart raced, and she tried to call for help, but one fast slap hard on her face and a hand around her throat, followed by a warning to shut up or get hurt, silenced her. The smaller man squeezed in beside her in the back seat, and the other got into the driver's seat. She heard them say, "East Port Commercial Shipyard, gate Y." Then they took off.

***

Greg followed Thomas through traffic and, totally against his promise of confidentiality, phoned Dugud as arranged. Medical ethics did not presume confidentiality if another life was at risk, and his judgment was that Thomas and Katie needed the full support of the police. That was why he'd contacted Dugud while he was driving to Thomas's home a few minutes earlier.

Finally, there it was, the main entrance to the East Port Commercial Shipyard. This was the port that everyone knew, but pretended not to know, was run by organized crime, Satan's Bikers. Probably most illicit products, especially drugs, came in through this port and made its way across the country. The business was carefully managed by a boss no one ever crossed, at least not twice. It was a huge port facility—dark, old, and cluttered with crates, containers, forklifts, rail lines, trucklines, and cranes—and Greg, still following Thomas, counted a line of twenty-five piers running perpendicular from the quay road that ran along the shore. The dock had to be a mile long, he surmised, and it looked like the piers were each identified by a letter. He could see Alpha, Bravo, Charlie, and Delta from his car. Not wanting to get too close, he stopped his car just out of sight, hoping not to lose Thomas. *What pier should I be watching?* he wondered.

He looked for any activity that might not be related to loading or unloading, and then as he watched, a black, nondescript sedan drove right past him and headed down the quay road from which all the piers projected. Greg slid out of his car and followed in the shadows; then he saw Thomas, holding his cell phone to his ear, start up and follow the sedan.

Greg whispered into his phone a terse phone message for Dugud and then slowly crept down the road, trying to keep his eye on Thomas. *Do not be obvious; do not let yourself be seen*, he said to himself. He saw the black sedan far ahead and noted that he had passed O, P, and Q piers—Oscar, Papa, and Quebec, the marine phonetic alphabet running through his head. Then he saw the sedan turn onto a pier.

Suddenly worried for Thomas, he started to run down the road to catch up without being seen. *Hardly obvious*, he thought: *a guy in a gray suit and blue tie with shiny black shoes running down a commercial loading dock where every other person is in overalls and an orange hard hat.* A moment's thought, and he realized that totally contrary to character and a lifetime of training, he was acting on fight-or-flight impulse, didn't have any weapon, and since he was six years old, had never been in a fight. The cars had driven onto

Yankee pier, and he slowed as he passed W pier. *Whiskey*, his mind said, and then he cautiously approached Yankee Pier.

***

Thomas stopped as instructed and watched as the black sedan also stopped, but it then did a three-point, 180-degree turn, ending up with the car positioned for a quick getaway facing back to the road, down the pier. Thomas's car, as directed, faced the ocean.

"Stay exactly where you are," said the voice on the phone. "Do not move."

The back door of the sedan opened, and there she was. A gun pointed at her head, wrists tied, Katie stumbled out of the car. Tears streamed down her face, and she had a look of terror.

"Give me the computer," said the car driver, who had moved ahead of Katie.

Thomas had been clutching the computer as though it represented life or death. He shook his head and said, "Not until Katie is in my car."

The big man stuck his huge square face through the window and glared at Thomas eye to eye. Thomas nodded as best he could with his head pushed back against the headrest in a failed attempt to move away. The man reached through the window and ripped the computer out of his hands.

"Stay here in your car and await my confirmation of the information," growled the man, who looked like an unshaven football player.

When the huge goon pulled his head away, Thomas saw to his horror that Katie was being pulled down the pier, and the goon, now with his computer, ran after them. They were taking Katie! Forgetting his orders, Thomas leaped out of the car and sprinted down the dock after his daughter. He was still thirty feet away when he saw the Zodiac dinghy's dock lines being cast off. The goon handed the computer over the edge into the grasp of the sedan driver, who was in the dinghy. Katie was already in the dinghy.

Unnoticed by the others, Greg had caught up to the car, witnessed the computer grab, and joined Thomas in the chase for Katie. Before the goon could jump into the dinghy, Thomas and Greg together threw themselves at him in a football tackle. They were too close to the edge of the dock, and the three of them careened forward, fell, and splashed into a diesel film of cold ocean water an arm's length from the already-moving dinghy. As they struggled to swim, they saw the goon grab the dinghy lifeline and pull himself headfirst into the boat as it picked up speed. The two stern 250 outboards were engaged into full thrust.

Katie and her wet captor were both flung awkwardly into the stern as the boat accelerated. Full throttle, it slammed into the waves. Katie tried to get her balance, but with her hands still bound behind her back, she was flung backward and slammed into the stern station. The Zodiac banged into and over the waves and picked up speed until finally, it started to plane atop the water. *Mission accomplished*, thought the driver—he had the computer and the kid and knew that no one could catch them at this speed. They could hide in any of a multitude of small inlets, and if all went well, they'd deliver their package of kid and computer to the waiting freighter steaming just outside the three-mile international limit.

***

It was the kind of moment Max liked: action and tension. He stood at the top railing of a nondescript rusty-brown freighter flying the Panama flag, and he was listening through his earphone to a blow-by-blow description of the events as they unfolded on the dock. Max and his money had a special relationship with Panama, and he was pleased to be standing beneath that country's flag. *Yes*, he thought to himself, *the canal means something different to international bankers and accountants than it does to the ocean-freighter business.* He was, as usual, in control. He had the chip and the hostage to ensure he would get the entire chip information.

Now, he mentally reviewed the next step. How to disappear? Taking out a new burner cell phone, he alerted the crew leader to prepare for the next step.

"A dinghy with three people will approach the port beam. You will take them aboard. They will have a laptop computer, and it is the critical thing. You must, above all, obtain and keep the computer. As soon as you have the laptop and crew, sink the dinghy. Rip open the inflatable sides, ignore the engines, and attach the spare delta anchor to the dinghy to take it to the bottom. This boat must disappear fast and without a trace." Order confirmed, he spun his burner phone into the sea. *Another burner phone for the seabed*, he thought. *How many phones have I wasted over the chip and the Jags?*

Then he retrieved from his satchel yet another phone and ordered the freighter captain to get ready to launch the tender that would deliver him to his meet-up point ashore, just a nice three miles up the coast from the shipping port. Yes, he mused, no one could ever connect him with any of the events, and soon he would have the computer analysis, and then, yes, finally he could initiate the real plan with the info on that computer. *This is the moment.* He had waited for more than a year to act on the chip and now the computer information.

***

Dugud was at a loss. His day had started at five in the morning, and he had been pulled in too many directions because of his caseload that was totally screwed up by the Jag family mess. He'd finally been able to head home after another long day and was alone in his car when he'd received a series of terse messages from Greg and suspected that something serious was happening. He needed more detail before he could call for backup. The team would respond to a backup code request, but across the jurisdiction, many essential police activities would be interrupted. If the backup was unnecessary, his reputation would never recover.

He knew the port, but he was in the dark figuratively and now literally because it was dusk. The docks were quiet, with hardly anyone around. He could not see any signs of loading or unloading activity. Pondering his next step, he remembered the coast guard rescue station a short drive up the quay toward Alpha dock and sped to it. Coast guard rescue was always at the ready and could act without unnecessary disruption to the police, so after some quick paperwork, he commandeered the crew. Within minutes, they were off on the rescue hovercraft heading for Yankee dock. In keeping with his training, Dugud informed police communications of his location, destination, and plan.

***

The backwash wave from the dinghy takeoff flung Greg into the cutwater edge of the pier. Desperately he grabbed the metal ladder and pulled himself up. Thomas was frantically but futilely trying to swim after the Zodiac that had Katie.

Up on the pier, Greg searched for some means to assist or rescue Thomas; then the coast guard rescue hovercraft came speeding in. The glare of its searchlight almost blinded him, but they saw his sign when he pointed to Thomas, who was now flailing ineffectively in the water. The rescue headlamp focused on him, and Greg saw them pull Thomas onto their deck. He screamed and waved to get the helmsman's attention; though soaking wet and cold like Thomas, he wasn't going to be left behind. When the craft maneuvered back to the pier, he virtually slid down the ladder onto the hovercraft and held on. Now they were in a chase after the boat that had kidnapped Katie.

"Go! They have Katie! Go, go!" Thomas was yelling at the driver as he wrapped himself in the blanket that was handed to him. They had lost precious time getting him out of the water and Greg off the pier and were far behind.

The hovercraft accelerated, its multiple engines all roaring; they rose onto a plane and flew over the waves. The noise of waves and engines muffled any attempt to converse, and the crew knew this was a real rescue, not another training mission. Thomas, Greg, and Dugud were required, like all crew, to don personal floatation vests, each with the mandatory whistle and MOB (man overboard) LED light.

"We are gaining on them; I don't think they've seen us yet," Greg yelled into Thomas's ear. "They are too busy driving to look back."

"We're faster, and they don't know we're after them," Dugud shouted. He alerted Special Forces that he was in pursuit of kidnappers who might be armed and were in a speeding boat heading out of the port.

***

A quick look behind confirmed to Katie's kidnapper that he was being followed, and he realized that it was a coast guard hovercraft bearing down. Alarmed, he gunned the engine to maximum and made for the freighter. This easy delivery was now becoming a bit messy. His orders were to make his delivery and get out of there without being seen. And now he'd been seen.

"Damn it," he swore aloud. The freighter he was heading for had already weighed anchor and was moving into the commercial shipping lane. He knew it would continue to accelerate until it reached full hull speed, and he would have to unload his cargo onto a moving boat whose deck was the equivalent of a two-story building above sea level.

***

"Keep him in sight," shouted Dugud as both boats spun between the maze of anchored and moving ships. The boat with Katie was dark. It did not display the required port, starboard, bow, or stern navigation lights. The light was fading, and a rolling fog repeatedly obscured their visual contact with the Zodiac. A phosphorescent spray of its bow wave was its only giveaway. Then it disappeared.

Oh my God, Thomas thought in panic, *it sank!* There was no sign of it. Dugud had the hovercraft slow down and search with its spotlight, but there was no sign of the dinghy or of any wreckage, and they then realized that the headlight was of no help other than to identify their location to the kidnappers. Looking around, they could see lots of moving green starboard and red port lights in the distance and some white anchor lights near, but no hint of the Zodiac with Katie. Waves, freighters, ferries, water, fog, and sky, but no dinghy.

"Here," said a crewman to Thomas, "take these night-vision ultraviolet binoculars and search. I'll do the same with the thermal-imaging infrared ones."

It worked. As he focused on one of the moving freighters, Thomas saw unusual activity on its port side. "Look!" he yelled and pointed. "That freighter is lifting something up over its port side."

It was now dark. Greg and the coast guard officer were both searchings with binoculars, and at Thomas's call, they also saw the same activity. The crew member with the UV binoculars reported, "That freighter is under power and heading this way. It has an emergency boarding ladder swinging down. I see the dinghy, and I think it's attaching to the foot of the ladder. Yes, someone is trying to climb out of the dinghy onto the ladder."

The hovercraft roared to full speed, but as they approached the freighter, they heard rifle shots and were suddenly blinded by an explosive flash. The fuel tank of the dinghy that Katie had been abducted in had suddenly exploded. Further shots holed the inflatable sides, and the dinghy sank, dragged down astern from the weight of the two outboards. Gunfire—Dugud made another report to the station. Police helicopter 841 was en route, and he was connected through.

The freighter was gaining speed, leaving the port and heading for the open ocean. Thomas could see the rope ladder swinging back and forth like a pendulum across the hull, and near its foot, splashing in the water where the dinghy had been moments before, there were three people on the rope ladder. Katie, the last one on the ladder, was struggling, kicking, and screaming.

"Why didn't she jump?" Thomas wondered; then he saw that she was being held and pulled by her hair and coat by the man above her. The first person was climbing the ladder, carrying a package that Thomas guessed was the laptop. Katie was fighting back, causing the rope ladder to swing even more wildly. The freighter was gaining speed and turning at them, an eight-story building plowing bow first right at them, and they were not able to see Katie and her two abductors on the ladder. Suddenly the hovercraft didn't seem so safe and secure. They were about to be run over or swamped.

***

On the freighter deck, the crew was trying to hoist the ladder and get all three people onto the ship. Eighty feet of rope ladder is heavy for one strong man to lift when the freighter is stationary, but a swinging ladder with two bulky males and a kid attached to it had the crewmen struggling to get the ladder to move at all. The ladder was swinging, and they were straining to get it up. More crew were called to assist the ladder raising, and four of them finally started to make progress hoisting the ladder. Then they saw the last person drop like a stone into the dark ocean.

***

A quick spin—port engines forward, starboard astern—and the hovercraft whipped around out of collision course and then slammed forcefully into the port side of the freighter's hull. After multiple sweeps with the boat hook, they were finally able to grab the lower end of the rope ladder.

Dugud jumped up and caught the bottom rung, pressed his feet against the hull, and pushed out, forcing the ladder to twist so that he and the lower man, instead of facing the freighter hull, now had their backs to the hull, and the lower man was off balance. A grab and tug from Dugud, and he fell. Then, using the momentum, he kicked and pushed off the freighter to spring higher up the ladder and grab the belt of the laptop man. Together they fell backward and crashed in a mass back onto the hovercraft. Dugud landed atop his prisoner, his high-neck collar and floatation-vest padding breaking his fall. The prisoner was not so lucky. He was moaning, his left arm was bent at an odd angle, and he was having trouble breathing. Dugud reflexively searched and removed the handgun from the prisoner's jacket. He grabbed the laptop, which the prisoner had been clutching to his chest and, as they fell, had been trapped between the two of them. It had survived the fall and seemed to be in one piece.

Thomas ignored the drama on the ladder and reflexively dived over the side to rescue Katie. Katie was trying to survive by swimming like a porpoise and treading water, because her wrists were tied behind her, and she couldn't use her arms. She treaded water as best she could, but the waves kept breaking over her head, forcing her down;

she was sinking. Thomas dived out of the boat and grabbed at her to save her, but he could not get down deep enough in the water because his floatation vest kept pulling him back up. She was sinking out of reach. He tried and tried, but she was always just a few feet deeper than he could reach.

He desperately tore at the clips and zippers of his life vest to remove it so he could dive down and save Katie. His daughter was drowning! Then suddenly, the full power of the freighter's stern propeller wave lifted Katie up toward the surface, and he grabbed her. They broke the surface, with Katie taking deep, wrenching breaths of life-saving air.

The hovercraft, still attached to the rope ladder, was being towed and was now a football field's distance away from where Thomas and Katie were working to stay afloat. The lower man that Dugud had kicked off the ladder had been able to grab the lower rung and got back up just as the crew unhooked the rope ladder and dropped it. The freighter, now heading into international waters, plowed full speed into the night.

***

The freighter's yellow tender, indistinguishable from every other freighter's tender, had earlier been lowered off the leeward deck and had already delivered its only passenger to shore. Max was safely sitting in the back of a limousine listening to his phone. He ground his teeth as once again he heard the description of another Jag chip-recovery disaster.

"Will this chip and Jag thing never end?" he said aloud to no one. Always careful, he would be dropped off not at his home but at a bus depot, where he would catch a taxi for a few blocks and then call an Uber to take him within walking distance of his home. Even the Uber driver would not know where he lived.

As he settled into the comfort of the back seat of the black car, he pondered the strange turn of events that had him participating in today's mission. He ran businesses in many cities and several countries, but the goddamn Jag family was blocking his every effort to get his chip information. Did he really care? Well, he admitted to himself that he loved the adventure.

What a day, manipulating the container, and then the sea chase. He had known for years that he was two people inside one brain. Mrs. Jag and that little girl somehow exposed the drive for life and sex, and that was what Mr. Freud would have called his ego side. His other side was his urge for destruction and death, his Thanatos. Somehow, days like today stimulated both sides of his brain.

His memory took him back to those days as the kid who was ignored by everyone. Even older, he was the last to be chosen for anything, the useless kid. Now he was the top of an almost invisible corporate pyramid, but unlike most successful corporate CEOs, he hid from publicity. Four men reported to him, and they did not even know one another. Down the pyramid of control, few knew who was the boss of their boss. What they did know was that they were more likely to survive and get rich if they didn't inquire. Street drugs, big pharmacy, munitions, precious metals, and robotics—he was on top of a lot of deals, and nobody knew.

Could it all unravel because of one computer chip? he wondered. That chip might have his image on it. He wasn't sure, but he knew it had the ability to take a photo image of anyone who held it. But now he had the chip, so presumably, he was still invisible. Safe.

Max didn't smile much, but now he leaned back and smiled at the secret pleasure he got from escaping his computer and hidden life to again experience operations. *Yes*, he said to himself, *I ran the crane, and there was a thrill directing operations from the freighter.*

Chapter 28

Janeva was still in her private and police-guarded hospital room, and now, late at night, and to the expressed inconvenience and displeasure of the hospital staff, Deputy Sheriff Dugud, Thomas, Greg, and Katie were all crowded into the room. As soon as she had entered the room, Katie had broken down into tears and embraced her mom. They both cried. They had survived their own life-threatening, close-to-death crisis.

Dugud coughed to get everyone's attention and then said, "I know, I know that you all need to erase this horrible memory, but I absolutely need your information now when it's fresh, and you should know that until this is resolved, your lives are all still at risk." He emphasized the word *all* by looking at Katie then directly at her parents one at a time.

"We need to work together, and we need to act fast. We have reason to believe that you have become ensnared in the machinations of a ruthless organized crime syndicate. We think that its operations include some large, reputable retail, manufacturing, and energy companies whose senior management probably don't even realize that they launder money or produce materials for organized crime. Unsuspecting low-level people take orders from someone in the syndicate, perform seemingly irrelevant actions, and provide information that cumulatively assists the syndicate to manipulate markets and high-level people.

"The problem that you have, all of you—let me repeat, all of you, even Katie—the problem that you have is that you are now a threat to the syndicate's operation. If the syndicate knows you have already told your story, then it has less reason to harm you. It cannot control you with threats. That means you must disclose all and any information you have to me now. Note that I'm recording what I've said, and now each of you, please say clearly that you know you are being recorded and that you are telling the truth."

They all agreed. Dugud neglected to tell them that people who upset the syndicate just seemed to disappear.

"OK," said Dugud, "let's start with Katie. Katie," he said, "I'm sure you've been taught to never get into a stranger's car, so tell us, how did you let yourself be abducted?"

Her eyes welling up with tears, she sobbed, saying, "Terri told me that Mom had asked her to pick me up and that it was possible I'd contracted some infectious disease from a mosquito when we were in the Caribbean. It started with a *Z*, and I needed to get into the health-care van that was right there at the school. She told me that they were taking me to where Mom was; Mom was also being tested. So I got in. I thought it was an ambulance because it had a cross on the side and no windows."

Katie sobbed and turned to her mother. "Terri is your friend; she works at the yacht club. We saw her in the BVIs—" And at that, she broke into full sobbing and crumpled into her mother's arms.

"So Terri took you in the van?" asked Dugud.

"No, I never saw her again. The paramedic person gave me a pill as soon as I got in, to swallow with a drink of water, and then I woke up in a hospital bed." Sobbing harder, she said, "It wasn't a hospital; it was a motor home! I saw it when they took me out."

"Did they hurt you or ask you questions?" Dugud asked.

"They took my blood to test and asked me about the computer chip. That is all I remember. When I woke up, a nurse was taking blood, and I remember the doctor was taking a video message on his iPad. He told me what to say."

Thomas broke in, saying, "He wanted the computer chip—you know, the one Katie found last summer at Chatterbox Falls, and you returned to her."

"Of course, but that chip was a dud. There was nothing of value on it," the officer said, baffled. "Where is the chip now?"

No one said anything. Then Thomas said, "To save Katie, I was ordered to leave it in an envelope at the yacht-club reception desk…someone took it. I don't know how they took it so fast. Then I heard from the same automated, disguised voice that it was a dud or empty, as you said, but they were still convinced I had the real one."

Janeva, whose voice was still hoarse from her choking and fall, spoke up. “And, well, we think that the chip did have something on it. When we were in the Caribbean and I was doing the catamaran inventory, I found a black box in the tool kit that I assumed was a battery charger, so I attached it to our travel laptop. All we used the laptop for was to play spider solitaire and watch movies. And it turned out that in the BVIs, we had so much to do and so many real distractions that we rarely used the little travel laptop.

“I noticed that the black box had a USB port that was the same size as a chip, and the only chip we had was Katie’s, so I tried it. When I inserted the chip into the black box, suddenly and for only an instant, the chip and black box both flashed, and then the smooth, black surface of the box lit up and flashed green computer code and random numbers. I remember thinking that the chip did something, but then you all came back and needed me to grab the dinghy line. And, well…I put the box and chip away and rushed out with towels. Katie was shivering.

“Then I was too busy with work, the yacht club, and all the Betty stuff, and I just forgot about the laptop until Thomas came in a panic because the chip was empty, and Katie was going to be…” She trailed off, unable to finish the sentence. After a time, she continued. “Until that moment I just never thought to tell anyone what had happened; then when I did earlier today, Thomas figured out that I might have transferred the data from the chip and downloaded its contents onto our travel laptop.”

Seeing the quizzical look on the deputy sheriffs face, she added, “The catamaran we were using belonged to Lorenzo before he was murdered, and if he developed the computer chip, it would make sense that he would have a means to transfer the data."

Dugud was busy taking notes. As he looked up and started to speak, Janeva briefly wondered what had happened to the travel laptop. Then she forced herself up into a painful sitting position and said in her croaking, pained voice, "Oh my God, Terri is here and not in Europe! I remember Wiffy mentioning Max. Is Max the syndicate that you're talking about?"

Deputy Sheriff Dugud nodded and then held up his hand, signaling her to hold on for a moment as he answered his phone. He reported that the coast guard was tracking the freighter they had identified trying to abduct Katie. It had already disguised its name and flag. Greg and Thomas both admitted they had never seen a name or flag on the freighter, and it looked much like all the other freighters anchored in the bay.

The hospital-room door opened, and the police guard, now unnecessary because Dugud was with them, walked in with a welcome tray full of fresh, steaming coffee and cookies and scones he'd picked up from Starbucks. Everyone now realized that they were in for a long night of interrogation.

Thomas explained that his company was involved in some special and confidential CIA and US military research related to laser drone surveillance, and he assumed that was why his office had been broken into and searched. All this, he assumed, was associated with his job, and until Janeva's abduction in the container and Katie's kidnapping, like Dugud, he hadn't thought that the chip was relevant.

"Just explain to me now," said Dugud, "how did anyone know how to find you in the Caribbean? This is important because it sounds to me like you were being watched or followed."

The group looked at one another in silence as they pondered the question; then aloud they speculated about Jeff, the blond guy who always seemed to be close.

Thomas blurted out, "There is one other connection. Trent. He repeatedly wanted to know our location; he showed up at every crisis moment; he was at the yacht club when someone lifted the chip envelope."

"Trent's a harmless busybody." Janeva hesitated, then added reluctantly, "And he is our friend, but Thomas is right. He always seems to turn up! And now that I think of it, Wiffy, Trent's wife's, was…" Janeva trailed off and then quietly added, "Wiffy was one of the people on Betty's list; it was her name that made me think the list might be important."

Quietly Dugud was busy conveying orders to the night staff at police headquarters to pick up both Terri and Trent for questioning. Then he hesitated, changed the request, and ordered that Terri and Trent be picked up *immediately* for questioning. Terri had certainly collaborated in Katie's abduction, and Trent's association was suspicious enough that he would be interrogated. Seeing that Janeva was almost asleep and Katie was fading, he told the assembled Jags and Greg what he was doing and that they could return home. Greg, Thomas, and Katie were under police protection until further orders, and Janeva was restricted to her hospital room. He wanted them all back in the hospital room at ten o'clock the next morning for more questioning.

***

The next day, as required, they gathered back in Janeva's room after the in-house hospital staff had finished rounds and declared Janeva well enough to return home. She had physician's instructions and a prescription.

"They have promised us the use of this room until one o'clock," Dugud said, "so let's get started. Now that you have all had a night's sleep, is there anything else to add?"

He looked in turn at each of them, waiting until they had each said a verbal no. Then he continued. "You'll be interested in learning that Terri has been under interrogation for more than an hour already. Terri knew she was caught, and she admitted that all she did was what her husband, Chad, had demanded of her. She did not know who gave him orders. It wasn't a big deal; she was helping Katie, after all, and what if Katie had contracted the Zika virus? All she was to do was to let Katie know she could trust the people in the ambulance, because they were going to take her to her mom, Janeva, to be checked."

With that, he visibly squared his shoulders with a look of resignation. He looked directly at Janeva. "I understand that the hospital has released you. We still have some leads to follow up, but I believe you hold the key to this. Please think about what I have confided in you today, and please, all of you, report in tomorrow at thirteen hundred hours—that is one o'clock p.m.—at the station. We require your written statements." With that, he closed his leather portfolio, stood, and with a nod of good-bye, left the room.

It took a while to arrange for the wheelchair, but finally, Thomas checked Janeva out of the hospital, and Katie maneuvered the chair, with her mom uncomfortably sitting in it, leg propped up. Greg and Steph were waiting for them when they arrived home. The smell of fresh coffee dripping cheered Janeva, and after the group had full coffee cups, they seated themselves around the Jags' kitchen table and got down to analyzing and exploring all the questions of the chip and Betty's murder.

***

As required, they all met at the police station the next day to document their statements. They were crowded in a small office, made more awkward because Janeva was in a wheelchair. Dugud reported that their crew had boarded the freighter, but it was outside territorial limits, so they could not retain it. The freighter captain had agreed to let them search it, but they'd found nothing of interest.

"How can you search a huge container ship?" he said. "In a ship that size, you could probably hide almost anything. They did not have the chip and did not know what the chip did or why it was so valuable."

This time it was not the self-appointed sleuth, Janeva, who started the questions but Katie, who said, "I just don't get it. What does any of this have to do with the chip?"

At Dugud's request, Thomas had worked on the laptop information late into the night and thought he had some exciting news for the group. He had refrained from telling them until they were together and Dugud could take notes. He was smiling.

"Here's what I found, and here's my theory," he said. "The file was saved on the hard drive, but it didn't show up in the finder. It was hidden by a password, what we thought was the bar code."

"Bar code?" Greg asked.

"That's right; it turns out that those numbers on the chip were—"

"That's right; I remember the detective asking us about them, the numbers on the chip," Katie interrupted excitedly, "but they didn't relate to anything."

Thomas, with a nod to his clever daughter, said, "All those ones and zeros embossed on the chip were a code."

He opened the small laptop, let it power up, and then continued. "That's right. Remember, before we went to the Caribbean, and after Janeva and Katie were interrogated at the police station, we were at the club and talking about the chip. Trent asked about it, and Katie pulled the chip out to show it to us. I admit, I thought the chip was a bit of nonsense. I meant to investigate it but forgot until last night when I was searching the laptop hard drive. Look here; I printed it out."

He brought out a sheet of paper. "The numbers were mostly unreadable, but on the laptop, I found a file named this: 00110110 00111001 00001101 00001010. At first, I thought like the police that it was a bar-code method to categorize the chip for storage and recovery. If you had a factory that made chips for different purposes, then you would need some way to recognize them, and this would certainly be better than putting them in a labeled envelope, because every chip appears to be an identical twin of every other. But then I opened the file." He turned the laptop around to show the group the map of North America with red pins on it.

Leaning over, Katie exclaimed, "Look!" She pointed to the pins on the map. "That's Princess Louisa Sound, where Chatterbox Falls is, and Anegada Island."

"Other than the fact that we have been to both those locations, how are they connected to the chip?" Greg asked.

"Good question; I wondered that as well. I studied the code on the computer, and it jumped out at me that it was binary code, so I ran it through a binary-to-text converter, and it came out Tm69."

"And," said Janeva, "the significance of Tm69 is?"

Katie jumped up, raising her hand like she was in class. "I know, I know! It is an element in the periodic table. We studied the periodic table this year. It's atomic number 69—a rare-earth metal. I don't remember the name, but it starts with *T*."

Thomas and Katie fist pumped. "Right on, Katie," her dad said. "It's thulium. This element is found only in trace amounts in the world, and it is an absolutely critical element in lasers and in brachytherapy radiation, which is now the standard treatment for prostate and other cancers. Interestingly, it is also one of the compounds my company uses in our SLARD project, the Stealth Laser Augmented Reconnaissance Drone. And Katie, I know, will appreciate this: it's a small but essential element in the semiconductors of many electronics, including your iPhones. It is relatively harmless, but it does give off alpha-decay radiation, a proton emission. None of this made any sense until I compared the thulium and the places where Katie saw a flash, and it occurred to me that maybe the chip was able to detect the alpha wave of thulium. Could Lorenzo have produced a chip that could be activated by thulium? I wondered. However, that would require a power source, and there wasn't one."

He looked at the others; then with a smile, he said, "We couldn't see the flash because we were inside. Katie saw the flash because she was in sunlight. Solar power. When the chip was charged with solar power, it could pick up a thulium proton if it was close enough. If the chip located a thulium deposit, then you knew you were atop a fortune. No gold mine could compete dollar for dollar with a thulium deposit of any size."

"I guess the legend was right," Katie announced. "Remember at the powwow, the Indians' story said that an eagle created the bay below the Chatterbox Falls? I bet that was a meteor collision."

"Well," her dad said, "neither First Nations nor any other life was around when it happened, but thulium is not a decay product of our earth mantle. It probably, like other rare-earth metals, was deposited by a collision with an asteroid or even a supernova a billion years ago."

Katie interrupted him. "Finally you believe me. I saw the chip flash when I first found it, and that must have meant we were near or on a deposit of thulium. The second flash was when we were at Cow's Wreck Bay in the Caribbean, and everyone knows the Caribbean is the result of a giant meteorite strike. Dad," she almost shouted, "where's my chip now?"

"Sorry, honey," her father said gently. "This computer has the data from the chip, but only the chip can locate the thulium, and it's gone. Max has it."

"So does that mean the chip still works?" Katie asked.

"Excellent question. Probably; I just don't know. Hmm. I wonder if it will work for Max or…" Thomas trailed off.

It was Greg's turn to bring them back on track. "So how is this all related? If I understand the sequence, presumably Lorenzo developed a chip that identified a rare-earth mineral, he was murdered for the chip, and Wiffy, Trent's wife, who we now know probably had some expertise in subatomic physics, was the prime suspect in his murder, but she died. Could she…" He let his voice trail off as well.

"Trent and I both remember her mentioning Max when she had us at gunpoint, so of course we can project that she might have been working for, or with, or been a blackmailed pawn of Max," Janeva said.

"Yes, we've speculated endlessly about the relationship of Wiffy with Lorenzo and Max, but what about Betty's death?" Greg said. "Does this relate to anything? To the chip? To Wiffy? I am now convinced that Betty was murdered. The suggestion that she was planning to drown herself ignores that she was on deck, at night, in a storm and was prudent enough to be wearing a floatation vest."

Janeva opened her large purse and brought out Betty's Surface laptop.

"Janeva, I thought you gave that to the lawyer," Thomas chided.

"I was going to, but then I found this file and told Deputy Sheriff Dugud about the list, and I got to wondering if there was anything else important on the computer, an—"

"OK, OK. What list?" Thomas put his hands up in surrender.

"Well, I found this list that I felt was significant." She scrolled through the computer files until she found the photo of the handwritten note that Betty had found on Terri's desk. She turned the screen around for the group to see.

"Wow! Those are club bigwigs," Steph exclaimed. "What was the list for? And what do you think Terri meant by, 'Chad, here's the list of contributors that I promised. Don't forget to emphasize the big dividends'?"

"The use of contributors and dividends is interesting—almost sounds like Chad and Terri are exploiting members," Thomas pondered.

"And there's more, in the 'Yacht Club History' file. I was going to ignore it because I know most of the club history, but I scanned it to see if my grandfather was mentioned. Betty had added some notes to the effect that Terri and her husband, Chad, were promoting big investment in the energy sector. She noted that Chad was promoting shares in an oil-production organization in Alberta, Canada."

"Didn't you say that Betty had worked in the oil industry?" Steph asked.

"Yes, when I looked up Betty's past employment history, it turned out that oil industry was her field of expertise, and she had managed a major drilling company in Edmonton, Alberta. According to her notes, it looks like she did some research and became suspicious of the project Chad was promoting. Look here."

Janeva opened a new file. "It sort of looks like she was either gathering data or keeping a journal of sorts. Here she has made notes from a discussion with some of the members on that list whom she could trust and found that

Chad's selling point was that the Canadian Native Indians, or First Nations, as they like to be called, were sitting on a treasure of oil but didn't realize its true value. This treasure could be grabbed for next to nothing. Or relatively next to nothing, because the number of shares was fixed at one hundred, and they were ten thousand dollars each. One million Canadian dollars in total. A deal. That would give ownership to the land and mineral rights.

"Betty's research revealed that the company's credentials were highly suspicious. In Canada, unlike the United States, the government owns almost all mineral rights including petroleum, even on private land. Mineral rights must be obtained through a negotiation with the government, and the quick profit from shipping the crude by pipeline that Chad was promising was in truth an agonizing political nightmare. Plus, the First Nations would never agree to a pipeline and oil freighters in their sacred inlet."

Dugud collected the Surface laptop from Janeva; then he said to the group, "Thank you for this. With Terri's statement, we were able to locate Chad, whom is now in our custody and is being questioned; this information is critical to our investigation. Our preliminary investigation had already linked Chad to a Ponzi scheme, an international consortium built on the promise of huge profits from the export of petroleum products from the Alberta, Canada, oil sands. It was a shell company named MAXX Global Inc., but there was no money trail. We had no proof. Apparently, he was convincing members of your yacht club that he had insider information into a fantastic oil-producing-and-exporting scheme that was going to make them all extraordinarily rich.

"Like the classic Ponzi scheme, he was selling the same oil-company shares to multiple people, and they all believed they owned real oil-producing property. They were sucked in by tempting dividends that were in fact from money invested by the next level of investors. We think that he probably pocketed millions. The plan was for the company to file for bankruptcy and blame the Canadian First Nations group for blocking the project in the name of climate change and pollution."

"So it was my book report that gave you the clue," Katie gloated happily.

There was silence as everyone absorbed the information. Janeva summarized her understanding of the case. "So Chad was using his wife's inside knowledge to target potential victims, stealing yacht-club members' money in a Ponzi scheme."

Dugud nodded.

"OK, I get that now about the chip; was Lorenzo working with Max? Lorenzo developed the graphene chip, so why was Max so determined to get it?"

"I told you that the person you call Max"—the policeman smiled—"is or owns MAXX Global Inc., the shell company." Then, seriously, he continued. "Regarding the chip, we are dealing with an international criminal organization. We don't think that Lorenzo was working with or for Max. Instead, it is our working theory that Max wanted the chip and Lorenzo refused to give it to him, so Lorenzo was probably killed for it. We do have evidence that at least one branch of the MAXX organization is selling military equipment, and I did not appreciate until now that the automated weapons probably depended on the rare-earth mineral thulium."

Katie was frustrated by all the oil company and Ponzi scheme mumbo jumbo that didn't interest her and that she didn't bother to understand. When Dugud paused, she asked, "How did Betty die?"

Dugud tapped Betty's Surface laptop. "These files are pretty convincing that Betty uncovered the Ponzi scheme. Terri has admitted in questioning that Betty confronted her about the list, and she reported to her husband, Chad. Now, it is just speculation, but if Chad reported up the line that they were exposed, then it is typical of organized crime to eliminate any risk."

"Chad killed her," Katie clarified, clearly frustrated by his convoluted answer.

"Yes, that is correct," Dugud replied with a kind smile; he wasn't in court, after all. Then he added for her benefit, "You are safe now; we will arrest Chad on charges of conspiracy, securities fraud, and now murder. He won't be getting out for a long time."

"Good. He should be in jail," she pronounced; then a moment later, she asked, "So how did Betty end up tangled up in our boat's kayak line?"

Deputy Sheriff Dugud cleared his throat, looking at Katie. "The local Caribbean police—you remember, the ones who interviewed you—said there is a back eddy in the area, and she most likely was caught up in it. It was pure luck that she ended up at your boat."

"Luck!" Thomas said quietly. "You call that *luck*?"

No one laughed, but out of politeness, they did try to smile.

Chapter 29

The sounding of a ship's bells is well rooted in the history and tradition of the maritime industry. Onboard timekeeping has been an integral part of shipboard life since the earliest days of long-distance navigation.

The maximum number of bells that can be struck is eight, hence the saying, "Eight bells and all is well." With the end of the watch, eight bells are sounded.

Ultimately the passing of a sailor is marked with the ringing of eight bells. The sounding of a ship's bell is a powerful reminder of the traditions rooted in this long-held maritime tradition.

It was as if Betty had arranged it. The day of her eight bells ceremony was clear and sunny. The Bay was calm, a relief for the many boats crammed with members out that afternoon to say good-bye. Sir Ford had flown in and was on the Jags' sailboat with the Writemans and Trent. All the club executives were on the boats that formed a rough circle around the Jags' boat. The honoree club minister stood on the transom of the Jags' sailboat and intoned in a voice that carried over the water.

"The ringing of eight bells is a ceremony to memorialize the life of our departed club manager. The eight bells signify the end of a person's watch on earth. Eight bells and all is well—a sailor's time for rest.

"Please observe a minute of silence in honor of Betty Rothman."

During the silence, eight bells were rung in pairs of two. Janeva swallowed back tears and put her arm around Katie, thinking about all the events that had followed Betty's death. The minister sprinkled Betty's ashes in the water and then stepped back to let Sir Ford walk forward and toss a large wreath into the water. One by one the rest of the boat's occupants did the same, but with single flowers, until the area was covered with floating flowers. Boats turned on their engines, heading back to the clubhouse, where the new club manager had arranged for food and beverages to be served. Janeva watched the flowers float away on the current and waves. For the first time in what seemed like years, she felt at peace.

Even though Max was still at large, Detective Dugud had confided that he was working with Interpol and other international law enforcement agencies to uncover and break up Max's criminal syndicate, and he was sure Max would be caught soon.

***

Max, however, was sitting on the aft deck of his luxury yacht in Tortola. Instead of enjoying the beautiful Caribbean sunset, he was staring at the small graphene computer chip held between his thumb and forefinger.

This chip has my photo on it. The one and only known photo of me in existence. I should destroy it. But even as he thought this, he knew he would not. This chip still had value. All he needed to do was find the right person to unlock the chip and extract the information. Then uncharacteristically he swore out loud and clenched his hand around the chip. That would mean exposing his face.

His decision made, he went inside to his onboard office and sent off several messages to his various organizations, looking for a computer expert. A disposable one. He didn't mention that the person would have to be eliminated after the chip code was broken. Damn the Jag family. He hated doing things twice. It was a bad practice. He knew he should just let this one go, but he couldn't. He needed the thulium. He had commitments too.

***

"The new club manager did a nice job of the post eight bells reception," Janeva said as she looked around the main dining room of the clubhouse.

"True," Steph agreed, looking around. "He's done a nice job of it, but something is missing. I can't put my finger on it, but…" She trailed off.

"Betty and Terri are what are missing," Janeva said bluntly.

With a sad laugh, Steph agreed. "I'm sure that's it. I'm missing Terri bouncing around introducing everyone to everyone else, even if they have known each other for years."

"And Betty triple checking everything, making sure it was all perfect," Janeva continued.

"I wonder what will happen to Terri now."

With a tap of her nose, Janeva leaned in conspiratorially. "So, last I heard, she agreed to testify against her husband, Chad, in exchange for house arrest."

"So she can be with her kids," Steph said hopefully.

"Yup. She has to wear an ankle bracelet and can only travel a limited distance, like to the kids' school, food store, and such."

The conversation was cut short when Sir Ford had ambled over to join them.

"Janeva," he said in his deep British accent. "Thank you! Words cannot express how much this ceremony means to me. It's just as Betty would have wished it, fitting and perfect. Thank you," he said softly as he worked to control his emotions.

"We were just saying how much she will be missed at the club," Steph said in her soft, gentle manner.

"What will you do now?" Janeva asked, thinking that he had aged in the past few weeks and looked years older. His stooped shoulders gave him a crumpled and almost dejected look.

With a ferocity that defied the look she had just witnessed, his eyes flashed. He squared his shoulders.

"Throw myself into my business. Ashton, my son-in-law"—he paused, seeming unsure how much to say but then continued with a half smile—"the little shit has lost a fortune and has run the business into the ground."

Janeva and Steph were astonished and unsure how to respond. Sir Ford, seeing their discomfort, laughed, looking more like his old self.

"Don't worry. I built the company, and I will rebuild it again."

Nodding in agreement, Janeva said, "I'm sure you will. What about Ashton and Sylvia?"

"Ha. I haven't figured that out yet. I don't expect them to be happy about it, but I still have majority control." He grinned. "Fortunately, most of Ashton's deals were informal handshake deals, so he will be spending the foreseeable future talking his way out of those shady deals."

"Sir Ford." Trent joined the group, giving a quick nod to Janeva and Steph. He gently put his hand on Sir Ford's elbow to direct him. "I want to introduce you to—"

"Oh no, you don't." Thomas and Greg had appeared on either side of Trent.

Greg gave Janeva and Steph a wink as he pulled Trent away from Sir Ford under the ruse of official yacht club business.

Janeva and Steph's eyes met as they tried not to burst out laughing at Sir Ford's confused look. Thomas, with an eye roll, put an arm around them each, directing them away.

"Girls, it's time to go back to the boat."